THE
BASE
OF
REFLECTIONS

TOMORROW'S ANCESTORS:
BOOK 2

AE WARREN

'Adapt or perish, now as ever, is nature's inexorable imperative.'

- H.G. Wells

ONE

Elise stood on the pebble-strewn shoreline and peered into the lake. The surface was still and reflected a mirror image of the snow-capped mountains behind it. The weather had warmed up in the last few days and she hadn't washed properly since leaving Thymine Base—she had a horrible suspicion she was beginning to smell. Stepping back, she shuddered at the thought of letting even a drop of water touch her.

Next to her, Luca gave an identical grimace. 'So, let me get this right...you're telling me not only can we drink the water, we can swim in it as well?'

Luca was running his hand over the back of his head. His shaved hair was beginning to grow out and his blond, baby curls were forming once again.

'That is correct,' Samuel said, his previously patient tone beginning to crack. 'The chances of a mutating virus are slim to none. As I said, the fear of untreated water is instilled in you from birth so you become reliant upon the treated water. They then limit its supply, which means leaving the base you grew up in is never an option. It's quite clever, really.'

'Or tyrannical,' Elise said, still peering into the water. Even dipping an investigatory toe went against everything she'd been taught from birth.

'Yes, that too. You are fine to swim in untreated water but you should always boil any water you intend to drink. The viruses in your bedtime stories might not exist, but that doesn't mean there isn't a rotting animal carcass at the bottom of the lake or upstream in a river.'

Luca turned to Elise and raised an eyebrow. 'I think he's trying to kill us.'

'If it's so safe, why don't you go in first?' Elise said to Samuel, still unsure whether she believed him.

'If that's what it takes,' Samuel said, beginning to unbutton his shirt.

Luca raised both his hands. 'At least leave the pantaloons on.'

'I was going to! And they are not pantaloons. They are standard-issue, mid-line middies...and you accuse me of overusing Pre-Pandemic terminology?'

Elise turned from Samuel to give him some privacy while he undressed. Shielding her eyes from the sun, she smiled back at Georgina and Kit, who were sitting next to each other with five-month-old Bay propped up between them. Elise tried not to stare at the prominent, keloid scar that zigzagged its way from the outer corner of the nurse's eye, tracing its way down to her chin.

Elise glanced at her own arm; the only mark was the mandatory tattoo on the inside of her right wrist, which she'd been given when she was fourteen: Elise Thanton, 17 February 2250, Thymine Base, Sapien.

While she waited for Samuel to undress, she inspected

the index finger and thumb on her right hand. They had started to heal but still ached continuously; it would be a few weeks until she knew how much movement she would recover. This was the price she had paid for escaping Thymine. The person who had broken them, Fintorian, had paid an even heavier price.

The splash of Samuel kicking in the lake made Elise turn back again. When he was farther away from the shore, he stopped and floated on his back, the water gently rippling around him. He looked at peace, no hint of the strained expression he had worn since leaving Thymine. Elise knew he felt responsible for them all and she wanted that to change as soon as possible, to share his burden.

'Oh, why not...' Luca mumbled to himself as he started tugging off his boots.

Sighing, Elise walked farther along the shoreline before peeling off her clothes; she had to force herself to go against her instincts if she wanted to unravel all of the misconceptions she had grown up with. The loud splash of Luca belly flopping into the water made her grin, but she resisted glancing over at the two men and instead went back to her solitary thoughts.

The initial high of exploring the outside world was fading fast. The changing landscape as they continued northwards, woodlands to moors, grasslands to mountains, had held Elise captive and she'd thought nothing could replace that feeling.

But that had all ended a week ago, when she realised that it was her nineteenth birthday. She had spent the day thinking about what her parents would do to celebrate it now that she was no longer with them. Would they celebrate it at all? It was the first time she had spent a birthday away from them, the first time she had not opened her small gifts and let her younger brother blow out the candles on her cake.

Since then, she hadn't been able to shake the feeling that her family were not as she had left them. That everything had changed for them too. Day by day, this gnawing doubt increased, taking her attention away from her surroundings as her focus turned inwards.

What had happened to her family? She did not know. She hoped they had convinced the authorities that they'd disowned her before she did the unthinkable. But at night she would imagine that the Protection Department had come for them, as punishment for what happened to Fintorian. That they had taken her younger brother Nathan away. Her dad would have been killed in the struggle; he wouldn't have let Nathan go without a fight. Her mum? They could have told her anything about Elise and she would have no way of finding out if it were true...

The pebbles dug into her toes as she hesitantly dipped her foot into the cool water. Grimacing at the temperature, she stepped forward and her frown slowly receded. Back in Thymine, treated water was such a precious resource that their ninety-second, spluttering showers were on timers.

Now up to her chest in the lake, Elise took a moment to gaze around her in the fading light. The wind dropped and the lake became still again. If it weren't for the squawks and splashing coming from farther down the shoreline, she could have imagined herself the only person in the world. Instead, she settled on picturing her small group of friends as the only people in existence. She had not seen another sign of human life since leaving Thymine. It was quite possible that they were the only travellers who had stopped here in hundreds of years.

With only her head above the water, Elise tentatively

pulled her feet up from the bed of the lake and promptly felt herself starting to sink. She snapped her legs back down again and gasped as she tried to stop her head from going under the water. How was Samuel staying afloat? She resolved to ask him about it another time. She wanted to know everything now that her world had opened up. She surreptitiously listened to all the queries the others directed at Samuel and his informative answers, uncomfortably aware that her friendship with him was unequal. She didn't want to be his student any longer. Tilting her head up to the sun, she enjoyed the contrasting temperatures.

She would always remember the first time she was encased in water.

Later that evening, Elise built a large campfire by the edge of the lake. Although she had been teaching the others, she was still the quickest at creating a flame using only the iron pyrite and flint.

'How long until we get to Uracil?' Georgina asked, spooning mashed parsnip into Bay's eagerly awaiting mouth.

It was only in the last day that the group had started to believe that they would actually make it safely to Uracil. Consequently, they had begun to tentatively discuss their arrival.

'Maybe late tomorrow if we leave at daybreak,' Samuel responded.

'And you haven't been there since you were eighteen?'

'Nearly seven years now.'

Luca shook his head. 'I can't believe that all this time we thought there were only four bases, and now it turns out there's a fifth settlement hidden away that even the Potiors don't know about. Are there any other big revelations? Are you going to tell me that griffins really exist?'

'Griffins do not exist,' Samuel clarified, now at pains to clear up even the smallest of misconceptions after Luca had spent three days looking out for the Loch Ness monster.

'I hope the leaders of Uracil will let me stay; I just want somewhere safe to bring up Bay,' Georgina said, cradling her adopted daughter.

'She is not just yours,' Kit signed. 'She needs all of us. And I need her. We are the only two of our kind outside the bases.'

'I didn't mean it like that, Kit. I know she needs you just as much as me, more as she gets older,' Georgina said, smiling down at Bay, who made the sign for 'hungry' again with her tiny, cupped hand.

Elise glanced over at Kit, pleased that he had finally made his stance clear.

Dressed in Samuel's borrowed clothes, Kit did not appear to be that different to the rest of them. Elise thought he would only draw a few curious stares from anyone who encountered him; perhaps something about his unfamiliar features would hold their attention, but it was unlikely they would leap to the conclusion that he was a different species of human.

Kit was a lot shorter than Samuel, but that was an unfair comparison as Samuel was at least a foot taller than the rest of them. Elise and Kit were around the same height, but Kit weighed twice as much as her due to his densely packed muscles. He had a round, barrel chest and was one of the strongest men Elise had ever met.

Bay was also sturdily built, but as a female she was slightly less muscled. She had the same prominent brow bridge and wide features as Kit, but these were softened by her auburn hair, which Georgina had tied in a bow at the top of her head. It sprayed out and jiggled when she moved; Elise always thought it made her look like a pineapple.

The prominent lump of skull at the back of their heads, called the Occipital Bun, was more visible on Bay as her hair was thinner. Kit tied his long, straight hair with a leather strap at the base of his neck, which partially hid the differing shape of his skull. They both had light-coloured complexions and no more body hair than the rest of the group.

'What do you want to do when you get to Uracil?' Elise signed to Kit while saying the words at the same time so Georgina could understand her.

Kit fluently and eloquently expressed himself through sign language. Even though he could understand her spoken words, she knew he preferred it if she signed them at the same time. He had once told Elise he could read people's hands like their facial expressions, every gesture an additional indication of their meaning.

'I want to make sure Bay is safe. We didn't rescue her just to put her into another museum.'

'Then what?'

'Then I want to free as many of the Neanderthals from the other museums as I can.'

'If you want to go back to the bases, you're going to need some help,' Elise signed, fully aware of the consequences.

'Are you sure? What about your family, your brother? I thought you wanted to go back to Thymine as soon as possible for them, bring them to Uracil?'

Elise hadn't realised how much Kit had read her change of mood. She smiled at him; it was hard to keep anything from Kit. 'I do, and I will, but maybe we can rescue a member of your family on the way.'

Kit smiled at Elise in his own unique way, creasing the corners of his eyes until they disappeared and only slightly pulling up the edges of his mouth.

'I will come as well,' Samuel signed. 'It's the least I can do. But we can only extract one of them at a time. Leaving large gaps as well. If the Potiors find out what we are up to, they will come after us. We cannot risk Uracil being discovered. I will never let that happen.'

They all turned to look at Luca, who was spooning broth into his mouth.

He met each of their gazes. 'What? Course I'm coming. I'm not going to sit around listening to you all tell me about your latest, greatest adventure. Frack that.'

Kit scrunched his eyes and smacked Luca on the back, making the broth spill onto the ground.

'So, which base then?' Luca said, quickly spooning the soup into his mouth before he lost it again. 'I want to go to Adenine: "Guidance and Governance". I could see if I have any relatives left, find out why I was shipped over to Thymine as a baby.'

'I'm sorry, Luca, but it can't be Adenine,' Samuel said. 'As the capital of Zone 3, it would draw too much attention. We also have to aim for where one of the younger Neanderthals is held.' Samuel hunched forward. 'The older ones, well, they won't be in very good shape. Isolation like that doesn't play well on the mind.'

'Seventeen was fine until she got pregnant,' Luca said rather defensively. He'd looked after Thymine's other Neanderthal until she died in childbirth having Bay.

'Yes, but she had you and me. A lot of the other Companions and Collections Assistants are indifferent to the social needs of the Neanderthals.' Samuel sighed. 'It always seemed so obvious to me. If you put any human baby in a cage, told them their kind had previously been extinct, that they were now one of only a handful to be brought back, and gave them only one or two people for company, of course that baby would struggle to grow up without some sort of adjustment disorder. So, why do they think it's so very different for a Neanderthal?' Samuel glanced at Kit and hurriedly continued. 'I have always said that it's a credit to your strength of self that you have remained as you are.'

Kit nodded his acknowledgement.

'There are no Neanderthals left in Thymine and we can't risk going to Adenine. That only leaves Cytosine and Guanine,' Elise signed.

'Where is Twenty-Two?' Kit asked.

Twenty-Two was the twenty-second Neanderthal to be brought back through a process similar to cloning. In the museum, Kit had been named Twenty-One. Samuel had encouraged Kit to think of another name for himself to help with his sense of identity while living in near isolation.

'If I remember correctly,' Samuel said, 'Twenty-Two is a female. She was born only a few months after Kit, making her fourteen, and she is kept in Cytosine.'

Elise sat up. She had always been fascinated by the idea of visiting Cytosine: 'Ingenuity and Enlightenment'. It was the base that pushed the boundaries of scientific discovery. She used to wish she had been born there rather than Thymine, whose label was 'Purpose and Productivity', the essential, but stagnant, manufacturing base.

'Cytosine's south of Thymine, isn't it?' she asked.

'Yes, at the southernmost tip of Zone 3 and, consequently, the most isolated of all the bases,' Samuel responded.

'We should have gone there first, when we left Thymine. We have lost so much time,' Kit signed.

'We have to get Bay to safety. We can't risk her being recaptured,' Samuel said. 'We know Twenty-Two will be safe for the moment. Not free, but looked after. Let's just get to Uracil first, settle in there and then we'll decide on our next move.'

Elise smiled reassuringly at Kit. 'Try not to worry. I'm sure Twenty-Two is fine. The Neanderthal Project is important to the museums so we know she'll be cared for. And, anyway, we have to get through our arrival in Uracil first.'

TWO

T he next morning, they cleaned up the campsite twice as fast, making sure that there were no signs of their route that could be traced from Thymine. The threat of the Protection Department following them was always in their thoughts.

Setting off over the first of the hills, Elise thought about how much her brother would want to see Uracil. If only he knew of its existence. He would never be able to find her if she didn't think of a way to get to him. What if the Protection Department had expelled her family from Thymine? Where would they go?

She needed to distract herself from these circular thoughts.

'So, who lives in Uracil? Is it mainly Medius or Sapiens? No Potiors, I expect,' she asked Samuel.

'A mixture of Sapiens and Medius. Also a couple of Potiors, but not many. Some residents were born there and unbranded, like my mother. The people of Uracil don't live in a divided manner as they do in the bases. They try to teach that everyone is equal and encourage them to integrate, regardless of the genetic engineering they had access to. People learn quickly.'

Samuel glanced around at their group of two unenhanced Sapiens, two Medius and two Neanderthals.

'How long has Uracil been around?' Luca called out behind them.

'About fifty years now.'

'Do they use genetic engineering?' Elise asked.

'Yes, but it's limited to three traits, same as a Medius, and is open to everyone regardless of their circumstances.'

'So, your mum had genetic engineering?' Elise continued.

'Yes,' Samuel said, looking away. 'I think we're getting closer.'

'What other genetic traits were you given?' Luca asked Georgina, taking a moment to rest on the grassy incline. 'I know you were made to be "more aesthetically pleasing" and have a good memory, but what was the third?'

Georgina huffed and brushed her vivid, red hair out of her eyes. 'It was beyond ridiculous, as was the beauty. And that's already disappeared, thanks to this.' She pointed to the thick scar on her cheek.

'Tell me what "beyond ridiculous" is or I'll start guessing,' Luca said.

'Was it an enhanced ability to grow lengthy and robust toenails?' Elise said, stopping and turning around.

'How about the ability to raise your right eyebrow to an eye-wateringly high level?' Luca asked.

'Or the ability to feel mild annoyance ninety per cent of the time?' Samuel called out.

'Okay, no more guessing. I'll tell you.'

Georgina paused, unnecessarily fiddling with the straps

of the wrap she carried Bay in. They all stared at her in anticipation.

'Was it...?' Samuel said after a moment of silence.

'I said okay.' She raised her chin. 'It was strengthened tooth enamel.' Georgina looked around at their open mouths. 'I always said it was the choice of a half-baked drunk.'

'So, you're saying that your dad wanted you to have a thickened coating for your teeth?' Luca said. 'That's not the choice of a half-baked drunk. That's the choice of a someone glancing at the list of genetic enhancements, closing their eyes and pointing at one.'

'I know, I know. I think he associated good teeth with being a wealthy Medius. He thought the enamel would mean I could eat whatever I wanted and they would never get damaged.' Georgina shrugged. 'I've got no fillings, so it worked in that sense.'

Without waiting for a response, she strode off ahead and the four of them followed, trying not to laugh as they caught one another's eye.

'It's not her fault her dad was an idiot,' Elise said.

'No, of course not,' Samuel replied. 'And she does have nice teeth.'

Six hours later they had all, except Samuel, started to lag. His enhanced muscle strength meant that it took a lot to tire him; even though he had Bay strapped to him, he looked as serene as if he were taking a ten-minute stroll.

The light was fading fast and they picked up their pace, eager not to spend another night outdoors. Elise caught up with Samuel, used to the physical strain after years of her father's regimented exercise regimes. Samuel was standing at the top of the hill, Bay fast asleep, strapped to his back.

As Elise approached, she pulled her jacket tighter. The wind whipped around her head.

She took in the scenery and tried to imagine how it would have appeared two hundred years ago, before the Pandemic. 'It's hard to believe that all of this would've been pathways made of concrete and high-rise buildings.'

'No, not so much here,' Samuel said. He caught sight of her frown. 'I'm sorry. I know you're trying to learn everything and your rate of absorption is really quite remarkable.' He pushed his hand through his hair, a gesture she had become familiar with in the last few months. 'You are right that farther south it would have been covered in concrete, but this region was less developed. Settlements were sparse here, even two hundred years ago.'

In the final days of their seemingly endless trek across the length of Zone 3, Samuel had told her that all the idyllic scenes of forest, grasslands and moors had once been crisscrossed by lengthy, concrete strips. These were similar to the recycled, rubber pathways in Thymine Base but had been wide enough to carry millions of land vehicles. The strips of concrete had linked the thousands of settlements in Zone 3, some so built up that the concrete, metal panels and glass would shoot up to the sky. Elise had asked if these 'land vehicles' were like the small sailing boats that carried supplies around Zone 3; she had been secretly disappointed to hear they were much smaller and made from metal.

'Why didn't people want to live here?' Elise asked.

'I can only guess at their reasons. It used to be much colder up here two hundred years ago and most of the places to find work were farther south. But they certainly wanted to live here after the Pandemic. The rare survivors had fled the most built-up of the settlements and, terrified of reinfection, were drawn to the unpopulated wilderness.'

'So, where are the concrete pathways now?'

'When the Potiors took control, as you know, their attention turned to reversing the so-called wrongs of the Sapiens. Restoring the habitat to its natural order became one of their key projects.' Samuel glanced at Elise. 'A hundred years ago, thousands of Sapiens were sent out on work detail to dig up each concrete strip and tear down every Pre-Pandemic settlement. Whatever could be recycled or sold to the other Zones was sent off in sailboats. The rest was dumped onto a single island off the coast of Zone 3 called the Isle of Grey. It had a different name before the Pandemic; I forget what it was.'

They crested the top of the final hill in silence as Elise considered how much she knew of her real history. Everything they had taught her in school was designed to reinforce the wrongs the Sapiens had wrought. Her education had been presented from only one point of view.

'Well, there it is,' Samuel said. 'Uracil.'

Elise stared down at the vast, midnight-blue lake below. In the middle was an island so wide she thought it would take her more than an hour to walk from one end to the other. Probably longer, she reasoned, as there was a dense forest spread across half of the island's surface.

'It doesn't look like anyone lives there,' she said, while surveying the scenery and trying to locate any sign of human life. 'How many people are there supposed to be?'

'A few thousand,' Samuel responded.

'That can't be; there's no housing, no infrastructure, nothing.'

'Oh, there is; you just can't see it.'

Elise was about to ask more but was distracted by the others catching up with them, panting as they made the final climb.

'What? What are we staring at, Thanton?' Luca asked, bending over to rest his hands on his thighs. He flicked his head up again. 'Pretty, yes. But we've seen a lot of pretty in the last few weeks.'

'Apparently, that's Uracil,' Elise said, sweeping her arm out in front of her. 'A few thousand people live there, according to Samuel.'

'Are they underground?' Kit signed.

'Or underwater?' Georgina said, while checking on Bay.

Samuel shook his head, clearly enjoying the suspense.

'Come on, Samuel,' Luca said, trying to make Bay gurgle by booping her nose. 'You already know more than us about most things, but you're not normally smug about it.'

'Sorry, I know I shouldn't. I just admire the ingenuity,' Samuel said, clearly trying not to smile. 'There are small clearings dotted through the forest for the workshops and public buildings, but you can't see them. There are mirrors strapped into the tops of the trees and carefully angled so they reflect the other treetops. That way, it doesn't appear as if there are any breaks in the foliage surrounding them. I'll let you see their housing solution for yourself when we get there; I don't want to spoil the surprise.'

When they reached the edge of the lake, Georgina squinted at the progression of the sun. 'How do we get across? None of us can swim, apart from you, and even if it's shallow, it will take ages to wade through. I don't want to be in there with Bay when it gets dark.'

'Don't worry. They've thought of that too; we just have to find the right spot,' Samuel said.

He strode off, following the curve of the shoreline.

When they had been walking for thirty minutes and were nearly a quarter of the way round the lake, he stopped abruptly. 'I think it's here, if I remember correctly.'

He bent down, took his boots and socks off, and rolled up the bottom of his trousers. He then walked a couple of feet into the water. Instead of continuing farther in towards the island, he turned to his left and started splashing through the water around the edge of the lake.

'The beginning is around here somewhere. You should all take your boots and socks off too; you've only got one pair.'

He jabbed his foot out to the right.

Elise frowned at the water but bent to unlace her sturdy boots. She knew she had to keep forcing herself to break her beliefs or she might as well have stayed in Thymine.

As she unpicked the laces, a thought occurred to her. 'If we can drink the water, why did you make us carry litres of it out of Thymine?'

'We still needed water to drink and I didn't want to risk lighting a fire to boil any we found,' Samuel responded from farther down. 'At least treated water is safe to drink without boiling. It's why they put it in the streams in the pods, in case a Neanderthal accidentally falls in. The water's so full of chemicals no bacteria can survive to make anyone ill.'

He was advancing farther and farther down the shoreline, prodding the lakebed with his feet.

'Aha!' he exclaimed.

Elise watched wide-eyed as Samuel started walking towards the island. As he progressed towards it, he began rising gently, the surface of the water lapping at the tops of his feet.

He turned around. 'Come on then! It will be dark soon.'

Elise and Luca glanced at each other.

'It's new to us too,' Elise signed to Kit.

She looped around to follow Samuel, who looked as if he were hovering serenely on the surface of the water.

Clutching her boots, she tried not to wince at the chill of the lake. Unlike the one they had bathed in the day before, the water here was an inky grey and she suspected it was very deep.

When she walked towards Samuel, she too began to rise out of the lake, the platform beneath her feet concealed by the water.

Luca caught up with her, a big grin on his face. 'You can look smug this time, Samuel. This is bloody clever.'

Elise imagined how they appeared from afar, five figures advancing across the lake with the sun setting behind them. Each of them would appear to have mastered gravity, needing only to lightly touch the surface of the water to propel themselves forwards.

Once they reached the edge of the island, the platform descended down into the shoreline until they reached a sandbank. Samuel stopped at the first smattering of grass, unstrapped Bay, and wiped his feet to dry them before he put his socks and boots back on.

'You'd better take Bay,' he said to Georgina. 'They can be a bit abrupt until they've completed all the identity checks, so best I go first.' He rubbed his forehead. 'When you start down the path of sending out spies, you begin to worry about them coming in.'

It was nearly dark by the time they crossed the grass into the edge of the woodland. The noise of the lake lapping against the shoreline could no longer be heard and it was suddenly very quiet. The only sound was of boots stepping through the undergrowth as they moved farther through the trees. The light was fading fast and Elise knew they wouldn't be able to see their way soon.

'*Gah!*' Georgina shouted out as a figure dropped down next to her.

Elise whipped around at the sound of a loud, zipping noise. Without thinking, she hit out with her broken hand at the figure that landed by her side. It jerked backwards, narrowly avoiding her arm. She realised it was for the best; the impact would have damaged her hand more than she would have hurt them.

With a similar zipping noise, twenty more figures zoomed down from the treetops on ropes.

Elise reached for her sling but stopped once she heard Samuel's voice.

'It's all right. I am Samuel Adair, son of Vance, brother of Faye. I'm a few months early and I've brought some friends. But I'm sure all the necessary checks will confirm our identities.'

Without acknowledging what Samuel had said, silent figures grabbed their arms on either side and began marching them deeper into the woods. Elise tried to catch the eye of the man and woman striding beside her, but neither of them turned their head to meet her gaze. Three extra escorts led the way, with another five bringing up the rear.

As if sensing his friends' panic, Samuel glanced back over his shoulder. 'Don't worry; this is normal. When we pass the checks, we will be given a better reception.'

'What happens if we don't pass the checks?' Georgina called out from the back. The figure to her left yanked at her arm.

'No talking,' one of the people at the front of the procession said gruffly, without turning around.

Elise could see a single weak light up ahead. She concentrated on it as the panic began to rise. There wouldn't be a problem with her check. She had been born in Thymine, as her parents had been and their parents too.

Generation after generation stretching back to when the bases were first formed one hundred and fifty years ago. The mark on her wrist confirmed she was a Sapien. She reassured herself she had nothing to worry about, but she still felt uneasy.

As they got closer, the single light illuminated a figure standing stiffly, hands clasped behind their back. Elise thought it was a man as she peered into the gloom, either that or a well-built, female Medius.

Not concentrating on where she was stepping, Elise's foot caught in a tree root and she nearly fell. It was only the guard next to her holding onto her elbow that kept her upright. She turned to thank him but he didn't acknowledge her, instead increasing his grip on her arm.

'Found them advancing through the forest on the north side, sir,' one of the men at the front reported. 'Says he's Vance's son—'

'We were hardly "advancing",' Samuel interjected.

The figure stared at Samuel. 'I don't recognise him. Might be the beard.'

Samuel and Luca had been unable to shave, travelling as they had been for the past three weeks. Kit didn't need to shave yet as he was only fourteen, although his physique made him appear as if he were in his early twenties. Luca had a little patchy hair but Samuel had a full beard that reached up to his cheekbones. Elise thought it made him look much older than her and she hoped he would soon shave it off.

Samuel responded by rolling up his sleeve and angling his arm at the person manning the checkpoint. Instead of just reading the distinctive tattoo on his arm, 'Samuel Adair, 20 May 2244, Adenine Base, Medius', the man unfolded his screen and held it up to the tattoo.

After taking a reading, he scrolled down the screen, occasionally pressing his lips together. 'Reads as genuine. Don't run off, though; the Tri-Council will have a few questions for you.' He stared at Elise and the others. 'I thought you'd be coming alone.'

'I had to bring them with me. I'll explain everything to the Tri-Council as soon as I see them.'

The man ignored Samuel and gestured at Georgina to come closer.

'You know I'm a lottery baby, right? And that won't be a problem?' Georgina said, clutching Bay to her.

The guard gave no response and she reluctantly held out her arm to him.

He swiped the screen over her wrist and paused to review the information. 'She's fine too. Her brother's on the Commidorant List, so we'll have to speak to her about that later.'

'The what list?' Georgina said, glancing around. 'I can ex—'

'Not now, Georgina,' Samuel said abruptly. 'Just let them do the checks for the moment.'

Elise was next.

She fixed on her passive mask to shield her thoughts as she held out her wrist. Her fixed features did not allow any of the panic she was feeling to surface. The guard might as well have been scanning the items she wanted to purchase at the emporium.

After scanning her wrist, the guard scrolled through his screen. Elise busied herself rolling down her sleeve and took her time doing up the button on the cuff.

The guard nodded towards Kit. 'Next.'

Elise walked towards Georgina, who looped her arm through hers. The two young women huddled together for warmth as they waited. Elise didn't like that the man hadn't confirmed whether she had passed their checks. Still, she did not allow herself to appear uneasy. She concentrated on Kit.

Samuel moved towards the guards. 'He has no markings; he is a different species of human, a Neanderthal. You know they don't stamp them. I will go straight to the Tri-Council and explain. The baby with Georgina is also a Neanderthal.'

The guard took a step back before recovering. He stared at Kit's bent head. 'Pull the hood down then.'

Kit carefully pulled the hood away from his face and raised his head.

A few of the other guards moved around so that they could see him as well. One of them absentmindedly touched his own brow. Kit looked at each of their faces in turn, giving them his impassive stare.

Unlooping her arm from Georgina's, Elise moved towards him. 'He was in Thymine's Museum of Evolution. I was his Companion. We had to lea—'

'Stand back,' one of the guards said, only briefly glancing at Elise.

'I will take him and the baby straight to Vance,' Samuel repeated. 'He will want to meet them. Uracil has never had the opportunity to house Neanderthals before.'

'Vance left two years—' one guard said before abruptly closing his mouth.

Samuel tipped his head to the side. 'Faye, then. Take me to Faye. She'll help me get an audience with the Tri-Council.'

'Faye's now part of the Tri-Council.'

'Oh,' said Samuel, frowning but quickly recovering. 'Well, take me to Faye then.'

The guards stepped closer to Kit, each reacting in their individual way to this anomaly in their working day. They wore a range of expressions, from intrigue to fear to disgust.

'Isn't it my turn now?' Luca said, rolling up his sleeve. He held his arm right underneath the checkpoint guard's chin.

The guards glanced at each other; clearly, no one wanted to speak first and make a decision about what to do with Kit.

'Well, if you don't need to scan me,' Luca said, beginning to roll down his sleeve. 'I'll just go through then, shall I?'

'Oh no, you won't,' the checkpoint guard said, recovering. 'You'll all go over to the Tri-Council straightaway. Under escort.'

The guard scanned Luca's arm. Elise was barely paying any attention, slowly edging her way towards Kit.

'Except you,' the guard said.

Elise's head snapped around.

'You'll have to come with us,' the guard said, taking hold of Luca's arm. 'Your information doesn't match your markings.'

THREE

At the sound of the metal bars being pulled back, Twenty-Two automatically reached for her Companion's hand and clasped it tightly, trying to calm her. Sitting cross-legged with her back to the steel door, she did not move away or turn around.

She had learnt, after many weeks, that it was better not to engage. They didn't want to answer her questions and they couldn't understand her anyway. So, instead, she sat in silence with her linked hand hidden by the long blades of yellowed grass, listening for whether this was a delivery of food or something else.

For the first thirteen years, the packages of food and water had been delivered three times a day without failure. In the last year, since Marvalian had become leader of Cytosine's Museum of Evolution, the meals had become first irregular and then sporadic.

While she waited, Twenty-Two tried to ignore the clawing sense of panic that was spreading through her chest. It was so sharp that it made her breath catch in her throat. It had been two days since anyone had delivered food and she didn't know how much longer they could wait. To distract herself, she surveyed the once lush, green meadow that was now dried beyond repair. The flowers had long gone but she thought the hardier evergreens in the corner would survive a little while longer. The ivy that had covered the steel walls had wilted and then died, the only trace left of it was the sandy pattern that stubbornly remained. She knew it wouldn't be long before her home was a dried-out shell, full of scratchy leaves and dust, surrounded by thick, steel walls.

She stared up at the glass ceiling, high above their heads, so that she could tell what time it was. The sun was half way across its morning travels. That meant their visitor could be bringing a delivery of food, but it was a little earlier than usual. The thin rays failed to pierce the collection of leaves and mulch that had settled in the corners of the once transparent skylight. These corners of darkness were slowly advancing towards the centre where they would eventually meet. Along with the sprinklers that no longer came on at night, no one had cleaned her only glimpse into the outside world in the past three months and the pod was becoming darker every day.

The heavy door swung open, bending and snapping the dried grass on its way. Twenty-Two froze. She gave the small hand curled inside of hers two quick squeezes for reassurance while she listened intently.

Sometimes they remembered her and brought food and water. Sometimes she despaired that they would never come again. They certainly didn't want to see her, or listen to her silent pleadings. She had learnt this made them uncomfortable after they had withdrawn a few times, taking their trays of nourishment with them.

Twenty-Two tensed at the sound of a tray sliding across

the grass. She was perfectly still until she heard the door slam closed behind the giver of unknown gifts. Counting under her breath, one of the many things Dara had taught her in the idle hours, Twenty-Two waited a full sixty seconds before she gently released the hand and went over to inspect the delivery.

Her feet crunching through the dried grass, she scrunched her eyes in delight when she saw the jug and silver food containers. She broke into a little run. Her stomach growled, reminding her that she hadn't eaten for two days, and her usually dry mouth suddenly moistened with anticipation.

Trotting over, she began to slow. Something wasn't right. She peered again at the glass jug; she couldn't see the line of water.

It had to be empty.

Dara had explained to her once what it was like to cry, to be able to show how strongly you felt about something when no words could express what you were going through. Dara said that after the last couple of tears had dripped down her cheek, she would often hiccup and she would always feel a bit better afterwards. As if she had ended a chapter and could now face a new one. Twenty-Two didn't ask whether it was the hiccups or the tears that made Dara feel better; she saved her questions for more important matters.

Twenty-Two stared down at the empty jug and aluminium containers holding only chicken bones for a moment before squeezing her eyes shut and willing the water to trickle down her cheeks, as she had seen on Dara's face so many times. But nothing happened. She'd known it wouldn't; it wasn't anatomically possible. Tears could not be formed without tears ducts and she did not have them.

None of the Neanderthals did, unlike Dara and all the other Sapiens.

Twenty-Two coughed loudly a few times and tried to sneeze, but it didn't make her feel any better. There was no chapter change for her.

'Nothing for you today, Ned!' one of them called through the door. 'You were too close last time; we told you fifty feet minimum.'

Turning her back on them, she walked over to Dara, unwilling to ask her how far fifty feet was. Instead, she would make sure they stayed on the other side of the stream for all of tomorrow.

'Come on, hurry up. I'm starving over here,' Dara called out, shuffling around to face Twenty-Two.

'There was nothing. A new rule, I think,' Twenty-Two signed.

When Twenty-Two was growing up, Dara would communicate with her using sign language, but in the last year her arthritis had gotten so bad it hurt to try and twist and pull her hands around. Not that it mattered; Twenty-Two could understand her voice perfectly well. It was making the same sounds as her that she struggled with.

Dara's mouth turned white as she pinched her lips together and glared at the door. 'It was never like this in Mister Fintorian's day. Was a respectable position, being a Companion. Now they treat me like I'm one of those animals out there.'

Dara wiped her nose with the back of her hand and Twenty-Two watched as the tears began to roll, catching in the lines and funnelling across her cheeks to the bat-like ears pushing through her thin, silver hair.

'Worse even than them,' Dara continued. 'At least they get fed!'

Twenty-Two bent down and gently picked up her Companion, all knobbly knees and elbows, and held her to her chest. Wrapping her arms around Twenty-Two's once thickly muscled neck, Dara buried her head in Twenty-Two's soft tunic and openly wept.

Twenty-Two frowned. Dara had become lighter in the last few weeks. Despite her own lack of nourishment, Twenty-Two easily carried her through the meadow, past the wilting ferns and fruitless brambles, her strong arms cradling the gently hiccupping woman to her chest.

She hopped across the stepping-stones, over the flowing stream that cut the landscape of the pod in two. Her short, sturdy legs pushed her up the bank of the river into the sheltered sleeping area. She stopped for a moment to sniff the air. The strong smell of the pine needles blanketing the ground had the comforting effect she had hoped for.

Kneeling down, she carefully laid Dara on her sleeping mat. Twenty-Two then quickly pulled off her tear-soaked tunic and replaced it with a clean one. The last fresh one she had. Tugging the acorn-brown cloth over her legs, she kneeled next to Dara and tried to ignore the pine needles jabbing into her smooth shins.

Her hands now free, Twenty-Two signed, 'You can always leave. There's no rule that you have to stay.'

Pulling her hands out from under the covers, Dara gestured at Twenty-Two to take them in hers to warm them up. Her face relaxed as the heat transferred across the gnarled joints and a small smile crossed Dara's face.

'We've talked about this before. I'm not going nowhere whilst I'm still a Companion. I told Mister Fintorian on the day he left for Thymine Base that I would be a Companion until the day I died. And a promise is a promise. Been one for the last thirty years, oldest one and longest serving. Well, except for that dolt in Adenine. But he only started the week before me. Not my fault Adenine started hiring Companions before Cytosine.' Dara turned her head away as she muttered, 'One week, I give you, missed my name being known by every base by one week...'

'Perhaps you could go out and get us something to eat and—'

'In my state! Are you trying to kill me? I'm not going out there, I wouldn't make it to the end of the corridor without keeling over.'

Twenty-Two had asked Dara nearly every day if she could leave the pod to try and find food or someone to help them. But Dara steadfastly refused. Ever since her fall six months ago, she had clung to the pod; Twenty-Two had begun to suspect that she had grown afraid of the outside.

Trying to distract Dara, Twenty-Two signed, 'Tell me about Mister Fintorian again.' She said the name 'Fintorian' aloud, as she tried to do with all names, but she struggled linking the four syllables together.

She remembered Fintorian perfectly well but she liked it when Dara talked about him. Twenty-Two scrunched her eyes as she thought about him, the previous museum direc-tor. He towered above her, above everyone, but he always crouched down when he spoke to her so that they were the same height. He had been her favourite, alongside the Dara she had known before her fall.

A wistful look settled on Dara's face. 'He is the finest, most excellent man that ever lived. The best museum director as well. Not a bad word had anyone to say about him in Cytosine. A Potior, of course, but would talk to anyone. Would always have little discussions with me whenever he came to check on how you was progressing.'

Dara's brow furrowed and a small mole in the middle of her forehead disappeared into a deep crevice before popping out again. 'Paid more attention to you than was due maybe. Not that you'd notice when you was little. Always had a particular interest in the Neanderthals, he did. That's why he left us to become director of Thymine's Museum of Evolution. Bloody silver-nosed, we-live-in-a-perfect-valley Thymine had a female that was turning sixteen and he didn't want to wait for you.' Dara glared at Twenty-Two. 'Always been behind, you have.'

Twenty-Two stared across the pod, trying to ignore the words that hurt her more than anything else. It was her fault Fintorian had left them and gone to Thymine. It was when he left that the museum had stopped being interested in her, stopped caring for her.

Pulling her hands away, Dara turned and looked up at Twenty-Two, her milky eyes peering out under the folds of her fallen eyelids. 'Anyway, I can't leave because you've got to have someone with you. Can't be by yourself in here or you'll get suicidal like the others did. That's what us Companions do; we keep you going so you don't get depressed and drown yourselves. Like the first seven did.'

Dara smiled with pleasure at being able to remember one of the rules. Since her fall, she had struggled to recall most of them, and Twenty-Two had found she could now freely ask questions about previously banned topics.

Twenty-Two did not want to think about the first seven of her predecessors who had killed themselves. 'Can I show you the letters again and how they link up?'

She reached for her favourite drawing stick. She was determined that she would learn as much as she could over the coming months to make up for her previous failures. She didn't want to be behind. The long stick felt smooth in her hands and the pad of her thumb nestled into one of its curves, as if it had been shaped for her.

'Oh, go on. But hand me the last of the water first.'

Dara sighed and leant up on her elbow to accept the cup. She slurped it down as she watched Twenty-Two draw the letters of the alphabet into the pine needles and then spell Dara's name followed by 'Companion' and then 'carer'.

'You're getting much better,' Dara said grudgingly, holding the cup out for Twenty-Two to take from her trembling hand. 'Try a new one. How about "pony"?'

Twenty-Two sat back on her haunches. She tried to select the right letters in her mind before committing them to pine needles.

Taking the stick, she scratched out: 'P-O-N-E-Y'.

'No, no, no! There's no "e", girl. When a word ends with an "ee" noise, it's usually just a "y". Try again.'

Warming up to her role, Dara took the drawing stick from Twenty-Two, smartly rapped her on the knuckles and then held it out again for her to take back.

Twenty-Two sighed at all these little, illogical rules. She wished for the hundredth time that everything were spelt the same as it sounded. She carried on practising other words until she heard little grunts coming from her now exhausted teacher. After pulling the blankets farther up to Dara's chin, Twenty-Two stood and watched her Companion to check that she was fast asleep.

The sunlight was fading and it would soon be pitch black. There was no moon tonight. She crossed the pod in double-quick time, leaping effortlessly across the stepping-stones. When she reached the pod door, she stopped at the jug that was still defiantly sitting on the tray. Looking down, her mouth dried and her stomach rumbled again, thirst and hunger wrapped in one nagging pang.

She made her decision. If they cared so little about her, then she was going to break their rules.

Scooping up the jug by the handle, she tested its weight. It could be used as a weapon, but for the moment she had a more innocuous plan. Trotting over to the stream, she followed it down to where it ended in a small pool. In one of Dara's less cautious moments, she had told Twenty-Two that real streams in the outside world normally ended in the sea or a lake, but the pod that she occupied was entirely man made so the pool was where the water collected. Here it waited to be pumped underground back to the top of the stream where it would make its journey once more.

Twenty-Two took a moment to catch her reflection in the pond. It was the only time she could ever study her features.

She knew she was different to Dara, a different type of human, but no one had explained much more to her when she was younger. It wasn't until she turned eight that she realised that there was something very different about her existence. Why couldn't she follow Fintorian outside? Where did Dara go when she left her one afternoon a week?

Twenty-Two had begun to question Dara, who always evaded answering by distracting her with a new game or pastime. Dara would set them little missions to complete together: ten pots to be whittled in twenty days, two rolls of animal skins to be cured and prepared in the next three weeks. There was always some new order to fill.

That was the old Dara, though, the one who would laugh and dance with her, despite her aches and pains. That Dara had gone.

It was only in the last few months, since her fall, that

Dara had started answering Twenty-Two's questions unchecked. She had found out that the Neanderthals were a species of human that had died out around 30,000 years ago. She had been brought back through the benevolence of the Potiors, to correct the wrongs of Dara's species, the Sapiens. The Potiors kept her safe in Cytosine's Museum of Evolution. Twenty-Two was told that she was ungrateful when she appeared saddened or confused by the answers. Instead, Dara told her she should think about how lucky she was to have been brought back at all—hardly any other Neanderthals had been given the same second chance.

Kneeling over the silvered surface of the pool, Twenty-Two watched her image gently ripple. She touched her strong brow bridge. It felt hard and she traced her fingers to her wide nose and mouth. She stopped at her chin, which barely made an appearance and certainly didn't protrude like Dara's sharp, little point.

Twenty-Two knew she must be ugly; she was different to everyone she had ever met. There was nothing graceful about overhanging eyebrows or a wide mouth. Her skin was normally smooth and light-coloured, like a peach, but in the last few weeks it had lost its colour.

Twenty-Two pulled her hands through her normally thick, light-brown hair. Dara had always brushed it for her, using only her fingers, from when she was a little girl. A clump came away in Twenty-Two's hand. She carefully placed it on her knee and dropped her head as she studied it. She felt detached, as if it came from someone else. She knew her hair should not be thinning at the age of fourteen and she concluded that it was probably happening because she was slowly starving. The thought of food made her stomach knot and the pain made her gasp.

Dara had been Twenty-Two's Companion for as long as

she could remember and the first thing she had taught her was never to drink water from unknown sources. She was only allowed to drink the treated water that was delivered through the door and tasted so bitter it made her sneeze when she was a little girl.

She glanced around her. She knew no one was there but still felt the urge to check before tentatively dipping the jug into the stream. Holding the cold water up to her mouth, she prepared herself for her first taste of untreated water. She was so thirsty she didn't care if it killed her; she couldn't keep on giving all the treated water to Dara and go two, sometimes three, days without anything herself.

Tentatively, she swilled it around her mouth, ready to spit it out if needed, but it tasted exactly the same as the treated water. She allowed herself to swallow it and immediately her stomach demanded more. Gulping it down, she pulled the jug away from her lips. She suddenly felt sick. Her first thought was that it must be because it was untreated—the virus must be killing her. She couldn't believe how fast-acting it was. But after a few moments, she felt better and realised that it must be because her stomach was unused to so much content. She tried again, slower this time, until she emptied the jug.

She scrunched her eyes, her version of a smile, and thought to herself, *I'm a rule breaker now*.

Walking back to the sleeping area, she let her arms swing by her sides. She felt better than she had done in weeks now that she had sated her thirst. The pod was nearly completely dark, but she would know the way even with her eyes closed, never having left its confines.

Twenty-Two, The Rule Breaker.

She liked the sound of it and she allowed herself to add a little skip to her step. Just one, though; now was not the time for frolicking, as Dara called it. She had more important things to consider.

As Twenty-Two lay on her sleeping mat, she thought about the rules and how she could break them. Now that she had been taught the letters and how to put them together, she had started making lists of words in her mind that she could always pull back and read again if she needed them. She hadn't told Dara about this. She guessed that Dara would only say that it was another example of her being behind and that everyone could do that from when they were four.

She liked her lists, no matter how basic they might be. They meant that once she had learnt how to spell something correctly and written it down in her mind, she never forgot it again.

In her head, she sketched out the original rules and scrolled down the list, making corrections on the way:

1. Never drink the water ✓
2. Never ask about who she was and where she came from ✓
3. Never ask about the other Neanderthals
4. No biting, kicking, punching, scratching or harming of others
5. Never eat anything unless it came in the steel boxes from outside
6. Never ask about outside ✓
7. Never go outside

Ticking off the list in her head, she realised that she had broken three of the seven rules in the past few months.

Four more to go.

FOUR

'No, no, that can't be right. Check again,' Elise said. 'Luca's from Adenine; his surname's Addison. He has no parents. Came from there when he was young. He doesn't remember the journey.'

Elise desperately tried to remember everything Luca had told her about himself, which she realised was actually very little.

Luca opened his mouth to respond, but whatever he had been going to say was muffled by the hessian sack that was placed over his head by one of the guards.

'Please, no, there's been a mistake,' Elise said, taking a step forward.

'Luca was just a baby when he was brought over from Adenine. I've known him for the last three years,' Georgina said, clutching Bay to her side and joining Elise.

Kit reached out to try and pull the sack off Luca's head. Luca jerked his arms away from the guards. His captors curled their fists and their black, skin-tight gloves began to glow and pulse with a midnight-blue light. One of the guards caught hold of Luca and glared at the group; his gloves switched to an amber shade.

Elise took a step back. 'What's happening?' She stared at the guard's hands. 'Is it just for effect or do they do something?'

'It's definitely not for effect,' Samuel said, holding up his own gloveless hands in front of him.

The others copied the gesture, except for Luca, who was no longer able to move now there were four guards holding onto him.

'This will be resolved once we understand the exact discrepancies relating to Luca's information. It has to be a mistake. He's no spy.' Samuel met the gaze of each of the guards. 'I would never bring a spy with me.'

No one moved. The light from the guards' gloves began to fade away.

'I think we had better go straight to Faye, before this goes any further,' Samuel said to the checkpoint guard, who nodded in agreement. 'Perhaps we can bring Luca with us. I think the Tri-Council would want to know straightaway if we have an intruder.'

'I think they'll also want to know why you brought back half of Thymine Base with you,' the checkpoint guard responded.

After walking through the forest for another twenty minutes, they began to see signs of habitation. Up above, in the treetops, rope bridges stretched across their heads. The occasional octagonal boardwalk circled some of the thicker trunks.

Elise tried to reassure herself that the escort was normal and they just wanted to confirm whom Samuel had brought back with him. To distract herself, she tried to recall what else she knew about Luca, but she kept on drawing a blank.

She shook her head. Maybe Luca hadn't told her about himself because he didn't know much about his own past. She felt uneasy, glancing around at her companions. How much did they really know about each other?

She still hadn't told Luca that, for years, her father had relentlessly trained her in self-defence, which had increased her reaction time and helped with her perfect aim with the sling; only Samuel knew this about her. Only Samuel had she trusted with all her secrets. It was quite possible that Luca had hidden things from her in return.

A few faces in the trees above peered down at the procession. Most people were dressed in loose swathes of cloth that were wrapped around their shoulders and nipped in at the waist with ties, hanging loosely below their knees.

The observers above began following the trail of guards over the rope bridges and through the branches, knocking at their neighbours' doors on the way. By the time the procession on the ground reached a large clearing, several hundred people were filed around the edge of the circle. Those still in the trees allowed their legs to dangle from the branches as they took their seats. A few of them unwrapped packages of food; they looked as though they were settling in for the evening's entertainment.

Although the sawdust-covered ground was cleared of all trees, it was only partially open to the sky. Attached to the rigging high above their heads were long strips of reflective glass, each angled independently of one another. Through the criss-crossed strips of mirror came a waning moonlight that bounced around the reflective surfaces placed on the tree trunks. This tripled the light in the area and complimented the soft glow produced by the solar lanterns strung amongst the branches. In other circumstances, the setting would have enchanted Elise, but she was too unsure of what to expect to allow herself to relax.

The guards led them into the centre of the circle. Once the visitors were standing in a line, they melted into the crowds surrounding the clearing, taking Luca with them.

Elise tried to conceal her worry. She stood awkwardly between Kit and Georgina, waiting for what was going to happen next. She felt uncomfortable with so many eyes on her and tried to ignore them. Instead, she stared at the three tree stumps in front of them. Each one was still rooted in the ground and together they naturally formed a gently curved semi-circle.

Without any announcement, two men emerged from either side of the circle and silently made their way to the two outside tree stumps. Tucking their voluminously layered garments underneath them, they sat down. They looked like the archetypal Sapien and Medius from a children's textbook.

The Sapien was short, slightly overweight, with a double chin and thinning hair. Elise guessed that he was in his seventies, but he had an air of confidence she had rarely seen in a Sapien in Thymine. The Medius sitting on the other side appeared to be much younger, but Elise knew this could be the result of high-grade genetic engineering that slowed the visible ageing process. He was as tall as Samuel and had a muscled torso with a nipped-in waist. His features were strong and perfectly proportioned. He managed to appear effortlessly attractive, although Elise knew this was usually aided by a great deal of preparation. The only Medius she had met who wasn't interested in their appearance was Samuel.

Samuel took a step forward from the line and spoke loudly so that the gathered crowd could hear him.

'Flynn,' he said, nodding towards the Sapien, 'and Raul,' he continued, addressing the Medius. 'I am pleased to return and see that Uracil is thriving. I have brought some friends with me whom I hope you will be interested in receiving.'

Elise wasn't sure why their names only had one syllable; she had never met anyone besides Kit and Bay with a one-syllable name before. Kit and Bay struggled to link syllables together when they did try to speak, so Samuel had thought it best if they had names they could pronounce. Names were strictly controlled in the bases; Sapien first names had two syllables, Medius three and Potior four. It meant that a person's place in society could easily be deciphered if there were ever any question over how obvious their genetic enhancements were.

'Yes, we heard that you brought quite the troop with you,' Raul said, his gaze darting over each one of them in turn. 'Introductions, please. Quick, quick.'

Raul smiled around at the crowd in a knowing way and there were a few chuckles.

Standing, he took a step towards Samuel and clasped his hand between both his own. Samuel whipped his hand away and placed it behind his back. Elise winced as Samuel apologised, his face reddening.

'No need, Samuel. I had simply forgotten about your... preferences when it comes to greeting. Now, to your companions.'

Raul turned away from him.

Samuel touched his forehead. When he spoke, it was clear that he was trying to recover from his inappropriate reaction. 'Firstly, let me introduce Georgina. She is a skilled nurse and adopted mother of Bay, who is a Neanderthal.'

Samuel gestured at Georgina to come towards him. She

glanced nervously back at Elise and then stepped forward. She performed an awkward half curtsy and blushed when Raul smiled across at her in response.

'You are very welcome here, Georgina. We always need skilled medics,' he said, walking towards her. He tickled Bay underneath the chin. 'And this must be Bay?'

'Yes, that's right,' Georgina said, staring up at him. 'She has been freed from Thymine's Museum of Evolution.'

'Well, I am delighted to make your acquaintance, Bay,' Raul said, his gaze now sliding over to Kit. 'And you must be the other Neanderthal.'

Kit nodded.

Flynn pushed himself to his feet and joined Raul. 'You are very welcome, Georgina; we have much to talk about later, including your brother. And, also, what Thymine might do to recover two such unique individuals.' He looked pointedly at Kit and Bay.

Before Georgina had time to react, Flynn clasped her hand in his and pulled her to the edge of the circle, parading her before the audience.

'Enhanced or unenhanced, we welcome all to Uracil. What better way to display this than this Medius lottery baby and Neanderthal girl? In Uracil, they are washed clean of these titles and will be known simply as Georgina and Bay.'

The crowd cheered and a few people reached out to pat Bay. Georgina smiled back at them nervously.

Flynn led Georgina and Bay back to Raul, who was still clapping.

'And we are privileged to have Kit visit us as well,' Flynn said loudly, addressing the crowd. 'I hear that he is quite skilled in combat. To have survived all those years in near isolation, he must have the resilience of the stars themselves.'

Flynn's gaze swept across the crowd, seemingly waiting for their agreement. There was a rumbling noise as they gave it.

'We have much to learn from him. His species existed thousands of years longer than we have,' Flynn continued, adeptly taking the crowd with him on a journey into the past. 'Kit can rest assured that, in Uracil, he will be as free as he was 400,000 years ago.'

The crowd clapped wildly and a few whistles circled the clearing. Kit kept his face still, but nodded his acknowledgement.

'And who is this, Samuel?' Raul said, stepping towards Elise.

'This is Elise,' Samuel said. 'She is brave, loyal and resourceful. She is the one who believed that it was possible to help Kit escape. If it weren't for her, we wouldn't be here.'

Elise blushed and dropped her head, inspecting the sawdust covering her boots. But she couldn't just stare at her feet while all those eyes were on her; that was the old Elise, whose natural instinct had been to fade into the background.

She raised her head and took a step towards Raul and Flynn. Taking each of their hands in turn, she clasped them between hers, hoping that, in some small way, this would make up for Samuel's inability to have physical contact with them.

'Thank you for letting us into your home,' she said. 'I'd like to talk about our other friend, Luca. He was taken away in that direction.'

Elise peered into the crowd but couldn't see Luca's hessian-covered head anywhere.

'Do not be concerned, Elise,' Raul said softly, squeezing her hand. 'They have taken him to Faye, who has temporarily replaced Samuel's father on the Tri-Council.'

Elise stared at Samuel, silently encouraging him to help her with Luca's predicament. Samuel just gave a small shake of his head in response.

Raul began to walk around the edge of the circle, making sure that his voice could reach even those in the highest of branches. 'Thanks be to all of you for taking the time to witness this arrival. For we all know that if an act is not witnessed, it may as well have never occurred.'

Raul waved at the people as they began to disperse. 'Our guests will be tired, but I am sure that you will have the opportunity to meet them over the next few days.'

A few voices moaned. One or two of Uracil's citizens had hesitantly come closer but the last of Raul's words had them turn away.

'I will take them to the visitors' quarters,' Samuel said to Flynn and Raul.

They both nodded their agreement.

'Where did they take Luca?' Kit signed, as Samuel led them towards a narrow staircase that spiralled up the outside of one of the sturdier tree trunks.

'They took him to my sister,' Samuel signed. 'There is something wrong with his tattoo; it doesn't match up to the information they have about him on the system.'

'You don't believe he's a spy, do you?' Elise signed, pleased that they could have a relatively private conversation between themselves.

'No, of course not, but we need to hear what is on his records; their scanners are infallible,' Samuel responded.

'Luca does not lie about himself,' Kit signed.

Elise knew that Kit must be right. He was adept at reading people's body language.

Samuel did not respond. He led them up the tightly spiralled walkway that wrapped its way around the tree trunk; it was so wide that two people could comfortably pass each other. As Elise followed Samuel, she caught sight of a colony of ants also circling the bark around the trunk.

When she got to the top, she stood waiting for the others on an octagonal ledge that ran around the trunk of the oak tree. It was made from thick planks of wood and felt sturdy; there was even a rail around the edge to help prevent falls.

'You could stay up here for days if you wanted to,' Samuel said. 'Nearly everything you could ever need is above ground level.'

Elise looked around her while she waited for Georgina and Kit, who had stopped to lift Bay out of her sling. They were forty feet in the air. Swaying rope bridges, wide, wooden platforms and zip lines skirted off in every direction. Most of the trees held their own individually designed, wooden home. Some had constantly revolving wheels on the side, she guessed to generate electricity. Others had long, spindly arms shooting out through the roofs with solar panels at the end to catch the sunlight. One house was entirely covered in a multitude of knitted and crocheted panels that served as decorative insulation.

Elise smiled to herself; compared to the regimented housing back in Thymine, it appeared that if people could dream it, they were allowed to build it in Uracil.

Once Kit and Georgina joined them, Samuel led the way around the platforms and rope bridges, sometimes doubling back and apologising for not remembering the way.

'They really should get signs...' he muttered after his third mistake.

Everyone who passed them bowed at the group, sometimes addressing Samuel as 'son of Vance'.

'So, Samuel, are you some sort of prince in Uracil? And why didn't you tell us you had a sister?' Elise eventually blurted out, feeling more and more uneasy as increasing numbers of passers-by greeted them in this way.

'What? No, of course not. My father happens to be one of the three Elders, along with Raul and Flynn. But that is all. There are no hereditary titles in Uracil. They're only stopping to greet me because they want to stare at you three.'

'If there are no hereditary titles, why has you sister taken his place?' Georgina asked.

'I'm sure it's just a brief interim measure.'

Elise wasn't convinced.

'Why is it always "son of Vance" with people with a significant heritage?' Georgina whispered to Elise. 'Why do they change the order around like that, all pompous sounding?'

'Back in Thymine's Outer Circle, you'd be "Bob's son". Maybe "Bob's oldest son" if they could be bothered to remember your place in the family,' Elise whispered back in agreement.

'I like "son of Vance". It sounds significant,' Kit signed. 'If I have children, I shall call them "son of Kit".'

Elise laughed. 'Son of Kit sounds pretty significant.'

'Nearly there,' Samuel called out behind him. 'I can see them, three trees over in that direction.'

Elise hurried along. She was climbing across the final rope bridge when she spotted Luca seated on a stool, talking to someone hidden behind a tree trunk, his hessian sack now lying by his feet. When he caught sight of them, he waved them over.

'You all right?' Elise called out.

'Think so,' Luca called back. He grinned at them. 'Hey, Samuel! Why didn't you tell us your sister's a Potior?'

FIVE

Elise stopped in the middle of the rope bridge and turned to Samuel. 'Your sister's a Potior?'

She was struggling not to shout.

'Well not...not exactly,' Samuel stuttered. He ran his hands through his hair. 'She was born here, so she is not classed as anything. They don't have those classifications in Uracil. But our father is a Potior, so, yes, she looks like one.'

'*You lied to me.* Why didn't you tell me all this? After *everything* I told you about me?' Elise whispered, straining to keep her voice under control. The others had joined them now. 'What does this make you, Samuel? What are you?'

'Samuel, bring your friends around here and stop whispering in the trees,' a woman's voice called out from the other side of the tree trunk. 'You can explain yourself to your friend in my presence.'

Elise blushed. She had forgotten that Samuel had inherited a keen sense of hearing from his mother; his sister likely had the same abilities. She must have heard everything they said.

Pulling herself up, Elise fixed her expression so that her

thoughts were not visible and gestured at Samuel to keep on walking. She glared at his back.

When they passed Luca, Elise reached out to him and gave his shoulder a reassuring squeeze. For a brief second, she remembered her mother used to do the same to her.

Faye stood to greet each one of them in turn. She was seven feet tall, with tightly coiled hair that framed her ageless face. Not a mark or line marred the surface of her light, russet-brown skin. Even though she spoke animatedly, nothing was left behind when she finished speaking, no lines around the corners of her eyes or creases between her eyebrows. Her large eyes were streaked with gold and rested briefly on each of her guests, seemingly absorbing all the information she required about them before moving on.

She was dressed in layers of gauze that dripped and fell around her strong, lean limbs. When she moved between them, there was a tinkling noise from the gold chains that ran the length of her bare feet.

Elise blushed. Faye was only the second Potior she had met in person, the other being Fintorian, whom they had killed to escape Thymine—her experience with this species of human was limited to say the least.

Elise mentally shook herself and tried to maintain her composure as Faye moved up the line, stopping to speak with everyone. *She is not a different species; she is not better than me,* Elise repeated to herself. But after a lifetime of being told that's exactly what the Potiors were, Elise struggled to make her words ring true.

She watched as Faye effortlessly slipped into sign language when she spoke with Kit. Faye laughed at something Kit signed and he scrunched his eyes at her in return. Elise tried not to feel annoyed; it had taken weeks before Kit had scrunched his eyes at something she said.

'Samuel, it is so good to see you. I won't hug you; I know you wouldn't want that,' Faye said, stopping in front of her brother.

Samuel nodded his appreciation. 'It's good to see you too. There is much to catch up on. Is our father all right? Still making contact when he can?'

'Yes, of course. Such a worrier, Samuel. That hasn't changed as least. Seven years is too long not to see a brother, especially when so many changes have taken place. I feel as if I have to get to know you all over again. I hope to persuade you to stay by my side before your next assignment. But we will speak of this later. I still have one more to meet.'

Elise smiled up at Faye, who matched her smile with the same intensity and warmth that Fintorian had always displayed. Elise was cautious, though; in her experience, Potiors easily secured the trust of others. She didn't want to be fooled again. Perhaps it was because they were so attractive, or naturally charming, but she did wonder if it was a mandatory genetic enhancement that the other species of human did not know about.

Whatever it was, Elise was determined not to be the same gibbering mess around Faye that she had been with Fintorian. She decided to take the lead.

'Samuel has kept us all safe these past weeks. Without him, we'd never have known of Uracil. I can imagine how much you must have missed him.'

'And you have brought Samuel home to us earlier than we had hoped.' Faye touched Elise's arm. 'It seems we have at least one thing in common. I look forward to discovering more.'

Elise returned Faye's smile even though she was unsure of her meaning.

'Luca, come here,' Faye called out, as if he were a naughty child she had been saddled with for years. 'We have much to discuss, starting with your markings which do not read true. And, also, whether or not I am a Potior.' She raised an eyebrow. 'Issues that are linked.'

Luca raised his eyebrows and stood to join his friends.

'Don't worry. I'm not going to tell you that you're my other long-lost brother,' Faye said, gesturing for him to come towards her. 'Please, all of you, do take a seat.'

Faye nodded at a multi-tiered bench attached to the tree trunk before pulling out a screen that she started to tap at.

Ten seats of differing tiers were formed out of the trunk. Elise went for a high one that was carved into the side and pulled herself up. She tucked her knees up to her chest and waved down at Bay, who was seated on Georgina's lap below her.

Luca stared at the floor as he addressed Faye. 'I don't know why my markings would be different to what it says in your system. My surname's Addison so I must have been born in Adenine, just as Elise's surname Thanton means she was born in Thymine. I am not a spy; I'm just a Companion who used to work in the Museum of Evolution. Leaving Thymine is the biggest event of my life. I'm not hiding anything.'

Faye paced up and down in front of the group while she scanned her screen. Her elfin-princess appearance was at odds with the reams of data she was scrolling through at a lightning pace.

'I believe you,' she said, glancing up. 'Your markings are incorrect but that doesn't mean you have misled your friends. It is you who have been misled. It happens more commonly than you would expect.'

They all watched Luca, who raised his head.

'You have been taught since infancy that Sapien, Medius and Potior are three separate species of human. That genetic engineering created these different species, but this isn't true. Like the treated water, it is another example of the methods used by the leaders of Zone 3 to control their citizens.'

'If we aren't separate species of human then what are we?' Georgina blurted out.

'We are just humans, with different levels of engineering,' Faye said. 'Medius with their three altered genes, Potiors with their ten and Sapiens like Elise and Luca with no enhancements. You cannot create a new species of human by just enhancing ten of the thousands of genes we have. But if you tell someone something from the time they are born and prevent them from having any sort of education, then it's not surprising that people believe the theatre that is presented to them.

'This brings me to the creation of Uracil. Fifty years ago, two young people were desperately in love but knew they would never be allowed to have any form of relationship other than a nominal friendship. As anyone who has been in love will know, friendship is no replacement for the hidden treasures that desire and adoration promise. These two people avoided each other whenever they could, terrified that they would exchange an accidental look that would give them away. They had never even experienced the simple pleasure of holding one another's hand when they decided they could bear it no longer and would run away together. They have been here for nearly fifty years and built our community into the thriving alternative it is now. We have much to thank Raul and Flynn for.'

Elise had not realised that Raul and Flynn were a couple. Since birth, Sapiens and Medius were kept away from each other; they went to different schools, lived in different circles. They would only ever meet in their workplace. Any form of relationship was strictly prohibited—it would unravel all that separated them if they were allowed to mingle and merge.

'Our father, Vance, was sent to track Raul and Flynn,' Faye continued. 'He was a formidable hunter and classified as a Potior.' Faye glanced over at Luca and smiled. 'He found them on this island, but before he took them captive he agreed to listen to Flynn plead their case. Unknown to Flynn, he too was disillusioned with the world he was living in. After listening to Flynn, he agreed to report that they had both died. In exchange, they offered to make him a co-leader once he was able to safely return. He reported their deaths and then volunteered to travel to Zone 1 on a mission that would take him away for many years. After making the official crossing, the Potiors did not know that, in the dead of night, our father swam back across the narrow sea. He was an expert tracker and knew how to move without giving himself away. Only travelling at night, he made his way back to Raul and Flynn and together they established Uracil.

'Over the years, others joined Uracil. A few friends and relatives of Raul and Flynn to begin with, then a few others who had been banished from the bases and stumbled across it. Finally, a project was set up to monitor and extract some people from the bases. People who were disillusioned and deemed to be suitable. All were strictly vetted before being allowed inside. You can only join our community if you can bring some sort of skill or are willing to learn one. And you must work unless you are physically unable to. Finally, you must also swear to protect Uracil. These rules have remained the same since the beginning.

'Our mother was born here to Medius and Sapien parents, and she had the three genetic alterations that people of her parentage are offered in Uracil. When she was in her early twenties, she began a relationship with Vance that resulted in first me and then my brother Samuel being born. Both of us inherited our genes from our parents with no additional traits bestowed upon us; it would have been too much alongside the chance of inheriting our parents' gifts as well.

'When I was five, our mother left Uracil to infiltrate Adenine. She had separated from our father and wanted to see the rest of Zone 3. She could pass as a Medius and slip back into the bases. I, on the other hand, was unable to blend in so well, so I was left behind to be cared for by Vance. It wasn't until she arrived in Adenine that she realised she was pregnant again—'

'Can I not tell my own history, Faye?' Samuel said, his cheeks colouring.

'Clearly, you cannot,' Faye retorted. 'It was essential that you remained silent about this in Thymine, but you have been travelling with your companions for three weeks and have failed to update them on your history. There are no secrets in Uracil and I need to know that they are aware of the truth.'

Samuel blushed and dipped his chin.

'Our mother continued to live in Adenine and decided to wait to see whether Samuel could pass as a Medius as she could, or if he looked more like a Potior. He grew to be more like our mother than our father and was allowed to remain with her.'

Elise stared at Samuel, but didn't want to catch his eye. Thankfully, he hadn't raised his head.

'For Samuel, being able to pass as Medius has meant

that he has been able to continue in our mother's footsteps and live in the bases, only occasionally visiting Uracil throughout the years. But there is no Sapien, Medius and Potior division here, as it does not exist; the lines are blurred through inheritance of enhancements and we have all met Sapiens that look like Medius and vice versa.

'Which brings me to you, Luca. Our scanners are incorruptible and show that you were not born in Adenine, but Guanine. You were then shipped to Thymine. You might want to know the rest in private.'

Elise watched Luca, waiting for his reaction.

'No, no, whatever it is you want to say, do it in front of them,' he said, gesturing to his friends. 'I want them to know. There should be no secrets in Uracil,' he finished, glaring at Samuel.

'If you are sure,' Faye said, only continuing when Luca nodded. 'The Potiors' ability to master genetic enhancements is not infallible. A human genome is read not in absolutes, but in likelihoods. It is a combination of several alterations on the genome and some outside environmental factors that gives the strongest chance of predictable change. However, it does not always work. There are many notes in the chord and if one is slightly out of place, the results can be unwanted. An unforeseen mutation, even a lack of the correct nutrition at birth, can unravel even the most basic of enhancements.'

'What are you saying?' Luca said, standing up.

'There are hundreds, maybe even a few thousand like you, Luca. You are not alone in this,' Faye said.

'Just tell me what you are saying!'

'I'm sorry,' Faye said, her voice softening. 'You were most likely meant to be a Medius with three genetic enhancements. But, for whatever reason, one or more of them did not come to fruition. Zone 3 has a policy of removing these children as babies and shipping them to another base where they are brought up unaware of their origins. This is confused further by stamping them with another base's mark—even if you happened to return to the base you were marked with, you would never find your people.'

'My people...I have people?'

'Most likely, yes.'

'I have to find them, tell them I'm okay,' Luca said, stumbling backwards.

'Luca, please, sit down,' Samuel said, rising and walking over to him. 'Maybe you should think about this for a bit and we can talk about it later.'

'What? No. I have to go now, go to them!' Luca said, glancing around him for the route down to the forest floor.

Samuel stood in front of Luca, his back concealing the walkway that Luca was looking for. 'I'm sorry I didn't tell you everything about me on the journey. That was wrong. I promise I was going to tell you when we got to Uracil. But please don't do this.' Samuel lowered his voice. 'They don't always, well, they don't...your parents haven't been brought up free of all those terms and separations. Some of them, they feel having a Sapien child is something...something to be ash—'

Luca went bright red. 'It's all right for you. You're fracking awash with genetic enhancements. You're dad's a bloody Potior, for stars' sake! *You've had to hide your enhancements to blend in!* No wonder you could fight Fintorian and live. I knew that wasn't right!'

Luca rubbed his eye with the back of his hand. Elise ran over to him, Kit on her heels.

'No, no. I don't want to speak to any of you right now. I can't do this.' Luca looked around desperately for a way out.

'Let me take you to your tree house. Then I'll leave you alone, I promise,' Samuel said.

'Only if you promise not to say a word about this on the way. I don't want to talk about it.'

'I promise,' Samuel said.

Luca grabbed his backpack. Without turning around, he followed Samuel.

Elise sat back down again but kept glancing at the walkway they had taken, itching to follow them and speak with Luca.

'Maybe, sometimes, we should be allowed to keep secrets,' Kit signed so only Elise could see.

Faye folded her screen until it was the size of her palm and put it into a discreet pocket in the folds of her dress. 'Samuel was right to bring you with him. I can see that each of you contributed to your escape from Thymine. Without you, I would possibly never have seen my brother again. For that reason, I will speak with Raul and Flynn and request that you are given permission to remain. But I cannot guarantee it. You will also have to contribute to our group while you are here. Everyone has a role. After a few days, we shall start to settle you into each of yours.'

Kit raised his hand before signing. 'I am glad you will accept us, but there are others like me who need to be freed from the museums. I am happy to contribute to Uracil, but first I want to find more like me. There is a girl, Twenty-Two, in Cytosine. I want to find her.'

Faye stared at Kit for a moment. 'Before we continue, are there any other requests?'

'Nothing from me,' Georgina said. 'I just want Bay to be

safe and free. To be honest, I'd rather the rest of my family weren't here with me.'

Elise cleared her throat. 'I'd like permission to bring my parents and brother here. I had to leave them in Thymine. Before I left, I promised that I would find somewhere they would be safe, where we could all be together.'

Faye took a seat in front of the group of outcasts and rested her chin on her hand. 'What can you and your parents contribute to the group?'

'I was trained by my father for years in hand-to-hand combat; he could train others. And my mum is skilled, natural healer; she could help Georgina,' Elise said.

'I don't know what your medical supplies are like, but it would be good to have someone who could use natural remedies,' Georgina piped up.

Elise smiled at her.

'Our medical supplies are woefully short,' Faye said. 'We rely mainly on natural remedies. Everything else is sporadically smuggled over the borders when we visit the other zones.'

'You visit the other zones?' Elise said.

'Of course. We cannot manufacture everything here. We can talk about that another time, though. I think I have to make it clear that a decision was made three months ago that Uracil cannot expand any further. Even you being here will bring us over our maximum capacity. Raul and Flynn will not be happy.'

Elise's heart started to pound. She couldn't stay in Uracil if her parents and brother weren't allowed to join her. She couldn't just leave them in Thymine.

'If I cannot bring Twenty-Two here then I cannot stay here,' Kit signed.

Elise nodded her agreement.

Faye wrinkled her brow. Elise began to suspect that Kit was more precious to Uracil than Faye was letting on.

'Kit, you may try to bring back Twenty-Two. But she is the only one you can return with for three years. We cannot have the other bases suspect that there is a rogue group going after their Neanderthal displays. It would bring them to our gates. In three years' time, you can then try to free another.'

Kit nodded his agreement.

'We had planned to go with Kit to help him,' Elise explained.

'Of course. He cannot go by himself.'

'We were going to collect my family on the way back.'

Faye frowned. 'Elise, I'm afraid that it will not be so easy to admit three of your relatives. We are at capacity; there is no way I can agree to them returning. If you must leave permanently then so be it.'

Elise opened her mouth to respond but nothing came out; she didn't know what to say to change this woman's mind.

'There must be something we can do,' Georgina said, glancing at Elise.

Elise stood up. 'You would've let me stay if I didn't want to bring my parents back with me?'

Faye smiled at her. 'I'm afraid this is the way it has to be.'

'Then how about me for them? If I agree to work for Uracil, do whatever they want me to do out there, would you take my parents and my brother in? They could live in the home I would've been given. I'd hardly ever be in Uracil and I'd contribute outside of its boundaries.'

'You want to become a spy for Uracil?' Faye said.

'Whatever they want me to be. Ask Samuel—he knows what I can do.'

Faye looked at Elise steadily. 'You would work for us continuously. No breaks between missions. You will do whatever it is that we ask?'

Elise met Faye's gaze. 'Yes.'

'I will take it to Raul and Flynn,' Faye said, standing. Everyone followed her and stood as well. 'As long as you are as skilled as you say, it should pass. Your continuous allegiance, for your family's security.'

They all turned to Samuel as he loped back into the meeting area.

He raised his eyebrows. 'What have I missed?'

SIX

'Tell me about Ten and Twenty-Seven, please,'
Twenty-Two signed.

It was a week since she'd decided to start
breaking their rules and she was more restless with every
passing day.

'What? Why are you asking that?' Dara said, her gaze
darting up to the viewing platform that stretched the entire
length of the pod.

Twenty-Two couldn't remember the last time she had
looked up and there had been someone observing them.
When she was younger, she would catch sight of Fintorian
and he would wave at her and smile his big smile. She
couldn't copy the way he pulled his mouth up, so instead
she would scrunch her eyes towards him—her version of a
smile.

'I know that they live in the museum, in the pods across
from me, so I thought I would ask,' Twenty-Two signed.

Dara swallowed several times and Twenty-Two realised
that she was trying to remember if she could talk about the
other Neanderthals in Cytosine's Museum of Evolution.

'It's all a jumble...' Dara muttered, glancing up at the deserted viewing platform again.

Twenty-Two felt a twinge of guilt but she pushed it aside. She used her hands to add extra warmth to Dara's liver-spotted joints.

Dara's features softened and she shuffled closer. 'I haven't seen them for years, mind. Ten always seemed much older than she was. She just ate and slept her way through the day. She got wider every year and by the time she was fifteen, they had to employ two Companions just to help get her up from her sleeping mat. She must be in her late twenties now. Molly-coddling, if you ask me; one Companion is plenty enough for any Neanderthal.'

Twenty-Two mulled over this snippet of information. 'And Twenty-Seven?'

'I don't know, haven't seen him for years either. Must be six or seven now, I would've thought.'

Twenty-Two's eyes widened. 'Will they be doing this to the others? Not feeding them or looking after them? Or is it just me they are punishing? Because Mister Fintorian left because of me?'

Dara frowned and gestured for her to take her hands again.

'Did I ever tell you 'bout the inauguration ceremony for the first Companions?' she said, her voice brightening.

Twenty-Two had to force herself to remain calm. She reminded herself that this wasn't the real Dara, the one who had tucked her sleeping cover around her at night. This was the person she had been left with after the fall. Twenty-Two had decided months ago that she would honour her Companion's memory by taking care of this imposter.

To distract herself, she stood and began to pace while she decided what to do. What if Twenty-Seven was being neglected as well? He was only a child, not much more than a baby.

'Who is the Companion for Twenty-Seven?' Twenty-Two signed, still pacing.

'Why do you want to know about them? They weren't at the inauguration ceremony!'

'Have you met them?'

Dara relented. 'If it's the same one, I have. Sapien, of course. Woman in her forties, I would say. Was doing it for the tickets; she had seven children in the family.'

'How long ago did you meet her?'

'I'd see her at the monthly meetings before Mister Fintorian left...there's none of those now.' Dara began to gently rock from side to side. 'It wasn't like this before, not when Mister Fintorian was here—'

Dara was cut off by the sound of the steel bars of the pod door being pulled back. They both froze. They were sitting in the middle of the small paddock next to the door. There was never a delivery at this time, so they had taken the chance of enjoying the sunshine for an hour. They had broken one of the new rules.

Twenty-Two thought of the young boy across the corridor from her and she lost all thoughts of self-preservation. She bent and grabbed the glass jug she had been carrying around the pod since it had been left in there a week ago and ran towards the door. She would get them to speak to her, whatever it took.

'Don't leave me!' Dara shouted after her.

Twenty-Two ignored her and strode along the trodden, dust pathway that led to the only door. She breathed deeply through her nose, her eyes fixed on the pod entrance.

The door opened slightly and then stopped midway.

Twenty-Two broke into a jog and then a sprint, the

weight of the jug in her hand spurring her forwards. A hand came around the doorframe and Twenty-Two concentrated on it as she neared the door.

A freckled boy popped his head around the doorframe.

She skidded to a halt, the jug still raised in her hand.

His smile faded as he took in Twenty-Two's expression. He raised his hands and gingerly stepped sideways through the door, never taking his eyes from the jug.

'Who are you?' Twenty-Two signed with one hand. All her anger sparked and coursed through her without an outlet.

The freckled boy blinked rapidly.

'Hello, my name is Ezra,' he signed slowly. He broke out in a wide grin that stretched all the way to his eyes.

Twenty-Two dropped the jug.

'Have you seen Twenty-Seven or Ten? What's happening out there?' she signed, taking a step towards him.

Ezra took a step back.

'Hello, my name is Ezra,' he signed more slowly.

He gave his wide grin again, his eyes darting to the left and right.

Twenty-Two bent and picked up the jug.

'I,' he signed, pointing to his chest, 'happy hello...you.'

They stared at each other. Ezra's smile began to falter. Twenty-Two wondered how he communicated with people if he couldn't speak and his sign language was so poor. She concluded that he must be very lonely.

'You get away from her,' Dara shrieked, stumbling her way over the meadow. 'She ain't done nothing to you, so leave her alone!'

Ezra held both of his hands up again and stepped away from Twenty-Two, his back now against the pod wall.

He took two large gulps of air. 'I'm not here to hurt anyone. I just wanted to see what the pod's like is all.'

Dara nearly toppled over; Twenty-Two ran over and supported her the rest of the way. She felt a rush of love for her Companion. Dara hadn't walked that far by herself in weeks and she had done it for Twenty-Two.

'We don't need your help. I'm her Companion and we're doing just fine. She don't need another Companion; one's enough!' Dara said.

They reached the pod door and Twenty-Two patted Dara's arm to get her attention. 'We need help.'

Ezra stared at Twenty-Two's hands, following their movement.

'I only understood "help". Sorry, my sign language isn't very good. I didn't have anyone to teach me, always wanted to learn.'

He began to painstakingly finger-spell every word he had said to Twenty-Two, his brow furrowed in concentration.

Dara snorted. 'She can understand your voice, you carrot-bouffed, figurine-sized she-pup. You don't need to spell everything to her. She just can't speak back with her voice is all.'

'Oh.' Ezra dropped his hands. 'That'll make it easier.' He glanced around. 'Can I come in, please?'

Dara was opening her mouth to respond when Twenty-Two nodded.

'I have some food, if you want it,' Ezra said, pulling open his backpack and digging around.

Dara's eyes lit up but she quickly recovered. 'You can come in for a few minutes, but we'd better sit by the pine trees where they won't see you.'

Twenty-Two's stomach rumbled as she crouched for

Dara to clamber onto her back. She wanted to get to the pine trees as quickly as possible. Dara felt lighter than even a week ago and Twenty-Two tried not to think about what this meant.

Ezra pushed the steel door so it looked as if it were closed while still slightly ajar. Twenty-Two hurriedly walked to the other end of the pod where the trees still provided some cover.

When they were settled on the mats scattered around the trunk of the largest pine tree, Ezra handed them both packages of food. Dara tore off the wrapping and broke off small bits, which she fed to herself.

Twenty-Two stared at what Ezra had handed her. She didn't know what it was. She prodded it and the brown, spongy slice dimpled under the pressure before rising again. She dropped it.

'Is it alive?' she signed to Dara.

Dara chuckled. 'No, of course not. It's bread, isn't it! Haven't you ever seen bread before?'

Twenty-Two had never seen bread before. Dara had forgotten another of the rules. Twenty-Two and Dara weren't allowed any food in the pod that her species wouldn't have eaten thousands of years ago when Neanderthals last existed.

'Just try it,' Ezra said encouragingly.

Twenty-Two gingerly lifted it to her mouth, still put off by the fact it moved by itself. She wondered if it would taste like chicken. Chewing a small corner, she decided that she liked it; the texture was soft and the taste nourishing. She was surprised when it shrunk in her mouth. Twenty-Two scrunched her eyes as she checked off another rule from her list that she had broken.

She ate slowly, as her stomach had shrunk. Once she had finished, she signed to Dara, 'Will you translate for me?'

Dara sighed. 'If I must, but only for a few minutes. He has to go; he ain't meant to be here. One Companion is enough.'

Ezra looked between them both, not understanding.

'She wants me to translate for her,' Dara said.

'Why are you here?' Twenty-Two signed.

Dara spoke the words aloud.

Ezra drew a large breath before speaking. 'I started working as a cleaner in the museum a couple of months ago. Always wanted to work as a Companion, but I'd heard a rumour that you had to be able to use sign language. Being a cleaner was the closest I could get. They made me work at the other end, near the dinosaur displays.'

Ezra's gaze darted between them both before he continued, more slowly. 'They've been telling everyone that the Neanderthals have been moved to another base. That you don't live here anymore. It broke my heart when I found that out on my first day.'

Twenty-Two lowered her head. She had thought something like this had happened, but had always secretly hoped there had been a mistake. To hear it confirmed made the reality even more distressing. All of the Neanderthals had been abandoned.

'Not a walk-in job is a Companion; have to have the right skills, see,' Dara said, smiling at them both.

Twenty-Two ignored Dara and gestured at Ezra to continue.

'This morning I came down here just to see what one of the pods was like, where you would have lived. This area's off limits now but I used my pass to get in. That's the good thing about being a cleaner. Access to nearly everything.' Ezra smiled. 'Anyway, to see that you're still here and alive, well, that's just about made my year!' Ezra gestured up to the skylight. 'My life, even!'

'What about the others, Ten and Twenty-Seven?'

'I don't know; you're the first one I visited.' Ezra blushed and added with sudden solemnity, 'To meet you is the fulfilment of a life-long ambition of mine and today is a day that I shall never forget. Thank you.'

Twenty-Two glanced over at Dara, unsure if Ezra was unwell.

Dara briefly patted Twenty-Two on the knee. 'He's a Neanderfan. I used to get them coming up to me all the time in the early days when people actually cared about the displays.'

Twenty-Two was not reassured by the explanation.

'You have to go and check on the others. They might need help,' she urged.

'Anything you want,' Ezra said, jumping up.

It was half an hour before the crunch of dried grass signalled his return. Twenty-Two was already pacing, carrying the jug in her hand.

'It's just me,' Ezra called out when he saw her.

She gestured at him to come quicker and he broke into a little trot, his rucksack thumping up and down on his back.

He was so excited that it took him several gulps of air before he could order his thoughts. 'Ten's pod is empty. I searched it from one end to the other. I don't think it's been occupied for months; even her sleeping mats have been cleared away.' He swallowed down some more air and Twenty-Two willed him to hurry up. 'Twenty-Seven is definitely still in the other pod. As soon as I opened the door, he ran up to me, kicked me in the shin, and then ran away again. I followed him but he hid. There was no sign of his Companion.'

Twenty-Two chewed her lip as she watched Dara. Her Companion was struggling to keep her eyes open after eating more than she had done in weeks. Dara's eyes drooped until they finally closed.

Twenty-Two turned back to Ezra and spelt the words out on her fingers so he could understand her. 'T-a-k-e—m-e —t-o—h-i-m.'

Ezra gave his broad grin.

An hour later, when Dara was fast asleep, Twenty-Two stood facing her pod's door. She breathed deeply through her mouth and tried to calm herself. She had caught brief glimpses of the corridor before when the door had opened, but that was not the same as actually stepping out into the museum. Ezra waited patiently as she curled her fingers around the door. Counting to ten, she pulled it open and gestured for him to go out first. She hoped he had the sense to know she wanted him to check whether there was anyone in the corridor. Judging from their previous conversations, she wasn't sure that he did.

Ezra slipped out and disappeared down the corridor. Twenty-Two pulled the door farther open. She did not step outside. She stared straight ahead.

All she could see was grey.

She peered upwards and was alarmed by how close her head was to the ceiling. If she stretched, she would nearly be able to touch it with her hand. *It can't be safe to have something that close to someone's head.*

If there were ten of her teetering on top of each others' shoulders, she couldn't have reached the viewing platform and skylight in her pod. What if the ceiling in the corridor fell down?

The pit-pat of Ezra's feet drew her gaze in the direction the noise was coming from.

When he was in front of her, he said in a hushed tone, 'There's no one around; we should be safe. I'll pull the bars back on Twenty-Seven's pod, so it'll only take you a few seconds to cross.'

Within thirty seconds, Ezra had pulled back the three steel bars as quietly as he could. Twenty-Two still flinched at the sound, so much louder now that she was next to it. Pushing open the other pod's door, Ezra turned and gestured at her to cross the corridor.

Twenty-Two couldn't move. In all of her fourteen years, she had never stepped outside of her home.

She couldn't do it. The ceiling would collapse on her or the never-ending grey would seep inside and turn her to stone.

Then she thought of her list. Number 7: Never go outside.

Squeezing her eyes shut, she took three steps forward, only opening one of them when she bumped into Ezra.

Staring directly at his forehead, she began counting his freckles to distract herself. She didn't think she could move again; she would have to stay here, forever in limbo, not in one pod or the other.

The concrete felt cold on her bare feet. The counting of freckles was interrupted when her legs started to buckle underneath her. She closed her eyes.

'Come on,' Ezra said, grabbing her hand and pulling her inside Twenty-Seven's pod.

She stumbled forwards and he gently closed the door, just enough so they could still slip a finger round to pull it open.

A sturdy foot kicked her in the shin. 'Ooof!'

Her eyes snapped open.

'Oh no, you don't,' Ezra said, grabbing Twenty-Seven around the shoulders before he ran away. Still holding onto the struggling boy, he said to Twenty-Two, 'So you can make sounds then?'

Twenty-Two hurried over to the bundle of flying legs and grunts that was Twenty-Seven. He only stopped struggling when he saw her approaching. Once he had stilled, Twenty-Two knelt down next to him so that he was the same height as her. Just as Fintorian had always done with her.

'It's all right; we're not going to hurt you. I am Twenty-Two from the pod across from you. Where's your Companion?' she signed.

Big, brown eyes peered out from underneath a mat of hair that reached his nose. His tunic was dirty and torn and it was clear that he hadn't washed in weeks.

'So, if you can both make sounds, why can't you speak?'

Twenty-Two stared at Ezra.

He gulped again, as if he had to repeatedly take air in to be able to push words out. 'I'm sorry; I don't mean to upset you. I just want to know everything about you both.'

Twenty-Two sighed. She rarely spoke as she resented having to communicate in a way that was so jarring to her.

'Can...speak...one,' she said slowly, in a strained tone. Her voice was low and she struggled to succinctly end each word; they tended to catch in her throat and make a clicking noise. 'More, no link.'

Ezra smiled his understanding. 'I think you speak very well, if you don't mind me saying, that is.'

Twenty-Seven tried to move his hands and Ezra gently released him. Instead of signing, Twenty-Seven reached out to take Twenty-Two's hand. She clasped it in hers and scrunched her eyes at him.

He stared blankly at her in response and scratched his leg with his other hand. Twenty-Seven then turned to Ezra and kicked him in the shin.

Twenty-Two added a whole new rule to the list that she was going to break. After waiting for two hours for Ezra to return with some water and freshly laundered clothing, she cajoled the reluctant Twenty-Seven into washing himself and changing.

'You have to be clean if you want to come back with me. Dara won't let you in otherwise. You have to look your best,' she signed to the little boy.

She tried to push the hair away from his eyes but it would always eventually slide back, covering his strong brow ridge. His acorn-brown hair reached halfway down his face to his prominent nose and wide lips. Twenty-Two hadn't met another Neanderthal before, but she thought he was too skinny for a boy of his age. She would have to ask Dara if it was normal for his knees to poke out as they did.

Twenty-Seven gazed across his pod before motioning to be picked up. Twenty-Two obliged and carried him to the door. Before leaving, the two of them glanced back at Twenty-Seven's home. All of the Neanderthal pods were identical in design and this one had also been neglected for months. It was every shade of light brown, the only green outlined by the jutting pine trees in the corner. Twenty-Two waved at the pod. Twenty-Seven made a kicking motion with his leg.

This time, when Twenty-Two crossed the corridor, she

did it with her eyes open. She didn't want to fall and land on the boy. She stared straight at her pod door and didn't dare glimpse to her left or right, down the implausibly straight, concrete lines.

For the second time, the ceiling did not fall down on her, but she still felt relieved when she returned home. Gently placing Twenty-Seven on his feet, she took his hand and led him through the pod to the sleeping area. She motioned at Ezra to follow them.

Tapping Dara on the shoulder, Twenty-Two waited for her bleary eyes to open. Dara roused herself quickly and was propped up against the tree trunk in under five minutes. She peered at the two visitors.

'What's he doing here again?' she said, glaring at Ezra.

'He's brought us more food, water and clean clothes,' Twenty-Two signed.

'Well, I am a little hungry. Hand it over then.'

Ezra obligingly fished around in his backpack and produced more sandwiches and some treated water. Gulping the bottled water, Twenty-Two thought again about how it tasted the same as the water from the stream.

Dara peered at Twenty-Seven. 'Why's there a boy with you?'

'Dara, I would like you to meet Twenty-Seven. I think his Companion has left him and he could do with another one.'

A piercing scream echoed around the pod. Dara tried to scrabble to her feet.

Twenty-Seven hid behind Twenty-Two and even Ezra took a step back, his hands pressed against his ears.

'*You've broken the most scared of all the rules!* On my watch, as well!' Dara wailed, rising unsteadily to her feet.

'Ignorant, spiteful girl. Made my whole life's work a sham. What would Mister Fintorian say?'

'Why would Fintorian care?' Ezra said, blinking rapidly. 'He left for Thymine Base over a year ago, didn't he?'

'What if he found out?' Dara said, wringing her blouse between her hands and taking a step towards them. 'Neanderthals aren't supposed to be in the same pod as each other.' She frowned in concentration. 'They could argue, get into a fight and one could kill the other. Then we'd only have one Neanderthal left. *That is very bad Neanderthal arithmetic!*'

'That isn't going to happen with us, though, is it? He's too small to harm me,' Twenty-Two signed, ignoring the throbbing in her leg. 'And I would never hurt him. From looking at his pod, his Companion left him weeks or months ago. He shouldn't be this thin, should he?'

Dara hovered for a moment, clearly considering this before peering around Twenty-Two's legs. 'He's as thin as a Sapien boy, not sturdy like a Neanderthal child. He should be more muscled at his age. How old are you, boy?'

Twenty-Seven took a step towards Dara and raised his leg. Twenty-Two pulled him back.

'We don't kick Sapiens,' she signed, kneeling down. 'Or anyone, actually.'

Twenty-Seven stared at her blankly.

Twenty-Two waited patiently while Ezra gulped in some air. She had already gotten used to this ritual of his.

'If he's had no Companion for weeks or months, how's he survived?'

'He must have been drinking the water from the stream. We still get occasional food deliveries. He might have been getting double portions if they didn't know his Companion had left,' Twenty-Two signed.

Dara reluctantly translated.

Ezra broke into a wide grin. 'He's a little survivor, isn't he?'

He crouched down to smile at the boy.

Twenty-Seven jabbed his stumpy finger at Ezra, only narrowly missing his eye.

'No poking either,' Twenty-Two signed, realising she was beginning to set as many rules as she was breaking. She looked around at the others. 'We can't send him back. He's already been by himself for too long; he hasn't spoken once to me. He won't survive for much longer if he goes back by himself. He's slowly starving too. He needs the help and guidance of a Companion. A Companion who has been doing this for so long she was at the inauguration ceremony of the first Companions.'

'What would Mister Fintorian say, if he ever knew? I wouldn't be able to hold my head up for the shame if he disapproved,' Dara pleaded.

Before Twenty-Two could think about it, she signed her response. 'Why don't we go to Thymine Base to find out? They don't want us in Cytosine anymore and Ezra can't secretly feed us every day. Why don't we go somewhere we're wanted?'

In the early autumn before Elise's fourteenth birthday, her mum had caught her playing tag with some of the local Sapiens in Thymine's Outer Circle. It had been the last of the warm days and even though it was nearly dark, the group had continued with their game, oblivious to the dimming light. It had been an impromptu activity, brought on by the realisation that they would soon be leaving such things behind and entering a new stage of their lives at fourteen when they would be deemed adults.

None of her friends could keep up with her. When some of the faster ones came close to grabbing her, she was always able to dodge out of their grasp and circle back to the ancient oak. It was as if she could anticipate their next move and position herself just out of reach.

Elise had still been flushed with triumph when she caught sight of her mum, Sofi, standing at the edge of the clearing, staring at her. The look Sofi had given her had made her skid to a halt, even though she was in touching distance of a further win. Forgetting to wave goodbye to her friends, Elise had jogged over to her mother, already aware that she had made a mistake. She thanked the stars it was not her dad who had caught her.

Elise knew she was not supposed to be able to move that quickly. Her unusual reactions were supposed to remain hidden at all times. But she had let her guard down that day and Sofi had seen it. When Elise had reached her, Sofi could barely meet her eye. This hurt Elise more than any rage or ranting her dad would have produced if he had found out. Without saying a word, Sofi had started to walk back to their home.

When they had reached their front door, Elise had tugged on her mum's sleeve to get her attention. All Sofi could say was, 'How are we supposed to keep you safe, if you don't even take care of yourself?'

Elise was reminded of that evening, six years ago, watching Samuel's reaction as Faye recounted their agreement on the wooden platform where they had all learned about Samuel's past.

Samuel was next to Elise in a few seconds, his back to the rest of the group.

'*What were you thinking?*' he whispered, clearly trying to control his voice. 'She can't do it; it's out of the question,' he said more loudly, turning to Faye. 'No. We will find another way to secure entry for her parents.'

Elise bristled. She knew that Samuel felt responsible for her, for all of them now they had left Thymine, but that didn't mean that he got to treat her as if she was thirteen.

'It's not your decision to make,' she said. 'I'm starting my training tomorrow.'

'You heard her, Samuel. It is not your decision to make,' Faye said. 'Perhaps we should let newcomers make their own choices now they have left the bases.'

Samuel sucked in his breath and looked up at the tree's canopy before responding. 'Yes, you are right, sister.'

Elise returned Faye's smile. 'I think I'll get some sleep now, if that's okay?'

Faye nodded and turned to the others. 'There are tree houses for all of you in the visitors' quarters. I am sure Samuel will take you over.'

Elise avoided Samuel's gaze. 'Thank you for the offer, but I'll find someone else to show me.'

The next morning, before the dawn light had broken, Elise tried to get out of her hammock without spinning around and landing on the floor. Fast reflexes she had; gracefulness she did not. Teetering on the edge of the hammock, she launched herself onto the floor before straightening up.

As she fumbled for the light switch, a hand grabbed hers from behind.

Elise automatically shoved her elbow backwards, hoping to make contact. Adrenaline surged through her. She had already adjusted her balance to counter herself, so she didn't topple when she didn't make contact.

Spinning round to launch a kick, she stopped halfway, teetering on one leg as she felt a knife blade rest against the skin of her neck. If she had not stopped in time, she would have cut her own throat.

'That was pretty good, but we need better,' a female voice said.

The light flicked on and Elise held the gaze of the holder of the knife. She was a petite woman wearing a calm expression, even though she was holding a blade to Elise's throat. She had the appearance of always being in control.

'Move the knife and I'll show you,' Elise responded, staring down at the woman.

'There's no need for that. I just wanted to see what I was dealing with.'

The woman smiled, her broad lips revealing large teeth with a wide gap between the front two. Elise thought she was in her late thirties. Not that her smooth, cinnamon skin was weathered. Instead, she had a timeless look to her, like the Potiors.

'I'm Maya,' the woman said, tucking the knife into a side pocket on her trousers. She held out her hand. 'And I'm the person who's going to try and keep you alive.'

Elise reluctantly shook her hand. 'How long have you been in here?'

'Long enough to see that you've all the grace of a three-legged armadillo,' Maya said, taking a seat by the small table.

She never took her eyes from Elise, running her gaze up and down her several times before starting to unfold her screen.

'Can I at least have some privacy while I put some clothes on?' Elise asked, glancing down at herself. She was only wearing some pants and a t-shirt.

'Suit yourself. I'll meet you in the clearing at the north end of the island when you're ready.' Maya moved towards the door and opened it. 'You're leaving soon to rescue Twenty-Two. They'll probably send you on your first assignment straight afterwards. You've got, therefore, two weeks to get into shape. If I were you, I wouldn't want me to leave your side. After this, you're on your own.'

Elise walked into the clearing ten minutes later. Maya was standing perfectly still, waiting for her. She ran her eyes up and down Elise again and tapped something into her screen.

'Good. You do have the desire to train then?' Maya said, only briefly looking up.

Elise decided to ignore this comment. 'What do you need to know about me?'

'Nothing. Samuel filled me in last night. He asked me to be your trainer. Now that I've met you, I know the rest.'

'Samuel knows a lot about me, but he doesn't know everything,' Elise said, annoyed that it was only 6am and she already had to correct Samuel's assumptions.

Maya scrolled down her screen. 'You're five foot four. I'm guessing around sixty-one kilograms, and most of that is muscle. Your fitness levels are high but your upper body strength is pretty poor. Your legs are strong and you favour your left leg, even though you're right-handed. You broke the thumb and finger on your right hand—'

'Actually, Fintorian broke them for me.'

'Shall I go on?'

Elise realised she was being petulant. 'Sorry.'

'You've remarkably quick reactions, but these depend heavily on sight and you've not been trained to react without relying on this sense. These reactions extend to perfect aim with that sling of yours. Overall, you're a long-range fighter; at close quarters, you react defensively, but you've very few offensive skills. Your right hand is nearly useless at the moment, so we are going to have to teach you to block entirely with your left side...'

Elise didn't bother to add anything; Maya knew more about her current physical state than she did.

'In the fields of espionage, you can at least control your features so your thoughts are shielded but, like most people, you have no other skills.' Maya glanced up from her screen. 'Except for an above-average level of pluckiness.'

'In the spirit of pluckiness, can I ask why Samuel requested that you train me?'

Maya didn't release Elise from her gaze. 'I may be five foot one and only weigh fifty kilograms but I can disarm a man three times my size if required. You're no brawler, Elise; you haven't got the physique for it. And neither have I. But I can get in and slip out without anyone noticing and, if cornered, I can talk my way out of most situations. After that I have three black belts to fall back on if they're needed.'

'I get it; we match.'

Maya laughed. 'We don't match. In five years' time, we might match. Right now, you're where I was at age twelve.'

Elise blushed. 'Sorry, I meant that I can see that you're the right choice.'

'Samuel wouldn't make the wrong one, would he?' Maya said with a half-smile. 'Before we start, I need to ask you a question and you need to answer honestly.'

Elise nodded.

'Before Samuel told you about Uracil three weeks ago, where did you think he was taking you?'

Elise had not been expecting this. 'I don't know. I thought we'd find a cave or something. All of us live there, make it our home. I never dreamed that there was another fully functioning base that the Zone 3 leaders didn't know about.'

Maya studied Elise for a moment before nodding and walking over to a large crate at the edge of the clearing. She lifted the lid off and pulled out a few small boxes, checking the bottom of them before selecting the final one. Walking back to Elise, she gestured to her to join her halfway. She snapped open the box's lid. Inside was a solid, silver bracelet with a large amethyst held in the centre.

'You must wear this at all times. When you eat, sleep, shower. Even when you feel at your most safe, surrounded by a hundred fellow fighters, you keep this on. Understood?'

'What? Yes, if you say so. Is it some sort of tracking device?'

'Stars, no! If we could track you, it would mean someone else could as well.'

Maya popped open the clasp on the side of the amethyst. Inside was a tiny compartment that held a single capsule.

Elise peered at the innocuous pill. The capsule was clear and she could see the grains of powder inside it.

'If you're ever a hairsbreadth away from being captured, you must swallow it immediately. Don't think; just swallow. Agents have only had to use them a couple of times in our history, but that doesn't mean you should ever take this bracelet off. Wear the amethyst on the inside of your wrist. The clasp is designed to be opened with only your teeth if necessary. Means you only have to bring your wrist to your mouth to release what's inside. It will be exchanged for a new pill every time you leave Uracil.'

Elise frowned. 'Is it a suicide pill?'

For the first time, she began to question what she was getting herself into.

Maya stared at Elise. 'We're not that archaic. It won't kill you, but it will stop you telling anyone about Uracil. It might just save your life. More importantly, it will save thousands of others.'

EIGHT

By the end of her first day, Elise was fully aware why Samuel had requested that Maya train her. She was so fast that Elise had trouble tracking her whereabouts and she made no sound when she moved; surprise was a key weapon in her arsenal. On top of this, Maya knew the exact pressure points to completely disable someone. Twice, Elise had collapsed on the ground, unable to move for a full ten minutes.

It was not only Elise's body that was bruised. She always knew she could fight better than most people, but working with someone like Maya made her realise how basic her skills really were.

At the end of the first day, Kit came to meet Elise. Waving goodbye to Maya, they walked back to the main settlement in silence. Having spent sixteen hours a day together for six months, Elise realised that she missed it being just the two of them. The silences were never strained, each allowing the other to let their thoughts drift without explanation.

Wincing, Elise lifted up the side of her shirt as they

walked, trying to inspect the damage. Kit glanced over at her.

'I think I might've broken a rib,' she signed with one hand.

'I don't think so,' he signed. 'Just bruised. I saw the last bit of your training. When she circled around you, leapt onto your shoulders—'

'Don't,' Elise responded, still wincing. 'I've already been sufficiently pummelled today. What've they got you doing? They're not studying you or anything, are they?'

Kit scrunched his eyes. 'It is me who is studying. I went to school today. You can go to school for years here if you want to; you don't have to leave at sixteen like you did.'

Elise smiled as she pictured Kit sitting at a desk. 'Most of my classmates left at fourteen. They had to get jobs. My parents were determined that I'd stay in school as long as I could. Dad took extra shifts at the factory...' Elise felt a pang of guilt and changed the subject so Kit wouldn't be able to read her. 'So, you're finally learning to read and write then?'

'Yes. It is only my first day, but the teacher said that my memory is very good—'

Kit stopped abruptly when they reached the main entranceway to the raised tree houses. He pulled the hood farther over his face as they passed people on the spiral staircase.

Elise waited for a few moments before signing, 'Why are you covering your face still? You shouldn't be ashamed; everyone here wants to speak with you, get to know you.'

Kit stared at her. 'I have never been around so many people before. I am not covering myself so they cannot see me. I cover my face so I cannot see them.'

'Stars, I'm sorry, Kit. I didn't think. You're doing so well, being out of the museum; it's hard to remember that it's still all so new to you.'

Kit nodded. 'It will take time. Shall we visit Luca in his tree house? I have not seen him all day.'

Elise was happy to agree; she hadn't seen Luca since he'd found out that he had been born in Guanine.

When they reached Luca's room, she knocked tentatively on the door. She could only guess that he was inside, as the small blind was closed.

'Go away!'

He was definitely in.

'Luca, it's me and Kit. We want to come in, just to say hello. We don't need to talk about anything that happened yesterday!'

Silence. Kit signed at Elise and she translated for him. 'Kit says you can poke me in my bruised ribs and see how high I squeal!'

There was some shuffling around inside and then the door swung open. 'How squealy are we talking, Thanton?'

'Pretty squealy. Can we come in?'

Luca held open the door.

'What happened to you?' he said, rubbing his eye. He looked like he had just woken up.

'It was her first day of training,' Kit signed. 'She did not win.'

He scrunched his eyes at Elise so she would know he was only teasing.

'It's true.' Elise said, making a snap decision. 'About that. In the spirit of secrets being frowned upon, I've got a few things to tell you both.'

It felt good to finally tell her friends about her years of brutal training, exceptionally fast reflexes and perfect aim.

After spending all her life trying to hide it, she wanted to feel comfortable with who she was.

'So, that's why you joined us at the end? Because you had to leave to protect your brother?' Luca said, sprawled across his bed.

'Yup,' Elise said, sitting on the floor and leaning against the wooden wall panels. 'My mum punched me in the face so we could show the neighbours they were disowning me. I also shouted out that my dad wasn't my real father so they wouldn't think Nathan could do what I can. It's the reason my aunt and uncle were taken away when they were our age. They could do the same as us. The Protection Department got them. No one's heard of them since.'

Luca gave a low whistle.

'What is the Protection Department?' Kit signed.

'They work for the base leaders, supposed to keep us all safe. But, really, they just keep the Potiors' hands clean, so they can give off the appearance of being benevolent. Peaceful even,' Elise signed. 'All these years, Kit, I thought there was something wrong, but I blamed the Sapiens for what they'd done to the world before the Pandemic. But I see it now; you should judge someone by their individual acts, not the overall actions of the group they fall into.'

'That means there must be good Potiors too,' Kit signed.

'I suppose so. But I've only met two Potiors and that's including Faye,' Elise signed.

'Faye's really nice,' Luca signed. 'She looks like a Potior, but she isn't really one. She has the genetic enhancements, but she's not out there trying to control four bases of citizens.'

Kit caught Elise's eye, but didn't lift his hands to sign. He didn't need to.

'That's what all the bases out there want to do. Keep

control,' Luca continued, his voice rising as he signed the words at the same time. 'Doesn't matter what it takes, who gets hurt...' Luca stopped abruptly. 'I've decided to join the guard here. I want to learn how to fight, protect Uracil.'

Elise wasn't surprised by his announcement. 'Do you think they'll give you a pair of those glowing gloves?'

'Stars, yes! I'm only in it for the accessories,' Luca said, smiling for the first time. 'I found out what those gloves do yesterday. When they put the sack over my head, I got a bit too close to the amber-glowing guard. They multiply the kinetic energy; a hit from one of those feels like someone has taken a run up.'

'Do you think I can get one to put on the end of my spear?' Kit signed.

Elise laughed, imagining a deflated glove loosely tied to the end of Kit's favoured weapon. He wasn't allowed to carry it with him in Uracil, but in the museum he would spend twelve hours a day practising with it. It was why Fintorian wanted to put Kit on display, so that he could show the public how Neanderthals fought 30,000 years ago.

Elise had also been ordered to join the display, practise with her sling and make fire to amuse the museum visitors— early Sapien and Neanderthal living side by side, just as they would have been tens of thousands of years ago.

Part way through their journey to Uracil, Samuel had let slip that the pod designers had even created costumes for her and Kit. When she had asked what hers had been like, Samuel had blushed and mumbled that it 'didn't leave much to the imagination'. She didn't want to think about it again. Helping Kit escape was one decision she would never regret; he'd been nothing more than another artefact to the museum and she had been viewed the same way.

'When do you start your training?' Elise asked Luca.

'Tomorrow,' he signed. 'I'm going to put in as much time as I can before we leave for Cytosine in two weeks' time.' Luca looked over at Kit. 'I'm sorry, but I wish Samuel wasn't coming to Cytosine. He's lied to us about everything. Didn't mention his sister being a flippin' Potior-type-human or his dad being one of the bosses here. Must have slipped his mind while we spent three solid weeks together.'

'He would have had his reasons,' Kit signed.

'And he's stopped wearing glasses. Since when could he see all right?' Luca signed.

'Does it matter?' Kit responded.

'He lied to me too, Kit,' Elise signed. 'Even back in the museum when he made me tell him everything about what I could do. He didn't tell me the truth about himself then.'

'He couldn't tell you in the museum; it would have been unsafe.'

'So, why didn't he tell us on our three-week journey?' Luca signed.

'I can guess, but it is not for me to say,' Kit responded. 'What you have to remember is that Samuel is a good person, just like you both are. But even the best of people sometimes do the wrong thing. You shouldn't judge them on that one action. Look at the whole instead.'

NINE

Dara's eyes lit up. 'We could see Mister Fintorian again? I could bring him two Neanderthals for his museum. He'd be pleased with that, wouldn't he?'

Glancing around her pod, Twenty-Two knew there was nothing left for them here. She nodded her encouragement.

'Can I come with you?' Ezra asked, sitting down and unwrapping a sandwich.

He held out a corner to Twenty-Seven without looking at him directly. The sandwich was silently removed from his hand.

'I don't think we'd get there without you. I don't know where we're going,' Twenty-Two signed, with Dara translating.

'There's no reason for me to stay if you're going,' Ezra said, holding out another corner of the sandwich to Twenty-Seven. 'I don't want to spend the rest of my life cleaning a museum that doesn't even have any Neanderthals in it. What sort of a Museum of Evolution doesn't have any

Neanderthals? I've got no family either, so there's nothing stopping me.'

'No family, you say? What's your full name, boy?' Dara said, fixing a beady eye on him.

'Ezra Thippen.'

'*I knew it,*' Dara exclaimed. 'I knew he wasn't Cytosine born.' She lowered her voice, adopting a conspiratorial tone and addressing Twenty-Seven, who just stared at her blankly while chewing on the piece of bread. 'It's in the countenance, you see. Thymine sticks their nose in everywhere because they think they live in a perfect valley. Forget that they're production-pluggers. They're not like Cytosine, who actually come up with the ideas!'

Ezra wasn't ruffled by Dara's tone; he was clearly used to being spoken to like this. 'I don't remember Thymine. I only remember the orphanage in Cytosine. They told me I was moved over here when I was a baby. I moved into the Museum of Evolution for my first job as a cleaner. Maybe if you teach me to sign, I can work as a Companion at the Museum of Evolution in Thymine Base.'

Twenty-Two scrunched her eyes in response. If they brought a Companion for Twenty-Seven with them to Thymine Base, they would be even less of an inconvenience.

'How old are you, boy?' Dara said.

'I'm fourteen.'

'I am fourteen too,' Twenty-Two signed, scrunching her eyes.

'A man then, if you're fourteen,' Dara said grudgingly. 'You should copy her sign language, she-pup, if you want to learn how to understand her. She said she is fourteen too.'

Ezra copied the movements Twenty-Two made with

her hands and repeated them several times until they were right.

'When will we go to see Mister Fintorian? Tomorrow?' Twenty-Two signed.

Ezra scratched his head. 'I've not left Cytosine since I arrived as a baby. You know we're not supposed to leave, right?'

Twenty-Two shook her head.

'Sapiens aren't supposed to travel between the bases unless they have permission to. Neanderthals aren't even supposed to leave their pods. We'll be breaking the biggest rule by trying to get to another base.'

'If we are travelling to see Mister Fintorian then we can explain everything when we arrive. He'll be glad we have come. He'll be sure to make you Twenty-Seven's Companion,' Twenty-Two signed, convincing herself of the truth of what she was saying.

Dara translated, though not appearing too convinced herself.

'Me? A Companion? I couldn't ever imagine anything better,' Ezra responded, a wistful look in his eye.

'You're doing the job already nearly, aren't you? You will definitely be made a Companion in Thymine.'

'But we don't have enough treated water. It's going to take months to arrange, even if we get the supplies together,' Ezra said, his voice starting to warm up to the topic. He took a few gulps of air and started to flap his hands. 'We need a tip-top plan, involving two or three back-up plans and maybe a zip wire.'

Twenty-Two began to panic. This was not what she expected. She didn't have months; she felt like she barely had days. 'We can come up with a plan tonight and then we can prepare to leave.'

Ezra stopped flapping his hands back and forth mid-waggle. 'We still don't have enough treated water. I only get enough for one person a day and I would have to share it with three others. How am I going to do that?'

'The water in the stream—it's treated. I've been drinking from there and it tastes the same as the treated water.'

Twenty-Two dropped her hands to her sides; she had not meant to say that.

'What! You've been drinking the stream water? *Rule breaker!*' Dara exclaimed.

'It's okay?' Ezra asked Twenty-Two, ignoring Dara.

Twenty-Two raised her head. 'I've been drinking it for a week. We've had no water for days and I gave the rest of the treated water to Dara. I'm fine, aren't I?'

She nodded at the same time, as Dara was too shocked to translate.

'You don't look like you have a virus. You're still very thin and your hair...'

Twenty-Two felt a tug on her tunic. She glanced down at Twenty-Seven, who met her gaze with his large, brown eyes. She couldn't understand what he was trying to communicate to her, but she could make a guess.

'Do you think that Twenty-Seven has been drinking from his stream? If no one's been delivering water and he has had no Companion, what would be stopping him? The pods are identical; it must be treated as well.'

Ezra studied Twenty-Seven, clearly coming to the same conclusion. 'Well, if it's good enough for you two, then it's certainly good enough for me.' He paled. 'I should test it too.'

His hand shook as he picked up the jug and went over

to the stream. After a few false starts, he tentatively dipped the jug underneath the water.

'More rule breaking!' Dara squawked before feigning a faint. When it was clear no one was listening to her, she sat up again.

'Here goes,' Ezra said, tipping the jug in Twenty-Two's direction.

He took a small sip and swirled it around his mouth before swallowing.

'It tastes exactly the same as treated water,' he exclaimed. 'I'm going to keep on having a little every day and see how I go. You know, you may have solved our water problem, Twenty-Two.'

She scrunched her eyes in response—now they could leave tomorrow.

'We still can't leave tomorrow,' Ezra said. 'I need to find out the way to Thymine and store some food...and we need to get you in a state where you can walk around without your eyes closed,' he finished, glancing at her. 'We'll have to take it in turns carrying Dara and making sure that Twenty-Seven is following. We can't do that if you're scared of going outside. It'll only draw attention to you and they'll see straightaway that something's wrong.'

Twenty-Two knew he was right. If this was going to work, she needed to try to pass as a Sapien.

Two weeks later, Twenty-Two was standing in one of the exhibition rooms with Ezra. They had taken it step by step each night, slowly working their way a little farther down the corridors until she felt more comfortable being outside of her pod. She still hated being in rooms or corridors with low ceilings, but she grudgingly agreed that it was unlikely that they would fall on her.

Despite the museum being deserted at three in the morning, she had still pulled the hood of her top up over her head. Ezra had cut her hair so that she had a long fringe covering her brow bridge and eyes. He had apologised when he had suggested it, quickly explaining that he thought her forehead was just fine as it was. He also made her promise that she would grow out the fringe when they got to Thymine.

'So, I brought you here because I thought you might be interested in the other species of human that existed at the same time your ancestors did,' Ezra said.

They were standing in one of the small display rooms off the main central atrium. These rooms held all the models of the species of animal that the Potiors had not managed to bring back due to the deterioration of the tissue samples or length of time since the animal's extinction. The Potiors were very strict on the order that they brought the extinct species back; haphazard was not their way. They worked in reverse chronological order.

The walls and floors of the room were painted black and there were ten lifelike models of different species of human who had existed over the last two million years. Each one was picked out by a single spotlight that gave them the appearance of floating men and women, nothing tethering them to time or space.

Twenty-Two scanned the placards, recognising the letters she had practised so many times, until she found the one that read: 'Homo Neanderthalensis'.

She stared up at the figure. This was only the second Neanderthal face she had seen. Even if it was only a model, it still helped.

He was much older than her. His only clothing was a simple piece of thin leather wrapped around his waist and tucked into the side to secure it. He held a sturdy spear in one hand and was smiling out at whomever was viewing him. His eyes were slightly glazed and he wore the expression of a trusting child. His long hair was pulled off his face and secured with a thin strip of leather. The prominent brow bridge dominated his face and his eyes disappeared underneath, barely visible. Deep lines were etched into his forehead and around his mouth.

'I don't have those lines, do I?'

Twenty-Two signed the words slowly, stopping to clarify each one if Ezra needed her to. She had found that this was the best way to teach him. Dara and Twenty-Two corrected Ezra's signs and made him practise again until they were right. Dara would then translate for Twenty-Two when they were together. When it was just Twenty-Two and Ezra, they would muddle along, finger-spelling any sign that Ezra didn't know. He was a keen student and determined that Twenty-Two would be able to communicate clearly with him.

Twenty-Two touched her face to emphasise what she was saying. Even Dara's wrinkles weren't as deep as the model's. Did she look that old? She couldn't be certain, as she only saw her reflection in the rippling pool at the end of the stream. Maybe the ripples covered the lines burrowed into her face?

'Don't worry,' Ezra said, staring at his hands as he tried to sign the words as well. 'You don't really look like that. I think they gave the model an "outdoors" look, as he would've been in the wind and rain all the time. You're paler than him, as you don't get much sun, and he's also much older than you are. I promise.'

Twenty-Two tentatively scrunched her eyes at him. She was relieved that she didn't appear the same as the model. She knew they wouldn't get very far if she did. Like Twenty-Seven, the months of not eating properly had meant that she had lost a lot of the muscle density she had before. Ezra was only able to bring them sandwiches and these were not helping her gain much weight. She felt less tired but she certainly didn't feel as strong as she used to. The weight loss did help her with trying to pass as a Sapien. But she missed the strength and confidence she previously had.

She knew it was important to pass as a Sapien as they were now visiting parts of the museum where there were cameras. They avoided the minute, winged machines at all costs. Whenever one did locate them in a corridor, Twenty-Two was under strict instructions to carry on as normal. Ezra would then lead them to one of the cleaning cupboards and, if the camera could be bothered to follow them, the only recording would be of two cleaners deciding which mops to take back out with them. The cameras were only programmed to follow someone relentlessly if their heartbeat increased or they panicked and ran.

'Why did we die out?' Twenty-Two asked, not looking over at Ezra.

She felt more comfortable asking these questions of him than Dara; she was still embarrassed by how little she knew about her own species. Ezra had told her he had spent whatever free time he had at school learning about Neanderthals from the prescribed textbooks. He knew things about her species of human that she had never even thought to ask. For the first time, Twenty-Two wished she had been able to go to school.

'We're taught that the Sapiens killed the Neanderthals,

hunted them to death,' Ezra said, staring straight ahead. 'I don't know how; you're so much stronger than us. But that's one of the reasons we have the Reparations. Because we killed your ancestors and countless other species of animals. Both on purpose and not on purpose.'

As well as recounting the Neanderthals' history in the evenings, Ezra had taken to explaining the Sapiens'. Their wars, famines, destruction of the environment and geno-cides had all been laid at Twenty-Two's feet.

'Tell me about the Reparations,' Twenty-Two signed, taking care to finger spell the last word.

'It's what the Sapiens live our lives by. We always follow the different Decrees. Now that we have the Potiors and Medius, they keep our base instincts in check. Without them, we'd probably be destroying everything again. There are twenty Decrees and they cover pretty much everything, from what we do with our time to the houses we live in.'

'I can't imagine you destroying everything.'

Ezra gave his broad grin before it faltered. 'No, I can't either. But I don't want to see whether I would. Could never forgive myself if I hurt you or any other living crea-ture. It's best this way. Nothing good came from the Sapiens.'

Twenty-Two silently agreed. Ezra was the kindest indi-vidual she had met, but that wasn't saying much. Besides Dara, the only Sapiens she ever saw were the ones who slid the trays across the pod floor before quickly closing the steel door behind them. She had learnt when she was little not to bother waving at them; she never got a response. She also knew from the evenings spent learning from Ezra that, as a species, the Sapiens were destructive, chaotic and cruel.

Twenty-Two moved over to the model next to her ancestor. She was drawn by his tiny stature; he only reached the chest of all the nearby models. He had large feet for such a small man and his gums were pulled back in a growl to show his wide teeth. His shoulders hunched forward, which made him seem even more petite. Like Twenty-Two, he had very little chin and a receding forehead. His skin colour was much darker than hers and he did not have her strong stature.

She crouched down next to the placard. It explained that this was a model of Flores Man or Homo Floresiensis. His remains had only ever been found on a tiny island in Zone 1, which used to be called Asia. Twenty-Two slowly read that they had had tools, used fire and hunted miniature elephants.

Ezra crouched down next to her. 'Look at this. On the placard, where it says that Flores Man was thought to have "become extinct 50,000 years ago".'

Ezra picked at a corner of the '50,000' and it peeled away. Underneath was another sticker with 12,000 on it and underneath that was one with 60,000 and then another with 12,000.

He smiled. 'Seems these things can change depending on their latest find, eh?' He carefully stuck the stickers back in the right order before continuing. 'It says here that they haven't been able to extract DNA samples from the remains they've found and that's why they haven't tried to bring them back yet. None of the bones they found had been fossilised; they were all too damp. But they're still digging through the island to find more remains. You'll be unique for a while then.'

Twenty-Two did not scrunch her eyes in response. The enormity of her situation, of being brought back from extinction, held all her attention. For a moment, she froze, unsure what she was supposed to do with this gift of life.

Ezra glanced at her. 'Come on, you need cheering up. It's nearly dawn so I'll take you to the main museum and you can see the displays waking up. It's my favourite time of the day. We'll then have to go straight back to your pod before the other cleaners start their shifts at six.'

Twenty-Two scrunched her eyes. This was what they'd been building up to.

Ezra led them to a closet hidden behind a panel. Inside, a light automatically turned on. He selected a broom for himself and a dustpan and brush for Twenty-Two.

'I found out in the first few weeks of doing this job that if I walked around holding a broom then I was left alone. It made me look as if I was busy and responding to a clean-up call.' He grinned. 'It's all about having the right props, you see.'

Twenty-Two nodded and pulled her hood farther over her head. She followed Ezra, shoulders hunched and head down, through the concrete corridors with their low ceilings.

Everywhere was deserted. It was 4am and most of the employees didn't sleep overnight at the museum. The few that did, some cleaners, canteen staff and rangers, were not awake yet. The only thing the two of them had to watch out for was a camera.

As they entered the main chamber from the south side, Ezra slowed down and nudged Twenty-Two, who tentatively raised her head.

She tried not to gasp as she took in the main museum. It didn't feel as if she were inside a building anymore; vast expanses of differing types of green spread in every direction. She pointed at everything she did not know the name of and Ezra spelt it for her. She committed these new words to memory, storing them for when she would see Dara and could ask what the sign for them was. Every night she went out, she came back with twenty new words.

Vast prairies and grasslands stretched off in every direction, so far that she could not see where they ended. In the far corner lay woodland and a small stretch of jungle. The entire ceiling appeared to be open to the sky, yet the air was completely still, as it was in her own pod. When she pointed up to it, Ezra told her that the ceiling was made entirely of glass, hundreds of feet in the air so that any sign of it or reflection was invisible to the naked eye.

Without saying anything further, Ezra led her up one of the steep, spiralling walkways. He stopped every few paces to pick up any pieces of litter that had escaped the attention of the evening cleaners. Twenty-Two followed his lead and only dared to take little glances around her whenever she straightened up. The spiral walkway had a coating similar to white granite, wide enough to take hundreds of visitors up and over the setting below. Similar walkways stretched across the entire museum.

As they climbed higher and the pre-dawn light started to filter down, Twenty-Two could make out the shapes below her beginning to move. The calls of the birds grew louder and some of the mammals began their low, morning rumbles.

She pointed at the different animals and Ezra quietly told her their names. She rolled these new words around her head, enjoying their uniqueness and unusual spellings. A young zebra shook its head and raced underneath their walkway, disturbing the stillness. It then stopped abruptly and raced back the way it came. Without thinking, Twenty-Two ran to the other side of the walkway to follow its path. She had never seen any animals larger than the few small birds in her pod. She soaked in everything and her attention was caught by the mammoths in the next pod. They raised their trunks and called to each other across the frosted tundra.

'Each one has their own pod. Specially designed for how they would have lived outside, either in groups or alone. They can't cross between the pods, or it would be mayhem,' Ezra explained, pointing at the zebra. 'There's invisible barriers, you see. It looks as if they're all living together but actually they're kept separate.'

Twenty-Two scrunched her eyes even tighter and started to head farther down the walkway. She could see a woolly rhino standing near a narrow stream.

Ezra caught her arm and took a gulp of air. 'I'm sorry, but we have to go. Everyone will start waking up soon.'

Twenty-Two knew he was right; she couldn't risk being found outside of her pod. She had no idea what the punishment for rule breaking was in Cytosine. She reasoned there was not much more they could do to her, but she worried that they might keep Ezra's food from him as well.

Following Ezra back down the walkway, Twenty-Two briefly turned to the impossibly vast, patchwork landscape of differing habitats. She silently wished that she could live there rather than her dusty, neglected pod. Twenty-Seven could live out there with her too and she wouldn't have to hide him away anymore.

Maybe she could ask to live in the main museum with Twenty-Seven in Thymine's Museum of Evolution? She pondered this as she followed Ezra down the corridors.

They were close to her pod when, without looking up, she froze. There were voices, coming closer from the other direction. These were the first people they had heard during their night-time explorations.

Ezra stopped to look around at her, panic contorting his features.

Without thinking, Twenty-Two turned and bolted. Blindly running down corridors, she pushed open doors at random, knowing she was heading in the direction of her pod but trying to lose them if they followed. At the last door, she tripped and stumbled, banging her knee as she fell to the floor. The dustpan and brush clattered to the ground in front of her.

The shock of the fall forced her to stay still. She listened intently for the sound of footsteps following her. She held her breath and reached out with everything she had. There was nothing.

Tentatively lifting her head, she glanced around her. She had stumbled into a room that was made entirely from concrete, apart from three huge panes of glass stretching along the length of each wall in front of her.

The room was deserted except for a few desks with chairs neatly tucked underneath. The door was still gently swinging. No one had followed her.

Pushing herself to her feet, she picked up the dustpan and brush. She knew she should get back to her pod, but she was drawn to the large, glass window to her right, stretching the entire length of the wall. As she walked towards it in a daze, the smooth, concrete flooring changed to metal grating. Her toes curled at the change in texture on her bare feet.

She traced her hands along the glass. The pod was different to anything she had seen before. It was still an enclosed, steel room, like her own, but it was entirely filled with water that gently rippled across the surface. Half of the viewing window was placed below the surface, the other half above. She crouched down and peered into the underwater section. There were some boulders scattered along the bed of the pod and a few underwater plants that gently swayed with the movement, but no animals that she could see. She thought they might be so tiny that they were hidden amongst the crevices and rocks.

She pushed her nose against the glass and breathed out, a round circle misting for a moment.

She jumped back.

An eye as big as her head, surrounded by a sucker, attached itself to the glass and blinked at her.

As quickly as it had appeared, it was gone.

Twenty-Two cried out.

Her breath came in short, sharp bursts as she looked around her. There was no eye anymore. She stumbled backwards until her shoulders hit the glass wall on the other side of the room.

She tried to calm herself as she stared at the lapping water on the other side, now empty of its occupant. She concentrated on the sound of her breath. In and then out. In and then out.

Three distinctive raps came from the glass behind her.

She froze. Her back was pressed up against the glass and she silently prayed to the stars that she had imagined it.

Tap...tap...tap.

Shaking, Twenty-Two took a step away from the glass.

Tap, tap, tap.

She turned around.

Her breath caught in her throat as she watched the tip of a giant, furry leg, the width of her arm, rap against the glass again.

Bracing, she took a step closer so she could see the leg's owner.

The creature was as big as the woolly rhinos she had

seen in the main museum. It had over ten oddly angled legs splaying out from its cylindrical body. Pulling its multitude of legs together underneath itself, it crouched and sprang into the air. The four eyes at the very top of its head were level with Twenty-Two for only a second before it landed thirty feet below on the ground.

The springy creature jumped up again. She realised that it was only curious about who had come to visit. When it sprang up a second time, she waved at it.

Twenty-Two scolded herself for being scared of what was just another exhibit. Not knowing the name for these creatures didn't mean she should be scared of them. She resolved to ask Ezra what they were called when she met up with him again.

The doors clattered open and she jumped.

Crouching on the ground, she began to vigorously sweep non-existent dirt into the small dustpan. She kept her head down and her hood slid over her face.

What if they spoke to her? They would expect an answer. *I can't just ignore them.*

'Are you okay?' Ezra whispered. 'I heard someone scream, thought it might be you. I came as quickly as I could.'

Ezra then screamed himself. His voice was higher than Twenty-Two had imagined possible. His cry ended with a final strangled note that hung in the air.

'Oh stars, oh stars, Jupiter, Mercury and all things above!' he stammered, his face contorted with fear. He was staring at the other glass window.

Twenty-Two glanced over. The eye was there again.

'It's just more animals,' she signed, walking over to pat his shoulder. 'That one just surprises you. He disappears and then flashes back again.'

'That's like no animal I've ever seen or heard of before,' Ezra whispered, his gaze sliding over to the opposite pod.

The leggy creature sprang into the air again.

Ezra mirrored its jump and added a yelp.

Grabbing Twenty-Two's hand, he tugged her towards the door. 'We have to go. We're not supposed to be in here. There's a sign outside that says no unauthorised personnel, and people are starting to wake up.'

The doors swung open before they got there.

TEN

Two weeks before her fourteenth birthday, Elise's mum, Sofi, had gotten up at 4am and hurried to Thymine's offices. She had wanted to reserve the first slot of the Marking Ceremony for Elise; she hadn't wanted her to spend her birthday worrying about how painful the tattoo would be. If she got it over and done with, then she could enjoy the rest of her day.

When Sofi had returned a few hours later, she had been pleased to report that she had managed to get the third available slot. Sofi hadn't counted on some of the Medius mothers also wanting the first slot, but for very different reasons. The Medius took pride in their tattoos, as the markings defined them as superior to the Sapiens. While nursing a cup of tea, Sofi had told Elise about the two Medius women in front of her in the queue. They had been sitting outside of the base's offices on small, foldout stools for the whole night to ensure their children were the first on the list. Sofi had rolled her eyes at this, but would have only made this gesture safely indoors.

Of course, the tattoo was painful, but Elise, like most

Sapiens, was not unused to pain. The limited amount of Medi-stamps meant there were no local anaesthetics if a Sapien needed stitches or a broken arm had to be reset.

So, when Elise was told a week into her training with Maya that something would have to be done about her tattoo, she was more intrigued than worried.

Maya was still pushing Elise every day, but she was careful not to hurt her like she had on the first day. Elise suspected that Maya had been tough on her so she would realise how much she had to learn and consequently throw herself into her training. If that was the case, it had worked.

'So, what do they want to do to my tattoo?' Elise asked, sitting down on one of the logs that marked out the edges of the sparring circle. She took a swig of water and swilled it around her mouth, still unused to the taste of it.

'It not just yours,' Maya said, standing in front of Elise.

Only the tiniest trickle of sweat had materialised on her temple. She pulled off her jumper and placed it next to Elise on the log. All her movements were tightly controlled; she would never casually throw the jumper down onto the log as most would.

A few days ago, Elise had dared to ask Maya why she didn't dress like most of Uracil in their loose, flowing robes. Maya had told her it was too easy for someone to grab hold of her if she dressed in that way. She had gone on to explain that she braided her hair tightly onto to her scalp and kept the ends short for the same reason. Elise only thought of it afterwards, but it was clear that Maya was always on her guard; she even took these precautions in Uracil.

'They'll also need to adjust Samuel and Luca's tattoos,' Maya said. 'They'll have to give Kit one as well. It's a huge strain on Uracil to falsify four sets of details and slip them into the system. They won't be able to risk doing this again for months; Kit must be very important to the Tri-Council.'

'What are they going to do to our details?'

'They'll read as if you're from Cytosine. You can't be Elise Thanton from Thymine anymore. There'll be a warrant for capture on all of their systems after what you did. Releasing all the animals in a Museum of Evolution, stealing a Neanderthal and killing a Potior—those things will not be forgotten.'

Elise frowned. In the space of a few months, everything had changed. She had gone from being one of the lowliest Sapiens from the Outer Circle to the person whom everyone would be talking about in Thymine. She imagined them, heads bent, in whispered conversations that trailed off when a member of the Protection Department came too close. She would be known in her base as 'the one who left'. The one who had run away with her band of misfit companions, each step ushering in chaos as they crossed from the centre of Thymine to the Outer Circle and then beyond.

What had happened to her family? Had they paid the price for her crimes?

She wished she could be the one who was forgotten, the one who pleasantly faded from people's memories. But that could never happen after what they had done. Being responsible for the death of a Potior—the high-ranking director of Thymine's Museum of Evolution no less—that was not something people would quickly forget. It was also not something that would be forgiven.

Elise shifted uncomfortably. 'Do you think what we did was wrong?'

Maya stared down at Elise before speaking. 'I think what you did was the best you could come up with in the circumstances. But it was noisy, disorganised and you put other lives at risk. If we have to kill people because our lives are threatened, we try to do it more discreetly or tidy up our mess afterwards. Samuel should've known better. And you can't continue in that way; you won't last long. Or, worse, you'll jeopardise the safety of Uracil.'

Elise dug her fingers into the palm of her hand and avoided catching Maya's eye. 'Do you think they've taken my parents and brother? As punishment for what I did?'

'I don't know. From what you've told me, it's unlikely. If the little stunt you pulled with your mother was believed then they wouldn't want to openly punish your parents after they disowned you. News of injustices like that spreads like wildfire. It can be the spark that starts an uprising. You know all about what happened in Thymine twenty years ago.' Maya took a step towards Elise and squeezed her shoulder. 'And you're going back for them soon.'

Elise blinked rapidly. The last time she had cried was when Fintorian casually snapped the bones in her finger and thumb; he had taken enjoyment from the action and taken his time twisting the bone to cause the most damage possible. The time before that had been when Bay's mother, Seventeen, had died. Now was not a time for tears; it didn't warrant them. In only a few days, Elise had begun to respect Maya and she didn't want her to think she was weak.

Elise sprung to her feet. 'Will you show me that move again?'

She was being trained in a martial art that drew on and combined many other, more ancient techniques. It had been created by Maya's trainer, who had studied illegal Pre-Pandemic recordings of fighting styles before deciding that this one best suited Uracil's needs. There was no spiritual element to this style; that had faded along with most religions following the Pandemic. Instead, it was brutal, dirty and designed to finish a fight as quickly and quietly as possible. Elise loved it.

She was only a beginner, but she had taken to it effortlessly after years of training with her dad, Aiden, in blocking moves. Combined with the gruelling cardio regimes, including running, skipping and whatever else Aiden thought would give her the hardest workout and, therefore, the best chance of escape, his coaching had given Elise a head start.

Her only weakness was her right hand, which had regained some of its dexterity but had not healed to the point that it could be used either offensively or defensively. Maya had told her that a skilled fighter would know straightaway that her hand was injured and would intentionally aim to make contact with it to cause her the maximum, debilitating pain. Elise could only hope that if she did have to fight anyone at the moment, it would be the knucklehead type.

In the afternoons, they switched from combat to the other myriad skills Elise would need for her assignments. She was relieved to discover that she was ahead of most trainees when it came to these at least.

Undercover work in Zone 3 consisted of less loitering on pathways and tracking targets than Elise had expected it to. Some volunteers, like Samuel and his mother, had to infiltrate one of the bases and start a whole new existence, staying there for seven years if necessary. Elise's role was different. She would be sent on collections and drop-offs, running urgent supplies or messages in and out of the bases to and from other undercover operatives. It was, therefore, essential that she could live for weeks outside of the bases and Uracil, travelling the terrain and circling the bases, waiting for a safe route in to open up to her.

This was where she excelled. She hadn't had the pampered life of a cosseted Medius. She was used to surviving on the same basic rations every day, sleeping on pallets and a certain amount of discomfort due to the lack of available anaesthetics and painkillers. On top of this, she could hunt, start a fire in less than five minutes and forage at a basic level. As long as she wasn't injured, she could live self-sufficiently outside of the bases for months.

After they had eaten their lunch in silence, Maya checked her screen. 'So, we still have tracking, building shelters, knots, on-body theft, impersonation and basic surgery left.'

'On-body theft?' Elise said, raising an eyebrow.

'That's pickpocketing to you and me. You might need to swipe someone's key card if you need to get into any of the official buildings in the bases.'

Elise sighed. 'Do you know what my first mission will be?'

Maya glanced up at her. 'I'm sorry. I don't decide the missions. That's for the Tri-Council. I'm being sent to Guanine around the same time as you, and I won't know until the morning that I leave what they'll want me to do.'

'Don't you get tired of it?' Elise asked.

Maya laughed. 'Of course I do. I've been doing this for fifteen years and my luck has come close to running out several times. But I believe that the people of Zone 3 deserve much better than the Potiors who run the bases are giving them. You'll find out more in the next few months, but the things they do to their citizens would make your hair stand on end. Separating children from their parents, like what happened to your friend, is only the start of it.'

Elise tried to keep her voice level and hide her frustration. 'But why do they wait until the morning to tell us what we're being asked to do? If I knew now, I could begin planning it with you.'

'You must be more careful, Elise. You flared your nose and it gave you away. You have to control the smallest of tics, remember?' Maya leant forward. 'They don't tell you until the very moment that you leave so that they can narrow down any leaks. They're always wary of betrayal. The protection of Uracil is always the first priority.'

'They want to narrow down the list of suspects if information is given away?'

'It works, as well. In the last fifteen years, only two operatives have been caught, which is a pretty impressive record when you think about it. And both of those instances were unfortunate cases of long-term, undercover operatives breaking under the pressure.

'You have to remember that agents like Samuel have to survive for seven years undercover. Alert to the dangers all the time. It takes a mental toll. Only the strongest of us can remain hidden but operate as normal for such a lengthy period. You have to fully believe in your role, become it if necessary.' Maya stood and stretched the muscles in each of her arms in turn. 'You have to remember that when judging him against what you'd expect from a friend.'

ELEVEN

That evening, Elise was about to turn off her light when there was a knock on her door. Pulling some trousers on, she answered it. Perhaps Maya wanted to start training her in the dark to improve her other senses.

Opening the door, she was surprised to see not Maya, but Samuel standing outside. She hadn't seen him once in the last week and had begun to suspect that he was avoiding her. Not that she had gone out of her way to find him.

'Shall I come outside?' Elise said automatically, remembering her mistake of inviting him into her room when they were living in the museum back in Thymine.

She had only asked him into her room out of politeness, but she'd forgotten that a Medius and Sapien being alone in a bedroom together, no matter how innocent the reason, would never be tolerated in the bases. What would be the point in regimentally dividing people by species if they were allowed to muddy those already tenuous lines?

Samuel glanced around him. 'I think it would be better if I came in, actually. That is, if you don't mind?'

Elise held the door open, careful not to touch him when he walked past her. Once she had closed the door, he closed his eyes for a moment before sitting down. The action was familiar to Elise; it was what Samuel would do in Thymine when he was checking for cameras.

Elise was curious when she realised that he was still taking these precautions, but she didn't say anything to him. Samuel knew what he was doing. If they were still at risk, the last thing they needed was recorded documentation of his suspicions.

Once his eyes blinked open, he took a seat and leant forward. 'I've been busy this last week, catching up on what has been happening whilst I've been away.' He pushed his hair away from his forehead and made the effort to look directly at Elise. 'I'm sorry that I haven't checked on you earlier, but I thought you might want some time away from me, after what I did. Or what I didn't do, to be precise.'

Elise opened her mouth to speak, but Samuel interjected. 'Just let me say this first. I'm sorry I didn't tell you about my background before we arrived in Uracil. I hope you can understand why I didn't say anything in the museum. But it was wrong of me not to tell you once we were safely out of it.'

Elise looked at Samuel clearly for the first time in a week. Once he had gotten them safely to Uracil, she had hoped that he would return to his collected self, but his features still wore that now familiar appearance of strain. He seemed more unravelled in Uracil than he ever had in Thymine. He hadn't shaved yet and a small line between his eyebrows was constantly present. She wanted to help him but she couldn't do that if he didn't feel able to speak openly. All she could do was relieve any anxieties he had about their friendship.

She took a risk and gently patted him on his trousered knee. He didn't flinch, meeting her gaze.

'Of course you're forgiven,' she said. 'Whatever your reason was, I'm sure it was the right one.'

Samuel broke out into a wide smile, the first she had seen in weeks, and pushed his thick, brown hair away from his face with both hands. 'It was never done to mislead you, but I had to mislead the people at the museum. They couldn't suspect that I was anything other than a three-trait Medius with a couple of additional gifts inherited from his parents.'

He leant back in the chair, the smile disappearing from his face as he stared at the ceiling. 'Fintorian guessed, of course, on our last day in Thymine, when we were on the platform above Kit's new pod. He knew that I shouldn't be able to do those things on top of the other traits he was aware of. As soon as he realised, I knew I had to do everything I could to leave Thymine. If I'd been captured...'

'Can you tell me why you waited? Why you didn't tell me on the journey?' Elise asked, careful not to raise her voice.

Samuel dropped his head into his hands. 'Stars, I don't know. I suppose I had spent seven years playing a role and I didn't know how to explain the truth to you. I was embarrassed as well, if I'm honest. I didn't want you...' Samuel stopped and corrected himself. 'I didn't want all of you thinking that I was any different. Because I'm not.' Samuel raised his head. 'There's something else I have to tell you as well. It's embarrassing, but I have to be honest with you.'

Elise took her hand from his knee and leant back in her chair, silently preparing herself for what Samuel was about to say. If he had a secret wife and child stashed away in Guanine, she wouldn't be surprised. In the last year, she had learnt to unravel everything she once thought was true and never automatically believe what she was first told.

'Whatever it is, I would rather know than carry on believing a lie,' Elise said.

'Yes, yes, you're right,' Samuel muttered. 'So, I should tell you then...'

Elise waited patiently for Samuel while he stared up at the hut's roof again.

He cleared his throat before speaking. 'I don't need to wear glasses.'

Relief washed over Elise. He didn't have an entire life hidden from her.

'I never did,' he continued. 'I wore them to look, well... I'm sorry, I was told to start wearing them when I went to Guanine on my first infiltration mission, when I started my university course. My mentor thought it would tone down the part Potior in me, make me look more vulnerable. I'm so sorry; I'm such a sham.'

Samuel's face reddened.

Elise frowned, remembering the conversation they had had when she had revealed her own hidden abilities. 'But your dad...you told me your father had dulled the gifts your mother would have passed on. That he had given you your bad eyesight...even that was a lie.'

In a second, Samuel was crouched down in front of her. She had forgotten how fast he could move. 'I know and I am so very sorry. It was the background story that I was given. A tale of two Medius parents, the mother with highly graded enhancements, the father an embarrassment to his offspring...the bad eyesight passed down the male line. I stuck to it, as I always had done. But it was very wrong of me to use it to try and win your trust.'

'You're probably the only person in Zone 3 who was

trying to downplay his attributes. Everyone else alludes to hidden talents but never produces them...' Elise said, not meeting Samuel's gaze.

'I'm not the only one who hid what they can do,' Samuel responded. 'You had to hide what you could do for years as well. Maybe we were the only two in Zone 3 who weren't fabricating talents or wearing lifts in our shoes to try and look taller.'

'But I told you,' Elise said, raising her voice before checking herself. 'Out of everyone, I trusted you and told you the truth. I've only just explained it to the others. It was always you, out of everyone I've met in the last year, who knew the most about me.'

Elise stared up at the ceiling of the small room, willing Samuel to move away. He slowly moved back to his seat.

'I promise that there will be no more secrets,' Samuel said quietly. 'Just give me a chance to make it up to you, tell you every small detail there is to tell.'

'Do you even remember who you really are?' Elise said, before glancing at him. 'Maybe, while you're in Uracil, you should take some time to think that over. Relax into yourself for a bit. It can't be easy coming out of being undercover for so long...'

She pressed her lips together. 'But you have to promise me that there'll be no more lies. I don't expect you to reveal all your hopes and fears and dreams to me, but I do expect you to unravel all of my misconceptions about you, and never present me with any more. If I find that there are others, then I will never, ever forgive you.'

Samuel nodded, before standing up. 'I think that's the best advice I've had for a while. And I promise that I will never take liberties with your trust again. Before I go, can I ask how your training with Maya is progressing?'

Elise turned around in her seat to face him. 'She's exceptional. The way she moves, combined with her calmness. What she can do, I didn't even think it was possible.'

Samuel smiled. 'I'm glad it's working out and that you two are getting along. She is one of the few people I trust with my life. She was my mother's best friend back when she lived in Uracil.'

'Your mum's best friend! But that makes her...'

'Nearly fifty now. She's a remarkable person, both inside and out. I'm sorry, but that's not my story to tell. I will explain everything about my mother, though, on our journey to Cytosine. My father too. I promise.'

Samuel walked over to the door but stopped before reaching to slide it open. He didn't turn around. 'I also wanted you to have someone you could speak to about what it's like out here. Outside of the bases. Someone I know would give you a truthful answer. I didn't want you to feel as if you only had me to question. Maybe you can tell me a bit about what you've learnt sometime.'

Before Elise could speak, he quietly slid open the door and disappeared into the warm, spring night.

TWELVE

A tall man entered the room with the glass walls. *'What's happening in here?'*

Twenty-Two crouched down as low as possible and carried on sweeping imaginary dust into the small pan, trying to steady her hands.

Ezra stood tall. 'We thought we'd start early today. Get ahead of the game, you know. Apologies if we startled you, sir, but she stood on my toe. Bit clumsy she is. We'll get out of your way.'

Ezra moved towards the doorway and Twenty-Two stood to follow him, careful to keep her head down.

The tall man blocked their path. 'You're not supposed to be in here. You can read, can't you?'

'Not especially well, sir. But I try and teach myself in my pod at night. I'm coming along, if I do say so myself. I'll soon be able to join up my letters if I carry on at this rate.'

The man didn't move. 'Why has she got no shoes on?'

Twenty-Two kept her head down, her heart hammering in her chest. She stared at her bare feet and resisted the urge to wiggle her toes. He was going to make her speak and explain her shoeless status.

'She spilt mop water over them yesterday, so left them out to dry. Only got the one pair, saving up for the next,' Ezra said, trying to step around the man.

Twenty-Two quickly glanced up at him. He was nearly as tall as Fintorian. He had thick, black, wavy hair that was pushed away from his face and stood almost upright. His expression told her that he was not convinced.

'What's your name?' he said to Twenty-Two.

'Mine's Ezra, sir, and this is—'

'Not you.' His gaze flicked from Ezra to Twenty-Two. 'I mean you.'

Her mouth dried. She thought she would bolt at any moment. She had to say something or it would all be over; she'd be put back in her pod, Twenty-Seven back in his and Ezra might have his food taken away from him as well.

'Two...two,' she said, stumbling to link the words together.

As soon as they left her mouth, she realised how stupid she had been. In her panic, she had tried to say her real name.

'Tutu? What sort of name is that?' the man said. 'These Sapiens...'

Ezra rested his arm on the top of his broom handle and leant in. 'She's a twin, sir. Her family's well known in the Outer Shoreline for it. Her mother called the other one Lulu and wanted a similar name for them both. Thought it would be charming.' Ezra scratched his head. 'Don't think her mum considered what it would sound like when she was an adult. Probably sound all right when she's ancient and lost her marbles. But the years between, well—'

'*Would you just stop speaking?*' The tall man glared at

Ezra. 'Stars, I can't believe I've wasted even five minutes on this inane chatter. Just get out. Both of you. Now.'

Twenty-Two didn't need to be told again. She stepped in front of Ezra and pushed open the door.

Without looking back, she went straight to the nearest cleaning closet and closed the door behind her, before Ezra could follow her inside.

She wouldn't open the door, even when Ezra tapped on it and tried to make her smile by calling her Tutu.

That evening, after Twenty-Two had made her way back safely to her pod, she stood by the door waiting for Ezra. Dara and Twenty-Seven had already gone to sleep. She hadn't told Dara about what had happened with the tall man; it would just bring on more shrieking. Instead, she had sat quietly all day, internally scolding herself. She wasn't sure who the man was, but she guessed that he must be someone important as he was so tall.

When Ezra still hadn't arrived by nightfall, she began to worry. Had she gotten him into trouble? Did he not want to see her again after she had been so useless? If Ezra stopped visiting, who would bring them food? It would be hopeless; she would have to go out into the museum by herself to find provisions for Dara and Twenty-Seven. She would eventually be caught...

The endings whirled around her mind and she thought that if she were ever going to cry, it would be now.

The noise of the bars on the steel door halted her. She looked up expectantly and was relieved to see Ezra's freckled face poke around the door.

Her hands were a flurry of movement. 'I'm so sorry. I

put us both in danger. I should have thought of another name. I was so stupid.'

It was only a half moon and she strained to see his reaction.

He carefully closed the door and turned to her. 'Slow down, Tutu. I'm still not that fast at following your speech either.'

He broke out his broad grin.

Twenty-Two felt a wash of relief and flung her arms around him. She couldn't help herself. Ezra stumbled backwards and a shy smile crossed his face. He quietly stood still while Twenty-Two rested her head on his shoulder, gathering her thoughts.

After a minute, she pulled away. She signed more slowly this time. 'Sorry, I just thought you might not be coming back and didn't know how I was going to look after Dara and Twenty-Seven without you. Are you okay? Did you get into trouble with that man?'

Ezra rubbed his nose before answering. 'I'm fine; you don't have to worry about me. Since working here, I've gotten used to dealing with those high-end, Medius types. He's the Collection's Assistant, name's Hadrian.'

'I thought he knew something was wrong. I was so worried. And it's all my fault.'

'He's got his head in other things, won't care about a shoeless, Sapien cleaner. They expect you to be inferior to them, so I just play up to it. Means they leave me alone as I've met their expectations.' Ezra grinned. 'You did really well linking those words together. But we might have to come up with another Sapien name for you.'

Twenty-Two nodded.

'Anyway, I've spent the day thinking about it and we should wait a while before leaving,' Ezra said, taking a gulp of air and continuing quickly. 'We need to get you to a point where you don't bolt anymore. We were lucky that we were in a part of the museum with no cameras. Don't get me wrong. I'd be exactly the same if I'd spent all my time in this pod. We also need to work on what you do if someone speaks to you. We'll cut the time we spend out there right back and only go out for an hour each night. That way we'll lower our chances of getting caught again.'

Twenty-Two stared at his features in the low light. 'Is there something wrong?'

Ezra gave a half-smile and shrugged. 'You can read people pretty well, can't you?'

Twenty-Two had never really thought about it. 'I suppose I can tell what someone's meaning is, even when the words they say are different. Can't everyone do that?'

'Not as good as you can. Maybe that's something Neanderthals can do better than Sapiens.'

'Maybe. But you haven't answered my question,' Twenty-Two signed.

They began walking towards the stream. Ezra had been drinking a small amount of the water from it every night.

He held up his hands. 'Okay, you've got me. I can't stop thinking about those things we saw in the room. They've given me the spinal cord shivers.'

'They weren't that bad. I think they are lonely. And not everything can be beautiful. What is the name for them?'

Ezra stopped part way across the stepping stones and turned to Twenty-Two. 'They don't have a name. They're not like anything I've heard of. That thing with the legs... that was too many legs. And the disappearing eye. Nothing that weird should be alive. They're not natural.'

Twenty-Two bristled. 'Some people would say that I shouldn't be alive. That I am not natural.'

'No, no, I didn't mean it like that. You're nothing like them. You've existed for thousands of years and they...well, they...I don't think they were put here by the stars. I think the Potiors made them.'

'How could the Potiors have made them? The Potiors can't just—'

Twenty-Two stopped mid-sign. Of course they could. They had made her, hadn't they? What was stopping the Potiors making other creatures as well?

'But they had something to start with when they made me. They couldn't just make something from nothing, could they?' she eventually signed.

'They probably had something to start with when they made them; they just changed the recipe's ingredients around a bit,' Ezra said. 'Made a ham sandwich instead of cheese.'

Twenty-Two stared at her feet. 'Do you think they might have changed the recipe for me as well?'

Ezra snorted. 'What? No way. They were obsessed with the Neanderthal Project; they would have made you as cleanly as possible. Don't you ever think about why they keep you locked up away from everyone? They want you to be untainted by the modern world. They want you to be just as you would've been.'

Twenty-Two thought about this for a moment before following Ezra across the stream.

They settled by its bank and Twenty-Two watched as Ezra made a face while sipping at a cup of water taken from the stream. He hadn't gotten ill from it in the last few weeks and her hopes were growing that it could be their water supply for their journey to Thymine.

'Why do you think they don't want me to be contaminated by what's out there?' Twenty-Two asked.

Ezra stopped grimacing and drank down the rest of the water. 'Who knows why the Potiors do anything? They're so enhanced that I couldn't even begin to think like they do. But they do like clear divisions. Sapiens and Medius aren't really supposed to mix and it's certainly illegal for them to marry or umm...spend time alone with each other.'

Twenty-Two didn't know why Ezra was blushing; he was clearly trying to hide something. She suspected it was something to do with people being alone with each other. She knew she didn't want to speak with Ezra about that sort of thing, whatever it may be. She would let it go.

'I can understand them wanting to keep me separate from the others out there; there's no point bringing us back if we're diluted,' Twenty-Two signed. 'But I do wish that I had been allowed to grow up with other Neanderthals. I think that would have helped us learn what makes us different. In here, brought up by Sapiens, who knows what bits of Sapien have rubbed off on me? Language, to begin with.'

'I never really thought about it,' Ezra said, stretching. 'Maybe you could persuade Fintorian to let you live with the other Neanderthals in Thymine. Show him how well you and Twenty-Seven have been doing together.'

'Do you know anything about the Neanderthals in Thymine?' Twenty-Two asked, hoping they would be around the same age as her.

'When I was in school, we were taught that there was a male and a female there. Twenty-One and Seventeen. The male would be around the same age as you—'

'And the female, Seventeen, she would be the one Fintorian left Cytosine to go and work with,' Twenty-Two signed. 'If only I'd been a bit older, he might have stayed and then none of this would have happened.'

'It isn't anybody's fault that they're the age they are.'

'Yes, but if only I'd been older...'

'Well, you're older now, aren't you?' Ezra said, brightening. 'Cheer up. You might be old enough for Fintorian to want to work with you now, like he did with Seventeen.'

Twenty-Two sat up and scrunched her eyes at him. This was the best bit of news she had received in weeks.

THIRTEEN

'You're flippin' right I'm not going to get an early night,' Luca said to Elise while adjusting his shirt collar. 'It's not like we're going to be breaking into Cytosine tomorrow; all we're doing is leaving Uracil. I don't need to be awake for that.'

'That's true,' Elise said, smiling up at her friend.

He was right; tomorrow it was only a matter of placing one foot in front of the other, which she could do on very little sleep.

'And a party's a party. And I've heard this one's not to be missed.' He gave Elise a broad grin. She was perched on his bed waiting for him to get ready.

'How do I look?' he asked, turning around. 'Actually, don't answer that. Do you remember when I asked Seventeen the same question before I went to that Fintorian-fest that Harriet organised back in Thymine, and all she could say was that I looked "better"?'

'She always told me that I looked like a boy,' Elise said.

Her hair now reached her chin and she hadn't had the

heart to cut it; Seventeen had always hated it when it was short.

Luca frowned. 'I still think about her all the time...still think about whether we could've done more to save her. I should never have let Fintorian do that to her.'

'Don't say that; you know it wasn't your fault. Fintorian manipulated her into agreeing to being implanted and having a baby. She was just another experiment to him. He wanted to see what a pregnant Neanderthal was like after growing all the others in labs. She was given the same care as a lab mouse and it ended up killing her.'

Luca nodded and tried to smile. 'Do you think Twenty-Two will be like her?'

'Who knows what she's like? Samuel can't find out much about her. All we know is she's a little younger than Kit.'

Elise stood and pulled at the skirt she had borrowed. It had a habit of riding up that she didn't like. It was only for one night, though.

'Stars, I hope she's had a decent Companion. I try not to think about what it'd do to Kit if she hasn't,' Elise said, still tugging at her skirt. 'I haven't said anything to him, but what if she's in the same state as some of the earlier ones? We'll never get her back here.'

Luca nodded and rubbed his hand against the back of his head. He'd shaved it again and he appeared older and tougher. Elise missed his baby curls.

'Let's not think about it tonight, Thanton. We've got four weeks to worry about it.'

'You're right. Look, why don't you go down and work out what sort of thing this is? I'm going to get Georgina. I've barely seen her since we got here and I think she's going to try and duck out of this if she can.'

'Sounds good. I haven't seen her either. I don't want her to become the weird hermit-lady of cabin thirty-one,' Luca said, sliding the door open for them both.

Traversing the wooden walkways in the treetops, Elise tried not to get flustered by the passers-by who openly stared at her. News of their forthcoming departure had already circulated throughout Uracil. She smiled at everyone she passed and stopped to chat if they spoke to her. It didn't come naturally, but she was trying to be more open instead of shrinking from this type of attention. Maya had already told her she would be given her mission details in the morning and she would be back again in less than three months, hopefully with her parents. She wanted them to be accepted by the Uracil residents, so she knew she had to try to get to know a few of them.

Not wanting to wake Bay up, Elise lightly tapped on the door. A few moments later, Georgina carefully slid the solid, oak panel open for her.

'Elise, come in. It's good to see you.'

Elise stepped through the door and into the darkened room. All of the cloth blinds had been pulled down and she had difficulty locating somewhere to sit.

'Here, over here,' Georgina said, clearing some clothes from a wooden stool.

'Do you remember your stool at the museum that you used to whizz across the room on?' Elise asked, smiling at the thought of the look of sheer glee that used to cross Georgina's perfect features.

'Of course. I loved that seat. It used to give me a rush of delight if I made it across the room in one go. Small things, eh? But enough of that place; I wanted to speak with you.'

Elise turned to open one of the blinds so she could see Georgina properly.

'No, no, leave it down. I don't like to be...'

Elise peered at Georgina. She knew that it wasn't for Bay's benefit that she left the blinds down; when Bay wanted to nap she could get to sleep no matter how bright it was.

'I know it's been hard...' Elise began, not knowing how much to say, '...with what happened to you at the museum. But you shouldn't hide away. Come down to the party with me; we'll get someone to watch over Bay. I think she'd have a stream of volunteers; they're fascinated by her here.'

Elise stood up and made her way towards the quiet sobs. Wrapping her arms around Georgina, Elise let her cry until she pulled her face away and shook her head.

A stillness came over Georgina's features. 'I've been thinking about it a lot, since we left, and I've decided to keep the scar. Even if they can mend it here in Uracil. I never wanted to be a Medius and now I'm not.'

Elise brushed back her friend's vivid, red hair. 'It's your decision to make and you're just as beautiful either way. But if the scar stays, you can't hide away like this. You should be proud of it. You got it in exchange for saving my life and I'll never forget that.'

Georgina sighed. 'You're right. I know I can't hide away. Look, let me just get changed and then I'll come down.'

'I'll go and find someone to watch Bay,' Elise said, leaning in to hug her friend. She stopped halfway when she saw Georgina's expression.

'Not so quick, sneaky-pie.' Georgina leant over and patted the seat of the stool. 'Sit yourself back down again. There's something else we need to talk about.'

Elise didn't like the sound of this, but she was willing to humour Georgina now that she was starting to sound like her old self.

'Why did you go and agree to be Uracil's retriever dog? They'll keep on sending you on their inane missions until you're worn down.'

Georgina watched Elise without blinking.

She was only a couple of years older than Elise, but she always made her feel like a much younger sister when she took this tone.

'Maya's been doing this for fifteen years and she's fine,' Elise said, trying not to sound like a twelve-year-old.

'Maya had a chance to have a life before she chose this one. I don't like it. Why did you suggest it?'

Elise opened her mouth to answer but was cut off.

'I know what you're going to say, to get your brother and parents here. What I mean is, why didn't you let us find another way to get them in? I don't know your parents, but if they are even vaguely decent human beings, they won't feel comfortable living in their luxury tree house, as free as a family of starlings, if they never get to see their other child because she's scampering all over Zone 3 on dangerous missions. So, I'm going to ask again, why did you suggest it?'

Elise stared at her hands for a moment before deciding to tell the truth. 'I've had this bad feeling for the last few weeks, that something's happened to them. I don't think we've got time to come up with another plan. And this training—what Maya's teaching me—it will be invaluable when the time comes. I need the training to help change—,' Elise gestured around, '—change, well, everything, I suppose.'

Elise knew she had never been good at making convincing speeches, but she also knew that it didn't matter when she felt this strongly about what she was doing. She knew it was the right thing and that's all that mattered.

She lifted her head. 'I want to be part of that change.

And I can't do that if I'm worrying about my family all the time.'

Georgina raised an eyebrow. 'Well, we both better start praying to the stars that you get back here with your family in tow. Then Maya can start working her magic again.'

Luca had been right; the party was not to be missed. It was a festival of lights. Every spare branch had a coloured lantern hanging from it. Their warm, golden glow illuminated the long tables laden with food. Guests wandered around, stopping to pick up morsels of food, their soft chatter ringing throughout the clearing. People were encouraged to mingle and switch benches, conversations weaving their way around the trees. Nothing was forced. It was the opposite of the segregated party Elise had attended at the museum the year before.

Like with the tree houses, the residents of Uracil were allowed to let their imaginations run free when it came to their outfits for the evening. There was nothing ostentatious or showy in the clothing they chose; it was more playful than that. Even Faye, who had a large concertina of material fanning out from the back of her dress, looked as if she were paying homage to a peacock's display rather than impersonating one. Some people chose colour themes and wore every shade of turquoise; others were swathed in robes with shocking shades of pink or orange hidden underneath, only revealed when they moved around. There was one man, nearly as tall as Faye, who had left his shirt completely open to reveal a network of tattoos that wove their way across his chest. Elise tried not to spend too long watching him, but she had never seen tattoos like them before; she thought they combined both beauty and meaning.

Elise's neighbour, Tilla, had persuaded her to dress up for the evening. She was one of the people Elise had been trying to get to know over the last few weeks. Tilla had dropped in on Elise before the party and been unable to hide her displeasure at the outfit Elise had chosen. She had called it 'unremarkable'. Elise guessed that in Tilla's view, this was as bad as it could get.

Elise was firm and did not allow Tilla to persuade her to wear a see-though, organza dress, no matter how much she pleaded. Tilla had sulked for a moment before pulling out a second and third outfit from the drawers in her small tree house. Elise had finally settled on a full skirt that reached her knees and shimmered in the light. She had been going to wear a loose shirt on top but Tilla had instructed her that, with a full skirt, she needed a tighter top, so Elise acquiesced. On her feet she wore flat sandals, which helped her keep up with Tilla, who never stopped weaving her way from one group to another.

For the evening's festivities, Tilla was wearing a floor-length, halter-neck gown that was completely backless and bright crimson. She was barefoot and skipped around the party introducing Elise to everyone she could think of. Elise had instantly liked this little ball of energy, whose mind flitted from one topic and idea to the next.

'Now it's my turn,' Tilla said, fluffing her wavy hair and pouting slightly. 'I'd like you to introduce me to someone. I'm too pretty to be alone.'

Elise laughed, used to Tilla's brazen humour. 'Of course, which one of my lovely companions are you wanting to meet? Luca has been watching you all night, if that is what's tempting you over.'

Tilla laughed. 'No, he's not the one. Guess again.'

Elise paled slightly. That surely only left Samuel. Was it Samuel that Tilla wanted to meet? It wouldn't surprise her; like Faye, he stood out from the crowd. He was taller than most and clearly muscled under his shirt. He was also Vance's son and Faye's brother. No matter how much Uracil preached 'equality', Elise was pretty certain that still held some weight.

Elise had caught Samuel watching them a few times during the evening, but she hadn't had a chance to say hello to him while Tilla pulled them first in one direction and then the next. When Elise had first spotted him, she had tried not to stare. For the first time since she had known him, he had made an effort with his appearance. He had shaved, had his hair cut and was wearing new clothes. Combined with the tan he had from being outside for three weeks, he was drawing more than a few admiring glances from the female residents.

Elise couldn't help but glance over at him during the evening; he had stayed by Kit's side all night to help translate for him. Elise suspected that it was also to help Kit surmount such a large group of people.

Staring at Tilla's perfectly curled hair and smooth skin, Elise hoped that Samuel hadn't noticed the additional attention he had been receiving. Realising that she cared so much made her uncomfortable. She had always wanted her friends to find someone; their happiness had never lessened her own. But not Samuel. She couldn't watch Samuel tentatively fall in love with someone. The thought of it brought a wave of loss over her; she tried to remind herself that nothing had happened to warrant this feeling of emptiness.

'Do I need to spell it out?' Tilla enquired.

Elise tried not to look flustered.

'I'm not sure who it is; just tell me and I'll take you over to them,' she said, glancing back at Samuel.

Tilla laughed. 'You like one of them, don't you? And you're scared I like the same one.'

Elise opened her mouth and closed it abruptly before trying again. 'No, no, not true at all.'

'Don't worry; you don't have to tell me. I can guess. But rest assured, I don't think mine is the same as yours.' Tilla grabbed her hand. 'Come on, let's help tidy the plates away and move the tables. We'll need a clearing if I'm going to show them how it's done.'

The dancing started an hour later. Elise had never heard anything like the percussion music before. The beat was strong and two female voices intertwined over the top of it. Elise spent most of the time next to Luca, who was one of the best dancers she had ever seen. He could adapt his style to any music and it wasn't long before the Uracil residents were starting to copy him. Kit came over and stood next to Elise, bobbing his head slightly out of time.

'I have never danced before,' he signed to her before scrunching his eyes. 'I suppose that is because I have never heard music before.'

Luca followed Kit's hand movements and came over to show him a few simple steps, signing encouragement along the way. One of the many benefits of sign language was that it didn't matter how loud it got; they could still have a full conversation.

Elise smiled. Kit was taking everything in his stride, his first time listening to music and dancing both handled with a sense of fun and adventure. She internally shook herself about her earlier feelings of imagined loss and told herself to stop being so self-involved.

She had been dancing for over an hour when she

decided to get some water. Taking her glass to a bench farther away from the clearing, she smiled as she watched her friends enjoying themselves. It was moments like this that she thanked the stars for intertwining her path with theirs. Luca and Kit had started a two-man dance group, a circle of people surrounding them and clapping; Kit's eyes were constantly scrunched in happiness. Tilla had pulled Georgina onto the dance floor and was twirling her around in between the two men.

Elise knew right then that she would do anything to protect this little world they had created together. She felt it so strongly that, for a moment, it took her breath from her.

'Can I sit?' Samuel asked.

Elise stared up at him; she hadn't heard him come over. He was wearing a light blue shirt and had rolled the sleeves up as he always did.

'Of course,' Elise said, suddenly feeling nervous.

Samuel stepped over the bench and sat down. He kept his distance and placed his glass between them.

They sat in silence for a few minutes until Elise couldn't take it any longer. 'It's a bit different to that party Harriet organised for Fintorian, isn't it?'

'It is,' he said. 'This one is much better; it doesn't feel like mandatory fun.'

They fell quiet again, until Samuel broke the silence. 'You'll be getting your orders tomorrow. How are you feeling about receiving them?'

'Not too bad, thanks,' Elise said, turning to face him. She concentrated on folding the material from her skirt between her fingers before going back to watching Kit spin Georgina around until she nearly toppled over. 'Maya thinks it will be simple data collection from one of the Cytosine homes. In and out. I should be able to do it after we've got Twenty-Two. I'll catch up with you on the way to Thymine.'

Samuel nodded. 'I've been thinking about it. We should leave Kit, Twenty-Two and Luca in the woodlands outside of Thymine. You and I should slip in together to get your parents. We can't all risk getting captured.'

Elise was touched. 'Thank you, but I think it'd be best if I went by myself. If any of my neighbours saw you...well, you don't look like any Sapien I've ever met in the Outer Circle. Your height alone makes you stand out.'

Samuel frowned and rested his hands on his knees. 'We'll talk about it more on the journey. We've got four weeks to work out our plans.' He smiled at her. 'I'm actually looking forward to it just being the four of us. I even miss arguing with Luca. Faye has me in constant meetings; she wants to know everything about the museum and the Neanderthal project.'

A thought occurred to Elise. She felt uncomfortable asking him, but she needed to know. 'Will they be sending you out to one of the bases for another seven years?'

Samuel didn't look at her when he answered. 'Something similar. The Tri-Council wants me to begin reaching out to our contacts in the other zones. It will mean I'll get to work alongside my father again. I haven't seen him in years.'

Elise felt the same wave of loss drag down at her chest. She hadn't thought about how much things would soon be changing—they couldn't stay like this forever.

'Maybe I could visit you when you're back in Zone 3,' she said, still watching Kit.

'Yes, I'd like that very much.' Samuel glanced over at her. 'I'm going to have to leave everyone behind again. Start all over. That's why I want to bring Twenty-Two here, so that Kit will have someone when I am gone.'

Elise leant forward and rested her head on her hands. She suddenly felt very weary. 'My parents will keep an eye out for Kit when they get here. I think he'll like my mum. But it won't be the same as having you; Kit looks up to you like an older brother.'

'I know, and I think of him as my sibling too. I just feel it's my duty to go back out again. Raul and Flynn's adopted daughter has been doing this work for the past eighteen months and they want me to join her. I haven't seen her for years either.'

Elise looked away. She had to let him go; she had to let them all go. She couldn't freeze their little world in this moment.

'What's wrong?' Samuel asked, sitting up.

'It's just...everything is changing so fast. Soon we'll be scattered all over Zone 3—you even farther. I can't imagine not seeing you every day.'

Samuel smiled at her and it reached all the way to his eyes before his face became serious again. 'People become separated in unsettled times like these. The mood is changing, both inside and outside of Uracil.' He rubbed his forehead. 'We could try and not become separated, though. If you wanted. But things between us might have to change.'

Elise stared at him; he was still looking in the opposite direction and she could see that his cheeks were red. 'Change how?'

Samuel spoke slowly. 'We could try and change together, change in the same way, maybe?'

Elise smiled. Then she slowly leant in and kissed him, right there, underneath the sycamore tree.

FOURTEEN

Elise had lived all of her first eighteen years within a five-mile radius. Inside that laced network of recycled, rubber pathways and wildflower roofs, she had rarely strayed from the Outer Circle. Elise's kind was not encouraged to wander—it was best if they remained in the life they were born into.

She had always known that she would never leave her base, but that hadn't tempered her inquisitive streak. Any chance she got, she would ask questions about the other three settlements, but she had to act carefully, showing only a passing interest. She would listen in on hushed conversations, a slightly bored look crossing her features if she was caught leaning in too close. She would take these small risks, if it meant she could learn a little more about the world outside.

Now, in her nineteenth year, she had spent more time outside of the bases than she could ever have imagined. Few Sapiens ever saw another base, yet, in only a few weeks, she would arrive in Cytosine. Perhaps she had always been destined for a different life to the one she had felt she deserved.

For a week, they had been retracing their steps south and she wasn't any less enamoured with the changing scenery than she had been on the first journey. She walked by herself most of the time, trying not to spend too much time with Samuel. If anything, she almost avoided him, acutely aware that their last night in Uracil had irrevocably changed their friendship.

They were trudging over a heather-strewn moor when Kit caught up with her. The two fell into step. She was always at ease in his company, and soon let her mind wander again.

'What happened at the party, was it a mistake?' Kit signed, jolting Elise out of her thoughts.

She stared ahead at Samuel, who was setting the pace; behind her, Luca was straggling, not having slept much the night before.

'What? How did you...?' Elise didn't bother to finish; she knew she couldn't hide much from Kit. 'No, it wasn't a mistake. It's just so awkward now, with the four of us.'

'You are hurting him, by avoiding him.'

Elise blushed. 'I don't mean to. I'm just not very... umm...experienced in this sort of thing. I don't know how we become something else when we've always just been friends.'

'And you think he does? The man who could not stand physical contact with anyone until you?'

Elise knew he was right.

That evening, she took the lead and sat down next to Samuel at the campfire. He looked over and gave her a half smile. Before he could move over to give her more space, she laid a hand lightly on his crossed leg and left it there. Her face burned but she hoped he couldn't see her reaction in the dim light.

Samuel smiled at her, wider this time, and caught her eye. She smiled back and they both broke into grins at the absurdity of the situation.

'Well, it's about time,' Luca said, peeling the meat off a cooked chicken leg.

Elise's face reddened farther.

'Better late than never,' she said as casually as she could.

'That's true.' Luca grinned. 'Now, if I can only convince the goddess that is Faye of my worth, I will die a happy man.'

'Umm...that is my sister you're talking about,' Samuel said, pulling Elise closer to him.

She was grateful that she had the darkness to smooth the transition.

'She's not really like a sister to you, is she?' Luca said. 'You didn't grow up together. And she's beautiful and... and...ethereal. And you're...well...you're neither of those things.'

Samuel laughed. 'And how do you think she sees you?'

'Hopefully not ugly and dumpy,' Luca responded. 'Or if she does, I hope that she finds ugly and dumpy irresistible.'

Kit scrunched his eyes.

'I bet you know what she thinks of me,' Luca said, pointing the now bare chicken bone at Kit. 'You could read her reactions straightaway.'

'I rarely see you together,' Kit signed. 'Anyway, it is not my job to interfere in such things. We are not children.'

'That is also true. Such wise words beside the campfire tonight!' Luca glanced at Samuel. 'Bet you could tell me a lot about her. You are her brother, after all.'

'I thought I wasn't her brother?' Samuel responded.

'Pleeeease...don't make me beg, I'm embarrassed enough as it is,' Luca said, leaning forwards.

At that moment, Elise realised that, in his own way, Luca was trying to help them both by admitting to his own fruitless infatuation.

Touched by the gesture, she grinned at him before turning to Samuel. 'Come on, you owe me a bit of background too.'

He smiled down at her. 'That is very true. Where to start?'

'At the beginning, of course,' Luca said, chucking the chicken bone into the fire. The flames spat at the unexpected addition and sparks circled up into the inky-black sky.

'Well, I suppose the beginning starts with our parents,' Samuel said. 'My father was on the Tri-Council in Uracil but he spent a great deal of his time abroad in the other Zones, obtaining supplies and making alliances. He would leave Raul and Flynn to run the domestic side of the base; he was always confident in their abilities and trusted them entirely. One year, he travelled all the way to Zone 5 and was gone for three years. When he returned, he thought that a new family had joined Uracil as there was a young woman that he didn't recognise.'

Elise raised her head, certain that she knew who that would be.

'He asked around and found out that she had always lived in Uracil, had been born there, in fact, but she had kept herself away from the main dealings of the base and lived at the edge of the forest with her family. She was beautiful...she is beautiful, my mother. Not in a Potior way or even Medius, really. She has a kindness and warmth to her features that I've never seen before in anyone. She always looks as if she is slightly smiling, even when her face is relaxed and her thoughts are far away.'

'I think Faye is like that too,' Luca said.

'Not quite the same, but I can see why you would think so,' Samuel said. 'For the first time in his life, my father didn't know what to do. He had never allowed himself to think of any of the residents of Uracil in this way. He was still acutely aware of the privileges he had enjoyed all his life as a Potior. He didn't want to be seen exerting his influence over anyone, especially someone as young as my mother was. She was twenty when he returned and he believed there was no hope that a woman of her age would genuinely find anything in common with someone with his history. He convinced himself that she would never be able to see beyond the Potior to the person below.

'According to Raul and Flynn, he was so withdrawn at that time they worried that he was preparing to leave Uracil for good. They eventually persuaded him to tell them about his predicament, and it helped. He realised that he didn't even know my mother and he couldn't fall in love just with the kindness displayed in her features; that was as insincere as his fear of her being enamoured only with his own Potior exterior. He had to know that the qualities he imagined in her were real as well.

'So he began to find excuses to spend time with her, much as I did with you,' Samuel said, glancing down at Elise. 'Everything went well for them at the beginning; she had grown up without the enforced view of the world so prevalent in the other bases and, consequently, treated him as just another person to get to know. She told me that even at the very start, she felt comfortable in his company. He never patronised her and was always keen to hear her viewpoint. In return, she knew her own mind and did not bend easily to his will. Before long, they were married and had Faye.'

Samuel leant farther backwards. 'But my mother changed in the coming years. She wanted to help Uracil and my parents would fight all the time about her desire to visit the other bases. He couldn't understand why she would want to leave what he perceived to be a utopia. In return, she couldn't be happy with such a small life when he was able to visit not only the other bases but the rest of the world as well. She didn't want to live her life in the back-drop to his adventures. It was a kernel of grievance that had always been there, but before they knew it, it was behind every argument, every distasteful glance. It came to a head one day and my mother left for Adenine when Faye was five years old.'

'That must have been difficult for Faye,' Kit signed.

'Yes, I suppose it was. My father stayed with her, though. He rarely left her side, only travelling when abso-lutely necessary and for the shortest amount of time. And then, when my mother arrived in Adenine, she found out that she was pregnant with me. She had initially only planned on leaving Uracil for a few months, but with my arrival, she thought that she had a chance of integrating me into Adenine in a way no one in Uracil had managed before. Faye had inherited my father's outward appearance and couldn't pass as Medius, but I could. I was tall but I didn't have that perfect, wax-like skin the Potiors, amongst other things.'

'I noticed that straightaway with Fintorian. So, they all have it?' Elise asked.

'Yes, most of their enhancements are mandatory. The height, skin, strength, intelligence and longevity...they all have to appear infallibly impressive or they would lose their hold. There are no exceptions. If they don't turn out exactly right...well...I don't know for sure, but my father told me that they weren't given a new life like you were,' Samuel said, glancing over at Luca. 'That's why he became so disillusioned. He had a child before he founded Uracil, you see, but all of the enhancements hadn't taken...'

They all fell silent.

'Stars, this world is a mess, isn't it?' Luca said, poking a stick into the fire.

'Perhaps it has always been imperfect in some way,' Kit signed after a while. 'Even when my kind was around last time.'

'Who knows?' Elise said, staring up at the sky. 'Perhaps we just have to concentrate on trying to correct the present, not distract ourselves with the past or the future. Both are only echoes of what is real anyway.'

Samuel smiled down at her and she met his gaze.

'I must get some sleep,' Luca said, rubbing the back of his shaved head. 'I can't have another day like today, felt as if I was wading through the porridge they used to serve in the canteen.'

'Me too,' Kit signed, before standing. 'But I do think tomorrow will be a better day.'

Before she knew it, Elise was alone with Samuel, their two friends having moved their sleeping rolls farther away from the main camp. It was a warm night and they had only needed the fire to cook with, not for its heat.

Without thinking about it too much, she turned to Samuel and kissed him lightly. 'I'm sorry for avoiding you. If it hurt you, I didn't mean to.'

'Apology accepted. It's not easy for either of us.' Samuel's gaze followed the still sparking flames. 'I hope, in the future, it will become as natural as breathing.'

Elise smiled at the thought. 'Can I ask you a question?'

'Of course. We have a new agreement. No lies.'

'Why is it that I can touch you now, when before you used to always avoid it. I remember when I touched your hand once in the museum and you actually flinched. You pulled away from me.'

Samuel drew her closer, as if to prove a point. 'It wasn't just you. It was everyone. I couldn't stand to have contact. You're the first person who has broken through that.'

'Why were you like that before?'

'I always have been. My mother said even as a young child, I never came to her for a hug if I had fallen or hurt myself. I don't know where exactly it comes from. Maybe knowing from a young age that I had a secret to hide. It was always at the back of my mind that I had to avoid being exposed. Maybe that's why I always kept my distance from people in Adenine and a physical manifestation set in as well. Or a symptom of social anxiety perhaps? I've always had difficulty reading social interactions, kept myself away from them if I could. I've read that it can be quite a common side effect with the higher IQ levels. I used to think about why I was like this all the time. I came up with many theories, but it's hard to be objective when you are analysing yourself, isn't it?'

Elise nodded.

'Anyway, all I am certain of is that there was a time, back when we were working in the museum together, when it started to change. But only with you. I understood for the first time why a person seeks another.'

With that, he rested his head against hers, and Elise silently thanked the stars for this gift she had been granted.

FIFTEEN

On the last day of the month, Twenty-Two shook Dara awake. The moon had passed the halfway point of the skylight and Twenty-Seven had already been awake for an hour, quietly sitting next to the elderly Companion.

No matter how much Twenty-Two tried to cajole him into talking to her, Twenty-Seven had remained silent for weeks. The only time he ever made a sound was when he cried out in the night. Twenty-Two would wake up to the sound of his screams and scramble over to try and comfort him. She worried about him constantly, afraid that the damage from his enforced isolation would be irreversible.

Every morning, she would usher him across the corridor to his pod so that he could wash in the stream. She hated having to take him back there, but with her stream being their only water source, she didn't want to taint their drinking supply.

Supporting Dara along the way, she would practically drag Twenty-Seven into his old home. There they would all clean themselves, as well as their spare clothes when needed. The constant cycle of laundry had to be taken care of most days, as Twenty-Seven would often wake soaked in sweat from his nightmares. A few times, he had even wet himself, and Twenty-Two had held him close as he stared glumly at his soiled sleeping mats. She knew they had to leave as soon as possible; she was not the only one hanging by a thread.

'It's time to go,' she signed to Dara. 'Ezra has got the eighteenth sandwich. That's more than a sandwich each a day if it takes us four days to get to Thymine.'

Dara didn't look convinced. 'How am I going to walk for four days?'

'You're not. Ezra and I will take it in turns to carry you. The other one will walk with Twenty-Seven. It will be fine.'

It has to be, Twenty-Two thought to herself.

It couldn't be that hard; Ezra had done it when he was a baby. It would be just like crossing the main atrium of the museum for four days. She could do that for eight days if it meant they would all be safe.

'Well, if it means that I get to see Mister Fintorian again...' Dara paused. 'It's just...it's just it don't seem right. Don't feel right and these thoughts...these thoughts...they keep on escaping me. It feels like we shouldn't be doing this. Not because it's wrong but because...' Dara shook her head and blinked quickly. 'I can't keep a hold of them. Do you understand? Am I making sense to you...am I still making sense?'

Twenty-Two nodded and scrunched her eyes. 'Of course you still make sense. You're just worried because it will be such an upheaval for you. It will all be fine. We just have to get out of the museum and everything will work itself out. We'll be with Mister Fintorian by the end of the week.'

Dara's eyes welled up. 'You're a good girl, trying to take care of us. I'll be sure to tell Mister Fintorian all about what you've done for us.'

Twenty-Two scrunched her eyes in response and felt a warmth deep inside that stayed with her as she began to pack up their belongings.

In the small hours of the night, they slipped out of the pod door, Dara on Twenty-Two's back and Ezra holding firmly onto Twenty-Seven's hand. They had decided that this was the best way to proceed; each Neanderthal would have someone with them who could answer any questions if they did run into anyone.

They were dressed in Sapien clothing to try and blend in. Ezra had struggled to find anything small enough for Twenty-Seven, so he was wearing a woman's t-shirt printed by the museum with a picture of a woolly rhinoceros on it. The t-shirt reached his knees, where they met a pair of Ezra's shorts that ballooned around his skinny legs. These flapping trousers barely grazed the oversized socks he was wearing in place of shoes.

Twenty-Two was wearing Ezra's smartest trousers, which were shiny and squeaked slightly when her thighs rubbed against each other. The trousers were for 'bests' he had told her. She had one of his warm tops on as well, with the hood pulled up and over most of her face.

On her feet she had Ezra's only other pair of shoes, which he had worn once before to a party at the museum. They felt tight and rubbed her heels already. Ezra had to do the shoelaces up for her, as she had never worn shoes before. She didn't like them. She had lost sensitivity to where she was placing her feet. They were so numbed to their surroundings that she felt as if the grey corridor were seeping upwards and turning her to stone. She had already promised herself that she would take them off as soon as they got out of Cytosine.

When Twenty-Two closed the door to her pod, she did not look back. She had already mourned the loss of her home as she had watched it wilt and fade over the last few months. She had no regrets or sentimental ties to this place; she'd had no real home since Fintorian left.

Dara shifted on Twenty-Two's back and wrapped her legs around her waist. Ezra had already gone ahead to scout out the first few corridors, leaving Twenty-Seven with them.

'I think you will like seeing the other areas of the museum, all the animals,' Twenty-Two silently signed to the young boy. 'There is so much life in the other pods.'

Twenty-Seven didn't follow her hands; instead, he stared intently down the corridor.

'Don't worry. He will be back in a moment; he's just checking that there's no one around.'

Twenty-Two tried to remain calm, but inside she was listening out for Ezra's footsteps returning as well. In a few moments, she heard them and sighed her relief. He stood at the end of the corridor and gestured for them to join him.

Twenty-Two took the young boy's hand and led him up the corridor, her eyes fixed on Ezra as she tried not to look up at the ceiling. Once they were a few paces from him, Twenty-Seven tugged his hand free and ran to Ezra, who gave his wide grin in response.

Dara opened her mouth to speak, but Ezra cut her off.

'No talking now; we have to be really quiet', he signed slowly. 'In five corridors, we will be out of the east wing and then the cameras are back in operation.'

Keeping close together, they silently crept down the first corridor with Ezra leading the way. The only noise came from Twenty-Two's squeaky trousers.

She had been this way before and knew that they were heading towards the main atrium. Each of the corridors consisted of the same grey walls, floors and steel doors leading off into unlabelled rooms. Occasionally, Ezra would stop and run his hands along the wall. Once he found the change in texture, he would increase the pressure. A door would then fully swing around, revealing a shorter, 'cut-through' corridor.

The tiny waft of air by her ear let Twenty-Two know that the first of the cameras had detected them and come over to investigate. It was only a small, black dot, but she knew that it was recording everything and feeding it back to the control tower in the main museum. Ezra had told her all about the cameras and she knew the only thing she could do was lower her head and carry on. It was important not to get flustered or panic. Without a word, she gently shrugged Dara off her back, as agreed—it would look less suspicious if she was on foot.

They were passing through the antiquities rooms now. Filled with rows of earthenware and weapons that had survived thousands of years out in the world. These preserved specimens were living out their final days in glass display cabinets, carefully labelled and evenly spaced from one another.

The sharp, electric lights clicked on as they entered another room containing fragments of pottery. Up ahead, Twenty-Seven visibly shrunk from the light and shielded his eyes. He glanced around at Twenty-Two and she scrunched her eyes at him for reassurance. She had also struggled with the electric lighting when she had first started exploring the museum.

At the end of the room, they stopped at the wide double doors.

'So, through here and then we're into the main museum,' Ezra signed. 'We'll use the viewing platforms to cross over the pods.'

Twenty-Seven shielded his eyes from the light and let go of Ezra's hand. He looked up at Twenty-Two glumly. She took his hand in hers and gave it two reassuring squeezes.

'I'll take Dara, if you want? I think that camera has gone now. We won't meet anyone in the main museum,' Ezra signed, while crouching down for Dara to clamber onto his back.

Dara's face lit up as she reached over Ezra's head to push the door open for them. With one hand, she used simplified signs to say to Twenty-Two, 'I've missed the main museum, would always do a lap around it when you were asleep as a little girl. I hope the porcupines are still there.'

Twenty-Two's step lightened as she followed Ezra through the door into the reception area. A large desk looked lonely without its three receptionists and a glittery sign above it confirmed that the Potiors had reached 30,000 years of reversal of extinct species.

In every direction, tantalising walkways scaled the heights of the museum so that visitors could view the animals safely from above. Ezra led them to the white entrance arch of the third walkway to their right. Twenty-Two was pleased that she could read the sign: To The Southeast.

As she walked up the gentle incline, Twenty-Two peered over the sides of the barriers. Most of the animals were either lying down or standing very still. She didn't know if they could sleep standing up or whether they were just resting. She realised that she didn't even know if they had personal names, like she and her friends did, and decided to ask Ezra about this on their four-day walk.

The air was perfectly still. The only sounds came from two birds calling to each other in a distant corner and Twenty-Two's squeaky trousers.

Twenty-Two scrunched her eyes and glanced over the side of the walkway again. Right below them were two woolly rhinoceros that she recognised from Twenty-Seven's t-shirt. Thinking he would want to see them, she picked him up and held him firmly so he could peer over the barrier.

Twenty-Seven looked over with interest and then froze, before letting out a blood-curdling scream that stretched across the grounds. As if recognising his meaning, the different pods came alive as warning calls were shot around and across the museum.

'Ooof.'

Twenty-Two received a kick to the knee and dropped the boy on the walkway. She watched in horror as Twenty-Seven sprinted towards the doors they had come through. Ezra was trying to set Dara down but his bag had become entangled in hers. He nearly pulled Dara to the ground before he realised his mistake. Untangling himself, he waved at Twenty-Two to go.

Twenty-Two ran after the boy but was slowed by her uncomfortable shoes. She didn't dare kick them off in case she met someone. Despite her awkward footwear, she knew she could catch Twenty-Seven if she didn't lose sight of him.

The sound of the swinging doors told her that he had made it back into the display room. She ignored the pain in her feet and picked up her pace as she raced after him. At the opposite side of the room, the swinging doors indicated that he had only just left. Without pausing, she followed his trail.

She was catching up now. With each turn of the corridor, she was closer, his short legs no match for her longer strides. Finally, up ahead, she saw him stop abruptly and enter a side door. A few seconds later, she entered the same room.

The electric lights automatically pinged on and she realised that she had been here before. Twenty-Two took a moment to check, but it didn't seem that any cameras had picked up their trail; they had been lucky.

The eye stared at her unblinkingly and she gave it a little wave as she made her way over to Twenty-Seven, who had both hands pressed against the glass. The springy creature had stretched up on his back five legs and placed two of his bristly limbs against the glass. He would have been touching Twenty-Seven if it weren't for the pane between them.

Twenty-Seven turned to her and scratched his leg before resting his forehead against the glass. The creature sprang in the air and Twenty-Seven scrunched his eyes in response. He then slowly crossed to the other side of the room and placed just one hand against the glass next to where the eye had been. The suckered eye momentarily flashed back against where his hand rested in three successive blinks. Again, Twenty-Seven scrunched his eyes at the creature before turning to Twenty-Two.

'Are they your friends?'

Twenty-Seven nodded slowly before staring at the glass walls and then the door.

'How long have you been coming here?' Twenty-Two asked.

She hadn't thought he had been leaving their pod, but he could have been when she was sleeping. They hadn't received a delivery of food for the last few weeks and Ezra had begun to leave the steel bars undone for them.

Twenty-Seven didn't respond.

'Are you worried about whether they are safe here? From what's in the main museum?'

Twenty-Seven nodded again.

'Even if they were moved out into the main museum, they would be safe; they're in separate pods from each other. It looks like they are free but they have barriers around each one that we can't see. None of the other animals could get to them.'

Twenty-Two didn't move. She watched the boy carefully. 'Do you want to come with us or stay here? It's your choice.'

Twenty-Seven stared at his feet. He blew up at his long fringe, momentarily adjusting it, before it swung back down to cover half his face again. He sombrely crossed between the two viewing platforms, touching each with his palm and tapping his fingers in a seemingly random order against the surface. The eye blinked back at him and the leg gave seven staccato taps in response.

The boy then hitched up his shorts and crossed the room. At the door, they took a moment before he closed it behind him.

'Come on. We have to go now. And no more running if you want to come with us,' Twenty-Two signed, trying to hide her frustration. She knew he was only worried about his friends, but if a camera had followed them, it would have been the end of their escape plan.

Twenty-Seven nodded.

Firmly taking his hand, she didn't let go until she pushed open the swinging doors leading back into the main museum. When they passed the circular, beech reception desk, Twenty-Two yanked the young boy behind it and crouched down low.

They were not alone.

She pressed her back against the inside of the reception area. Lifting her finger to her lips, she stared at Twenty-Seven. He nodded his response.

She peeked over the side of the desk for a split-second.

Dara and Ezra were standing under the arch of the walkway where she had left them. Except they were now surrounded by four guards. The tall man who had noticed that she had no shoes on was with them. She could barely hear what was being said but there was a heated discussion going on.

She ducked her head back down and strained to hear them. The animals were quieter than before but they were still ruffled, sending out low calls. These were pierced by the higher trumpeting noise of an animal that was more reluctant to believe that the danger had passed.

Frustrated at not knowing what was happening, Twenty-Two took a chance and peeked over the desk again. Two guards were standing directly in front of Dara and Ezra with their hands on their shoulders. The other two were scanning their wrists. Only Ezra was facing in her direction.

The double doors swung open and four more guards entered, accompanied by the tallest man Twenty-Two had ever seen. He was even taller than Fintorian. He had ash-blond hair that reached his chin; it contrasted sharply with his jet-black eyebrows. Twenty-Seven began to shake. Both still crouching, she tried to comfort him.

The tall man strode past the desk, scanning the area. Twenty-Two slid her hand over Twenty-Seven's mouth and pressed farther back against the inside cupboards.

Please let them go; please let them go.

She repeated the plea over and over in her head.

There were more mutterings and then Dara's piercing wail. Twenty-Two automatically began to rise and it was only Twenty-Seven tugging at her sleeve that stopped her. He was right; she couldn't help them if she was taken too.

The voices grew louder, along with the sound of twelve pairs of feet moving towards them.

'I saw him a few days ago in Lab 412 and now he's sneaking around in the middle of the night. That's why I called you out, Marvalian. I wouldn't have taken you away from your prior engagements if I didn't think it was important. I thought perhaps the two events of the evening might be connected?'

'You were right to do so. We cannot be too careful in these times,' the one called Marvalian said calmly. 'All anomalies must be investigated. Although I doubt it will come to anything. She can barely walk, so it's unlikely she has been sent from another base.'

'I ain't from no other base,' Dara squawked in indignation. 'Cytosine born and bred. Wouldn't have it any other way.'

'Make her stop. I do not want to hear her,' Marvalian said.

'What? No, no, don't do that...I'll be quiet. I promise. On Mister Fintorian's life.'

Feet trudged past the reception desk. Twenty-Two was torn. Should she join her friends, try and see if she could explain everything, that it was her idea to leave Cytosine? Or stay hidden?

'I wouldn't wait around if you think you're going to get much sense out of her,' Ezra said, as he walked past the reception desk. 'I wouldn't wait around at all.'

'Consider this your final warning too,' Marvalian responded.

There was no more talk as the procession trudged through the double doors.

When the door swung shut, Twenty-Two dropped her head into her hands. She had no thoughts; her mind was emptied of all hope and possibilities. She didn't know how long she stayed there, but it was still dark when Twenty-Seven tugged on her sleeve.

Lifting her head, she stared at him blankly.

He gripped her hand and tugged at her to stand. She plodded after him through the corridors, not even trying to listen for anyone approaching. She kept her head down and lost all sense of where they were going. Finally, they entered a large room with rows of tables and chairs.

She did not feel comfortable in this room of square objects; the unnaturally bright, electrical, strip lights made her blink. Glancing around, she decided that it was the worst room she had ever been in. There was not one thing that had been created by the stars.

The tug on her hand guided her past the straight lines of furniture. Why did they not just sit on the floor? She did not understand their ways.

Twenty-Seven stopped in front of a giant, metal box. It had cartons of sandwiches inside it. He pressed his nose against its glass window but nothing happened.

He had to be hungry. Pulling off her bag, Twenty-Two dug out one of the sandwiches and handed it to Twenty-

Seven. He sat down on the floor and began to unwrap his food. Twenty-Two slid down onto the ground to join him. She didn't know what else to do.

Twenty-Seven ate his half of the sandwich, while Twenty-Two picked at hers. When she was finished, she did not move.

Twenty-Seven stood, leaving the wrappings on the ground. He held out his hand and waited patiently for her to stand. Twenty-Two obliged; she did not want to stay in this overfilled room.

And then the thoughts came. A trickle at first, gathering pace, before they rushed into her, overcrowding her mind. She struggled to sort them and put them in order and slumped to the ground again.

It was not just this room that was unnatural. It was the whole of the museum. Her too. She did not belong here. She did not belong anywhere. She had been a failed project, one so insignificant that they'd not even bothered to tie up any loose ends. Instead, she had been discarded and not thought about again. Where could she go?

Her thoughts were muddled and she struggled to sort through them. Ezra had warned her not to wait for them when he had passed their desk. Did this mean he knew they would not be released straightaway? Perhaps they only wanted to talk with Dara and Ezra; then when they realised they hadn't been sent from another base they would let them go? Perhaps she should leave Cytosine and wait on the outskirts for her friends to be released. They could then travel to Thymine, find Fintorian and ask to be housed in the museum. Would it be unnatural too? Maybe, but as she wasn't meant to be, it would be the best place for her. There was nowhere else she belonged.

Rising, she slowly explained her plan to Twenty-Seven.

He followed the movement of her hands before pressing his nose up against the glass box of sandwiches. Still the sandwiches just sat there, refusing to come out.

Slipping through the corridors, Twenty-Two was aware of her surroundings this time. She had a plan and this increased her concern about her welfare again. Turning a corner, she stopped abruptly and stepped backwards. In both directions stood a patrol of guards.

'Hey, you! Stop there. Children are only allowed in the main museum during opening hours and never back here.'

Twenty-Two nodded and promptly turned back down the corridor she had come from.

'Wait, I'm not done with you yet!'

Twenty-Two started to walk more quickly. She began to run at the sound of feet following her. She did not look back.

Tugging Twenty-Seven along with her, she tried to lose the guard by ducking through doors, but nothing would shake him off.

A camera buzzed around her head, easily keeping pace. A second one joined it.

She sprinted round a corner and faced a dead end.

Both of the cameras circled above her head, locked onto their target.

'I said wait there!' the guard called loudly from around the corner.

There was nowhere to go.

This was it, the end.

A panel in the wall to the left of her swung open slightly. A moment later, a man's hand came out and grabbed her, tugging her inside. He was so strong that she couldn't struggle free. She tried to let Twenty-Seven go, so he could save himself, but he held onto her. She tripped and fell through the panel, bringing the young boy with her.

As soon as she entered the adjacent corridor, the panel closed behind her. She froze as she listened intently. There was no sound of feet from behind her; her pursuer must have run the other way.

She turned to face the guard who had finally caught her.

Lifting her face, she was met by four sets of eyes. None of these strangers were dressed like the rest of the guards.

A young woman moved towards her and Twenty-Two shrank backwards. 'Don't worry. You're safe now.'

'Did she bring any cameras with her?' a young Sapien said at the same time.

His hair was so short Twenty-Two couldn't tell what colour it was.

Even though the woman had spoken to her using sign language, Twenty-Two refused to respond.

They were all silent. The tallest man closed his eyes. Twenty-Two peered down both ends of the corridor. How would she get past these people without speaking?

'No, there's none nearby,' the tall man said after a few minutes. 'Please don't worry,' he signed to Twenty-Two.

Twenty-Two looked down, shielding her face; she had decided the less she engaged with them, the better her chances of leaving were.

'Are you sure it's her?' the young woman with brown hair said to the tall man.

'I think so; she's very malnourished, though,' the tall man said.

He pushed his hair out of his face.

Twenty-Two took a step backwards so that her shoulders were against the wall. She started sliding slowly to her right, hoping she would get far enough along to have a head start when she ran from them.

'Hello,' the young woman signed, crouching down next to Twenty-Seven.

She managed to dodge out of the way of his leg. For once, Twenty-Two didn't reprimand him.

'Twenty-Seven? Or maybe even a Sapien?' the tall man said, almost to himself. 'I don't know; both their faces are covered.'

'It is them. I can tell,' a shorter man signed. He too had his hood pulled low down over his face.

Twenty-Two stopped sliding her back against the wall and watched the shorter man. There was something about him that seemed familiar and she felt drawn to him. He lifted his hands to his face and slowly pulled back the hood of his jacket.

Twenty-Two stared at him, unsure what to say. He was like her.

SIXTEEN

E lise smiled at the girl whose light brown hair hung in a wispy fringe over half of her face. She didn't know how she had managed to get this far into the main museum without drawing attention. The girl was dressed in navy-blue, shiny trousers that didn't quite meet the tops of her pointy, plastic shoes. They had giant bows for shoelaces. Bright, lime-green socks bridged the gap between the two. She was nearly as slim as Elise, but her clothing swamped her body.

'Would you mind pulling your hood back for me?' Kit signed.

The girl bobbed her head in response.

When she pulled her hood away from her face, Elise tried not to react. Tight circles of hair were missing across her scalp. Her face was so thin that her cheekbones jutted out, drawing thick, sculpted lines to match the prominent bone of her brow. The whites of her eyes had a yellow tinge and the skin beneath was underlined with heavy, dark bags. Her lips were chapped and almost the same colour as her fair skin. She looked ageless, part way between child and old woman.

The little boy was in no better shape. He was as thin as a five-year-old Sapien and was missing three of his front teeth.

Elise fixed her features so they would not reveal her thoughts. She bent slightly towards the girl and signed, 'I am Elise. We are here to help you. What is your name?'

The girl peered up at her and glanced between their faces. She didn't respond.

Elise tried again. 'Are you Twenty-Two? You don't have to be afraid; we're not here to hurt you. We've come with our friend Kit, who is like you. He is also a Neanderthal.'

Twenty-Two stared at Kit, who scrunched his eyes in response.

'They have taken my friends,' she signed quickly to him. 'You have to help me get them back.'

Kit stepped forward slightly. 'I'm sorry about your friends. We have been trying to track you for the last hour and find a place that we could meet you safely.'

After three weeks of journeying, they had slipped into Cytosine that evening once the settlement had gone to sleep. Maya had given Elise a key card to access one of the back doors of the museum and they had crept through the corridors towards what they believed were the Neanderthal pods. After finding them empty, they had been circling the main atrium in an adjacent corridor when a loud commotion had let them know that not everyone in the museum was asleep. They had caught sight of the arrest and since then had been tracking the young woman with her hood pulled low over her face, trying to decide if she was Twenty-Two.

It would be light soon. Elise didn't want to rush the girl,

but she was anxious about the amount of time this was taking.

'Please, you have to help me,' Twenty-Two signed again.

'Who do you think took your friends?' Luca signed.

'The tall men. I think they are Potiors. They caught my friend and me before, a few weeks back, but they had guards with them this time. They let us go last time. But this time they took them away.'

'Where do you think they've taken them?' Elise signed to Samuel.

'It depends what they think they've done. If they had guards with them, they will probably take them for questioning in the containment centre. They won't be released for days, if not weeks. They won't accept their first answers.'

'Could we get in there?' Kit signed.

'I'm afraid not,' Samuel responded, glancing down the hallway. 'No one has ever broken into a containment area before. Well, only Maya, and she prepared for it for weeks.'

'I'll go by myself then. Please take care of Twenty-Seven for me,' Twenty-Two signed. 'I will meet you at the edge of Cytosine.'

'Which edge? It's a circle,' Luca signed.

Elise glared at him and he dropped his hands.

'If you go after them, you will not come out again,' Kit signed. 'We want to take you somewhere safe, but you will have to leave your friends behind. I'm sorry, but getting caught yourself won't help your friends. It may even make it worse for them if the Potiors find out they've been helping you.'

The girl was completely still for a few moments; she closed her eyes. When she eventually opened them, she pulled Twenty-Seven closer to her before answering. 'Help

me get outside of Cytosine; I will wait for them in the woodland there.'

Luca shrugged and looked around at the others. 'At least
it's a start. And we need to get moving. They might be
sending guards out while we're all standing around here
having a gab about it.'

Elise knew he was right. They couldn't help rescue
Twenty-Two's friends and at least this way they could get
her out of Cytosine. They could deal with convincing her to
travel to Uracil after they were safely outside the base.

'I've got one more thing to do here before I leave,' Elise
signed.

'I'll come with you,' Samuel responded.

'No, you have to help get them out. I'll join you in an
hour.'

'Will you come with me for a moment?' Samuel signed,
raising an eyebrow.

Elise followed him. When she had received her mission
details on the morning they had left for Cytosine, she had
been relieved to discover it was a simple one. She had to
find Lab 412 and record what was inside. There were no
cameras in this part of the museum, so Uracil had never
managed to hi-jack their feed and see what Marvalian's new
project was. One of her instructions was not to discuss Lab
412 with anyone. No one else could know what she was
doing. No one else could know about the lab.

Once they were a few steps away and had their backs to
the rest of the group, Elise signed, 'You know you can't
come with me. It's not how this works.'

'They would never need to know.'

'They might; they could have someone planted in the
museum. I have to do it by the book. I can't risk my parents
being turned away.'

Samuel sighed. 'Straight in and out, okay? I'll wait for you where we camped last night. Then we can put all of this behind us and begin making some far more interesting plans.'

Elise stared up at the man she had tentatively started to sketch a future with. 'I'll only be an hour behind you.'

She stretched up on her tiptoes and kissed him to seal the promise.

'I've got to get moving,' she signed. 'Take care of them; they're in worse shape than I thought possible.'

He kissed the top of her head before letting her go.

Turning, she signed to her friends that she would be one hour behind them and then walked quickly down the corridor in the opposite direction. She had been given a map of the museum, amongst other items, when she received the outline of her mission. On the journey down from Uracil, she had spent the evenings studying and memorising the map. Everything about the mission had to be committed to memory; she couldn't have any items on her that would give her away. The only thing she was allowed was the minute, winged camera that she would use to record the lab.

She was dressed casually as a Sapien museum canteen worker. She had even put some makeup on, borrowed from Georgina, and tied her hair into a high ponytail. She didn't want to draw any attention to herself and she thought that she looked just like one of the young women she used to see on their break. The canteen workers were among the few employees who stayed overnight, so she knew that at least she had a reason for being in the museum at this time of night. There was no valid excuse she could think of for being this far from the canteen and sleeping pods, though.

Thanks to the map, Elise knew exactly how to find Lab

412. Traversing the corridors, she slid through unnoticed by any cameras, pleased that, at this rate, she would be finished in half an hour.

Pushing open the doors to the lab, she smoothly pulled out a small box and released the camera inside. It flew directly upwards out of the box and began its lap of the room, slowly travelling along the glass windows. Elise pressed herself against the wall next to the door and tried to ignore the blinking eye and tapping leg across from her. They were like no animals she had ever seen, an amalgamation of familiar features that, together, did not sit right. She knew that they had to be something designed rather than born.

Five minutes later, she opened the box to guide the camera back inside.

It had only just begun its journey back to her when the door to the lab swung open.

A Potior with straight, blond hair walked in, followed by a tall man who was clearly a Medius. Five guards traipsed in after them and stood with their backs to Elise.

Concentrating on her breathing as Maya had taught her, Elise slowed her heartbeat. She started to inch towards the door, where she would try and push it open and slip outside. At the same time, she lifted the bracelet to her mouth, just as she had been instructed to do.

'Why would any base send those two to spy on me? They are the most ineffectual vagrants I have ever had the sorry opportunity of meeting,' the blond Potior said, staring at the blinking eye.

'I don't know. Diversion tactic? Deep undercover? Or maybe they weren't sent by another base and are just nosy museum employees. Maybe the tip-off was designed to ruffle you,' the Medius responded.

He hovered next to the Potior, his hands clasped behind his back.

Elise flipped the catch on the amethyst. The capsule was now resting on the end of her tongue, designed only to dissolve when it reached the acids of her stomach.

Still facing the interior of the lab, she started to push backward on the door, hoping it wouldn't make any noise.

'And what about the girl who is about to exit this room? Is she also a nosy employee?' the Potior said, still staring at the eye.

The guards and the Medius swung around and reached for their weapons even as the shock was still registering on their faces.

Elise only had time to swallow the capsule before fifty thousand volts of electricity hit her.

SEVENTEEN

She was alone when she opened her eyes.

Wincing at the bright, electric lights, she tried to sit up. Two wires, running from her forehead to a machine by her bed, pulled her back.

Succumbing, she laid her head down against the single pillow and shielded her eyes.

It started deep in her stomach, a gnawing doubt that grew in intensity until panic washed through her—she couldn't remember how she had arrived in this room. For a moment, she couldn't recall a single memory from before this point. She squeezed her eyes shut; the nausea made her head swim.

She. A girl. No, a young woman—that she was sure of.

Without warning, a name surfaced in her mind. Elise.

She knew her name was Elise.

Realising that this was a starting point, she held onto this scrap of knowledge tightly, her eyebrows pinching together as if her name—her self—could be clasped between them.

Elise bit the inside of her cheek as she tried to recover more about herself, the pain focusing her mind.

Her surname came next: Thanton.

Remembering the tattoo on the inside of her wrist, she glanced down at it for reassurance: Elise Cyton, 17 February 2250, Cytosine Base, Sapien.

'No, no,' she mumbled, trying to sit up again. She rubbed at her wrist, as if she could erase the error, but the tattoo remained firmly in place.

Another wave of nausea hit her. She pulled the wires free from the metal slat they had caught on—only just in time—and retched over the side of her bed. She stared down at the bucket someone had left there. Nothing had come up. She felt empty.

Elise became aware of a metallic taste in her mouth; she spat into the bucket. Throwing back the light sheet, she tried to place her foot on the polished concrete floor. Her hand automatically reached for the wires snaking their way to her temples. Her fingers traced the edge of the soft pad of plastic that covered most of her forehead. The pad was stuck down; she began to pick at the bottom edge. Slowly at first, then with an urgency when her skin couldn't be freed.

The sound of a bolt sliding back made her pause. Before the door to her left began to open, she sank back onto the bed, pulling the sheet back over her. She closed her eyes, but not too tightly.

Steps approached. One person. No, two.

'She hasn't come around yet. That's a relief,' a female voice said.

'When did they finish?' an older man replied.

'Ah...about two hours ago. We should bring her out of it, really. It's not good for them to be under for so long.'

'What do we tell her?'

'I always set the submersion so that it brings them back over the course of five minutes. Gives me enough time to leave. Best not to be here when they awaken. Too many questions.'

The man chuckled. 'That's clever. I'll use that.'

'You'll use everything I tell you. Remember you're the trainee. It doesn't matter that you were a Lead Nurse when you transferred from Epigenetics.'

'Sorry. I didn't mean to—'

'We all have to start at the bottom here. Just remember that.'

'Will do.'

One of them moved around the bed. Elise tried not to tense when they got closer. Some staccato beeps came from the machine to her right.

'Right, I've set it so that she will come round in the next five minutes. We better go.'

The footsteps left the room. One set more hurriedly than the other.

'Did they take everything?' the male voice said from the door.

'Shush...not now. She might be coming out of it.'

The door closed. Elise was alone again.

She tried to sit up, more carefully this time. Once she was leaning back against the wall, her hands were a flurry of movement as she checked her body from top to bottom. All was accounted for, from two ears to ten toes. The only thing that seemed different was her right hand; her index finger and thumb were bent to the side slightly. She didn't remember them being like this. When she held them up against her left hand, the difference was clear to be seen.

She hiked her paper gown up and examined her stomach. There was a light pink line stretching sideways between her belly button and the top of her underwear. She wasn't sure if it had been there before. She didn't remember it, but that didn't mean much right now.

Mind reeling, another wave of nausea hit. She stayed sitting up this time and didn't lean towards the bucket.

What did she last remember? Her brother. She had to leave her younger brother. Why? To keep him safe.

Where was he now? She didn't know.

Tears began to form and she breathed in deeply through her mouth. She pushed them back. This was not the time. She had to get out.

She surveyed the room and began to weigh up what to do. There was only one door and no windows. The room was big enough to hold several beds but there was only hers. She had to get to the door.

Elise pulled again at the pad on her forehead. It didn't budge. She got her nail underneath the adhesive and tugged again. It felt as if her skin were coming away with it, but she kept on pulling. Her eyes watered as the pad slowly peeled away. When the first part separated itself from the stretched skin, a pain in her belly erupted, increasing as the pad was removed. She gave a groan as the last bit came away with a reluctant snap.

Elise lay back on the bed again for a few seconds; she held the pad up and inspected it, turning it around in her hands. The two wires led back to the machine to her right where the beeping noises had come from. She had seen one of those before. She struggled to remember, but it didn't come to her. Hazy thoughts danced through her head. A woman with red hair. A deep cut on Elise's arm.

Elise looked down at both of her arms. There was nothing there. No cut or residual scar.

She examined the tattoo on the inside of her wrist. She

remembered getting that done. On her fourteenth birthday. Just the same as everyone else. Her mum had queued with her. Told her it wouldn't hurt. It had hurt, but it had been worth it—a rite of passage into adulthood.

Elise stared at the tattoo again.

The date of birth was correct; she knew that for sure. Her first name as well. But the surname and her birthplace, Cytosine Base—that couldn't be correct. She'd had that tattoo for five years; it was part of her now, and she knew every detail of it. It had always annoyed her that it was slightly off-centre. It was still askew but she was sure the name should be different: Elise Thanton, Thymine Base. That was where she had been born, had lived all of her life. She had never been to Cytosine Base. But then how could a Sapien travel between bases and have their stamp altered?

The nagging pain deep inside intensified for a second and she breathed in sharply. She had to get out, get to her brother. She shouldn't be here. What had they done to her? She pushed the thoughts away as the fear circled her mind, patiently waiting for a route in. Waiting to paralyse her.

Clutching her stomach, she allowed herself three deep breaths before she swung her legs over the side of the bed. Her bare feet tentatively reached for the floor, first one and then the other. The cool stone had a calming effect and she took another deep breath before standing.

She wobbled slightly and fell back onto the bed. Trying again, more slowly this time, she held her stomach with one hand and used her other arm to push herself up. She tested her balance before stepping away from the bed.

Staring at her feet, she placed one in front of the other. After a few steps, she realised that she could look up again; they didn't need her undivided attention. She slowly made her way across the room, allowing herself a brief smile in celebration of this small victory.

When she got closer to the door, she stopped for a moment. She had no idea what was outside. She took another step. Once she was next to the door, she listened closely.

Footsteps passed by on the other side. They were heavy but conveyed no sense of urgency. She held her breath, praying to the stars that the owner of the steps wouldn't come into the room. She knew she wouldn't be able to make it back to the bed in time.

The steps died away.

Elise remained where she was, waiting to see if another set would follow. Every five minutes, the same heavy steps would pass outside her door. If she timed it properly and left two minutes after they had passed by, she could maybe follow them and not be seen.

She allowed the footsteps to pass two more times while she built up the courage and reserves needed to leave. She placed her hand on the metal door handle and pulled, but it wouldn't open.

She pulled again, harder this time. It was locked from the outside. Frantically, she rattled the door, only stopping when the sharp pain became more persistent and she couldn't ignore it any longer.

She slid down against the wall to the floor and hugged her knees to her chest. It was only then that she allowed the tears to come.

EIGHTEEN

Twenty-Two would never have agreed to follow these strange men if one of her kind had not been with them. She trusted him to help find her friends.

Clasping hold of Twenty-Seven's hand and keeping her head down the whole way, she had watched as the floor beneath her changed from grey concrete to white, granite walkway, then springy, ochre, rubber matting to pebbles that were hard underneath her feet. Several hours later, the surface changed again and it was as if she were walking through her pod, before Fintorian had left.

They all moved quickly and in silence, the tallest one leading the way. They did not stop until they reached a small forest clearing.

By this point, Twenty-Two was exhausted. She couldn't remember ever having moved continuously for so long. The one that was like her helped pull the bag from her back.

'I should have introduced myself earlier. My name is Kit,' he signed with one hand as he placed the bag by her feet.

Twenty-Two was confused. 'Why are you called Kit? Is that your secret Sapien name you can tell people if you are caught? I thought they had to have two parts.'

Kit stared blankly at her before responding. 'No, that is my chosen name. My name when I was in a museum was Twenty-One. I am the one created just before you.'

Twenty-Two didn't know anyone else who had chosen their own name. Even though he was of her own kind, he clearly had some odd ways. She was too tired to ponder it further so she sat down and beckoned Twenty-Seven to come closer so that he didn't run away. There was no chance of that, though; he was just as tired as she was and compliant for once.

Grimacing, Twenty-Two pulled off the stupid 'best' shoes that had made her feet bleed. She wanted to launch them as far away from her as she could. Instead, she carefully tucked them into her bag. They belonged to Ezra and he would want them back. He only had two pairs of shoes and she couldn't be responsible for the loss of one.

Before she knew it, her eyes had closed. She drifted into a dreamless sleep, her hand resting lightly on the backpack that contained all of her possessions.

When she woke to the sound of her growling stomach, the sun was nearly setting. She must have slept for several hours. She opened her eyes and watched the men in front of her pace in circles.

'She should be back by now,' the tallest one said.

'It might have taken her longer than she thought,' Kit signed. 'Try not to worry.'

Twenty-Two pulled a sandwich from her bag and offered half to Twenty-Seven. They both ate in silence and watched the three men circle. When she had finished eating, she drifted off again with Twenty-Seven curled up in the crook of her arm.

When she next woke, she could tell that it was nearly dawn. She could also smell something that she had never experienced before. It was deep and woody. Aching from staying in the same position all night, she stood up and stretched. Twenty-Seven copied her movement and then scrunched his eyes at her. She returned the smile.

The tall man had gone and the other two were sitting staring at the most captivating thing Twenty-Two had ever seen. It was this that was producing the new scent; she was sure of it. Entranced, she walked closer and reached out to touch the marvel in front of her. She thought that it must be a sign from the stars that they were watching over her.

The one with no hair grabbed her hand.

'Don't touch. It's hot. See,' he signed with one hand.

He threw a twig and she watched it smoulder and disappear.

'And that goes for you as well, shorty,' the man signed to Twenty-Seven.

Twenty-Seven hid behind her legs and peeped out.

'You're scaring them,' Kit signed before turning to Twenty-Two. 'Sit with us if you want. The fire will warm you. We also use it to cook food, but don't ever touch the flames, as you will be in great pain.'

'Sorry, I shouldn't have snapped. I'm not myself what with Elise,' the shaved man signed, releasing Twenty-Two's hand. 'I forgot. Let's start again. I'm Luca.'

Twenty-Two nodded at him and continued to watch the dancing flames.

'What is Elise?' she signed after a moment.

'She is our friend; you met her earlier,' Kit signed.

'Have you seen my friends?' she signed to Kit. This was the only thing that could pull her gaze away from the fire.

'No. Elise hasn't returned either. She should be here by now. Samuel has gone back to Cytosine to look for her.'

The two men exchanged glances. Twenty-Two could see that they were clearly worried about Elise, just as she was about Ezra and Dara. Their ability to care for their friend made her feel a little more relaxed in their company.

'We saved you both some breakfast. Have some water too,' Luca signed.

It was the tastiest thing Twenty-Two could ever remember eating. The meat of the small bird was still warm and she scrunched her eyes in response.

Kit handed her a water bottle and she greedily gulped it down before spraying it out again, all over the fire.

The two men stared at her.

'It's not treated,' she signed. 'You know you should only drink the treated water. Did they not teach you that in your museum?'

'Don't worry. It's safe. We all drink it; it's as safe as treated water,' Kit signed, handing the bottle back.

She shook her head and walked over to her bag to collect her own bottle.

'We're going to have some trouble with this one,' Luca said.

'I can understand what you are saying,' Twenty-Two signed with one hand while staring into her bag. 'Don't worry; as soon as I find my friends, I will leave you.'

Twenty-Two decided that she didn't want to tell them any more of her plan in case they tried to disrupt it.

She quickly changed the subject. 'How long has Samuel been gone?'

'Nearly twelve hours. You've been asleep a long time,' Kit signed.

Twenty-Seven tugged at her hand. He needed to make water; she did too. When she returned, she settled down by her bag again; the flames had disappeared so there was no point in her sitting with the two men. She watched them while combing her fingers through Twenty-Seven's hair, just as Dara used to do for her when she was young. She wondered if Dara and Ezra had been released yet and whether they were making their way to her right now. She knew she could sit and wait for them for days; it's what she had done in her pod for years after all.

'We have to go. It's been twelve hours. You heard what Samuel said,' Luca signed to Kit.

'Maybe we could camp another night, wait for him,' Kit signed.

'That's not what Samuel said. We shouldn't have stayed here for a full day. It's not safe. We're too close to Cytosine.'

'You never listen to what Samuel says,' Kit responded.

'I do when it stops us getting captured.'

Kit glanced over at Twenty-Two. She quickly looked away. She did not want him to think that she was eavesdropping on their conversation.

'You are right,' Kit signed. 'We can't risk getting caught; we have to get them back to Uracil.'

The two men stood and started kicking dirt over where the flames had been.

Twenty-Two also stood up. 'Thank you for helping us out of the museum. I hope you have a good journey.'

His back turned to her, Luca stopped mid-kick.

'We want you to come with us,' Kit signed. 'You can't

stay here by yourselves. You have no supplies. You don't know when or even if your friends will be released.'

'But I can't leave Ezra and Dara. I have to wait for them right here so they can find us.'

The two men glanced at each other.

Kit walked closer. 'We have to leave them behind. I'm so sorry but they won't be released—'

'Right away. They won't be released right away, is what Kit is saying,' Luca interjected.

Twenty-Two stared at Luca.

'Why is he lying to me?' Twenty-Two signed to Kit.

'Great, they can all read minds. Good to know,' Luca said under his breath. 'Look, I'm sorry for lying to you. That's wrong. But we need to move now or we'll be caught. And all of this,' he gestured around him, 'losing Elise, losing Ezra, losing Dara, would have been for nothing. So, please, can we just start moving? We'll explain everything to you when it's safer.'

'But they are my friends. I can't leave them behind—'

'We will try to come back for them when Twenty-Seven is safe. I promise,' Kit signed. 'But you cannot expect Twenty-Seven to last much longer out here without proper supplies; he is already weakened. You are as well.'

Kit was not lying to her.

Twenty-Two looked down at Twenty-Seven. He was staring at Kit. She had to think of what was best for him now. What if they got caught? He couldn't go back there with no food or Companion.

'Are you Kit's Companion?' she signed to Luca.

'Umm, no. I was Seventeen's Companion. Elise was Kit's Companion,' Luca said, glancing at Kit.

'Where is Seventeen?' signed Twenty-Two.

'She, ah...she died. Last year,' Luca signed.

Twenty-Two could see that Luca missed her. She leant over and patted him on the arm. 'I am sorry she has gone. She is with the stars now.'

Luca nodded.

'Could you be Twenty-Seven's Companion?' Twenty-Two signed to Luca. 'Will you look after him?'

Luca raised his eyebrows. 'What? Ah, he won't need a Companion now he's free. But I'll be his friend.' Luca bent down to Twenty-Seven. 'If that's okay with you, little man?'

Twenty-Seven drew back his leg, but stopped when he caught Twenty-Two's expression. He nodded his head.

'Dawn has come; we should leave,' Kit signed, taking Twenty-Seven's hand before Twenty-Two could think any more about what to do.

She followed Twenty-Seven.

By midday, Luca and Kit had started taking it in turns to support Twenty-Two and carry Twenty-Seven. Their progress was slow but they did not stop walking until it began to get dark. They had spent most of the day travelling through exposed grassland and, after some discussion, the two men decided not to light a fire that evening. Twenty-Two did not care; she fell asleep as soon as she had eaten.

The following day folded into the next and it wasn't until the third that Kit and Luca started to visibly relax. That evening, they settled underneath a small copse of trees and told Twenty-Two that they were going to remain there tomorrow while Luca set some traps. Their supplies were getting low and they wanted to stock up on fresh meat.

The evening before they set off again, they ate well.

Luca had caught three rabbits and a pheasant so they had enough to keep them going for the next few days.

The hours of rest combined with the rich meat had restored a little of Twenty-Two's energy; she was beginning to become more alert to her surroundings and situation. After they finished eating, she did not fall asleep straight-away. Instead, after she had tucked Twenty-Seven into his sleeping roll, she returned to the fire to sit with Kit. Luca had gone to collect more water for them and she wanted to take the opportunity to speak with Kit alone.

'How are you feeling today?' Kit signed with one hand, feeding twigs to the small fire with his other.

'Not so tired, but not as strong as a year ago,' Twenty-Two signed.

'It will take much longer. You have lost a lot of weight,' Kit responded.

Twenty-Two looked away, unwilling to go into any details. 'Where are you taking us?'

'To Uracil. It is another base but it is very far from here. At our pace, we will be travelling for another five weeks. But there is no rush. As long as we avoid the other bases, we should be safe.'

'Safe from what?'

'Safe from being captured.'

Twenty-Two did not want to go into a containment centre. She didn't know what one was, but it didn't sound like a good place to be.

'Have you always lived in Uracil?' she asked.

'No, I spent the last few years in Thymine. Have you heard of it?'

Twenty-Two took a large gulp of air and it made her think of Ezra. 'Did you know the museum director? Mister Fintorian?'

Kit stopped feeding twigs into the fire and turned to face her. 'Why are you excited?'

'Because you know Thymine. That's where we were going to, the four of us. We were going to see Mister Fintorian. I grew up with him.' Twenty-Two stopped for a second. 'That's not quite right; he always stayed the same, but I knew him from my first memories. And then...then he went away to Thymine. There was another girl, like us, who was about to turn sixteen and Dara said he didn't want to wait for me. I've always been behind, you see. I think that she was Seventeen.'

'That is where you were going? To Thymine to see Fintorian?'

'Yes, I wanted to live at his museum. Maybe you could take me there instead of Uracil's museum.'

'We aren't taking you to a museum in Uracil, just Uracil. You don't have to live in a museum anymore. There isn't one in Uracil anyway.'

Twenty-Two dropped her hands for a moment. 'But where will I live?'

'Where everyone else lives, in little houses made for one or two people.'

'No, no. I don't like it. Take me and Twenty-Seven to Thymine tomorrow. I don't want to go any farther with you.'

'Try not to worry. I think you will like Uracil.'

'How would you know what I like? You only met me three days ago,' Twenty-Two responded.

Luca ambled back into the clearing carrying bottles of water under his arms.

Twenty-Two rushed over to him. 'Will you take me to Thymine tomorrow? I don't want to go to Uracil. It hasn't even got a museum. I have to see Mister Fintorian.'

'Mister Fintorian? Do you mean the museum director? But he's dead,' Luca said before Kit arrived at their side.

Twenty-Two stared at this man who used to be a Companion. He was telling the truth.

The world went black and she sunk to the ground.

NINETEEN

Elise remained in the small room for a further two days. Three times a day, the door was unlocked and a Medius would come in. It was never the same person, but they always had the same routine. After placing a small tray of food beside the bed, they would walk around to the other side to inspect the readings from the machine next to her. Each of them refused to answer her questions or even meet her eye; it was as if she were still sedated.

She was too weak to threaten or attack them; as soon as she moved, the nagging pain resurfaced and she was forced to lie down again. She spent the rest of the time alone, trying to piece together what had happened to her. Her memories had slowly come back: growing up in Thymine; joining the Museum of Evolution to work as a Companion; meeting Kit, Georgina, Luca and Samuel; the death of Seventeen; agreeing to help Kit escape the museum but refusing to leave with him; visiting her family the night Luca and Samuel were going to help Kit escape; hearing about what had happened to her aunt and uncle and the fate that awaited her if she didn't leave Thymine; her mum publicly disowning her in a staged performance to protect her brother, Nathan. And then...nothing. Not even the whisper of a memory about what had come next, nothing to hold onto and guide her.

Elise touched her cheek where her mum had hit her; it had completely healed. She tried to think logically. She was not sure how much time had passed since that night, but her cheek had healed and she had been in here at least three days. A fractured cheekbone did not heal in that amount of time without assistance.

It was a starting point.

She guessed that she was in some sort of medical facility, so maybe she had been brought here to repair her cheekbone. She didn't know how many Medi-stamps this was costing, but it was the last of her worries at the moment. She frowned, missing the time when preserving Medi-stamps, the healthcare currency, had been high up on her list of concerns.

On the third day, she had an unexpected visitor. Between her 1pm lunch and 7pm dinner, a man walked into the room and stood at the end of the bed. He had a slightly harried look to him and a thick line of grey hair sat close to his scalp. It was clear he did not want to be there.

When he addressed Elise, his gaze did not reach her; it was as if he were practising a speech in a mirror and she was sitting behind his reflection. As soon as he spoke, she recognised his voice; it was the man who had come into her room after her first new memory.

'You've had some time to recover now, so you'll be discharged this evening.'

He held up his hand when Elise tried to speak.

'I'm only told the facts so there is no point in questioning. We will do this much quicker if you just listen.' He scrolled down his small screen again. 'A little over three days ago, you were found in the Museum of Evolution in a prohibited area. You were apprehended and shortly afterwards you became delirious. You were unable to return to a lucid state so you were brought here to the containment centre's hospital wing. Your mental state deteriorated...'

He turned his screen around and Elise fixed her features so they remained neutral as she watched the short clip of recorded footage. There she was, balled up in the corner of a small room, repeatedly scratching at her tattoo with her fingernails. The recording zoomed in and she could see blood trickling down her wrist. Elise forced herself to keep watching.

'Oh wait a second...stupid of me,' the man said, adjusting the screen. 'You'll need the sound as well.'

'Not Cytosine, Thymine, not Cytosine, Thymine,' Elise repeated over and over again in the recording, timing her mantra with the destruction of her wrist.

'I think you get the idea,' he continued, rapidly turning the sound down. Elise's voice faded away, the mantra still continuing until the last moment.

'What is your last memory before waking up here?' he asked, cocking his head slightly to the side and meeting Elise's gaze for the first time.

Elise stilled her features and decided to be as vague as possible. She didn't want to bring her family into this—she still had to protect her brother. 'Being in the museum, before that recording was taken and then waking up here three days ago.'

The man pulled the page on the screen down. 'Shortly after this recording, you began vomiting and ran a fever that spiked at 102 Fahrenheit. You were still in a state of delirium so were unable to explain any further symptoms. Following observation, it became apparent that you were suffering from pain in your stomach as well. There's a recording of that if you want to see it?'

Elise shook her head.

'A few hours later, when you started to deteriorate even further, you were taken in for investigatory surgery. It was then discovered that your appendix was about to rupture. It was promptly removed, thereby saving your life.'

Elise nodded, unable to absorb that she had been moments away from dying. She was more concerned by the grounds on which they were still holding her here; she suspected she was in some sort of trouble if her parents hadn't been allowed to visit.

'It's a lot to take in. Why do you think that I was chanting that, back there in the recording?'

The man scrolled his screen up and down a few times. 'It happens sometimes, when the fever spikes. People become delirious; the words can jumble in their minds. I once had a woman swear to me that she had been in a prison all her life, when she had only entered the containment centre the day before.'

He paused when he scrolled farther down. 'Your readings say you've never been to Thymine. You were orphaned at a young age, brought up in care. You had just started a job at the museum as a canteen worker. We see that sort of delirium all the time in here; nothing new, I'm afraid. Maybe you had a dream of visiting Thymine, who knows?'

Elise nodded and tried to smile to hide the double blow. She had never been to Thymine. Her details on the system had been changed. Her mind went into overdrive as she tried to work out how this had happened.

The man stared at her.

Elise dipped her gaze. 'I'm just so embarrassed, watching all of that. Can I leave now? Get back to the museum?' She paused and took a gamble. 'Get back to Cytosine's Museum of Evolution?'

'No, the museum has severed your employment. There is also the issue of the Medi-stamps. You have none in your account; in fact, you have no tickets at all in your account—quite the little ticket spinner, aren't you? The Medi-stamps have to be repaid and you have no employment, so you will remain here and work as a cleaner until you have cleared your debt.'

Elise dug her fingernails into her palms to stop herself from scrabbling to the end of the bed and attacking him. Instead, she said in a calm tone, 'How long will that take?'

'Including paying back your board, food and a small stipend to keep you in toiletries and the like, around two years, I would think. But that is something you will have to clarify with your direct line manager. Nursing staff do not deal with such matters.'

Elise leaned back against the wall as she processed this. Two years? It took no time at all to decide that, at the first opportunity, she would leave.

TWENTY

That opportunity hid from Elise for the next week. As a cleaner, she was able to access most areas of the compound and she started to memorise the layout. By the second day, she knew for certain that she wasn't in Thymine. Although she had never been inside Thymine's containment centre, she had run past it every week on her way to and from the museum. It was a two-storey building with small, barred windows while this compound was all on one level and closed to the outside world. Since being inside it, she had not found a single window.

There was something about the coldness of the containment centre and the slight, damp chill that made her begin to suspect that she was underground. She knew little of Cytosine but recalled that it was perched on the edge of a cliff, overlooking a canyon. She had heard rumours that the residents lived in a network of caves dug into the cliff face. It was not beyond reason that the containment centre was also buried in nature's prison.

There was no way out, either up, down, or to the sides.

No fence to be hopped over or wall to be scaled. The only route out was through the main entranceway, which Elise had not even located yet. She tried not to despair and reminded herself repeatedly that it would take time. She pushed away the question of how she had come to be here and silently observed her surroundings and the patrolling patterns of the guards.

But it wasn't long before circling the containment centre's hallways started to bear down on her. She had no idea why she was in Cytosine and why her markings had changed. She could only guess at the possible reasons.

The most likely scenario was that, after helping Kit escape, Samuel had taken them to Cytosine. She must have then suffered some sort of breakdown in Cytosine's museum, maybe while trying to make contact with another Neanderthal.

In her darkest moments, she began to wonder if her Cytosine markings were real. Perhaps she had invented this colourful past full of intelligent Neanderthals and friendly Medius to counteract her disillusionment with the present. She quickly pushed these thoughts away. She would sign in the darkness at night, reminding herself that there had to be a reason that she knew this language. Surely she couldn't have invented a whole language to support her delusions?

She tried to distract herself by exploring her new surroundings. Within the compound were different zones: the medical wing where Elise had been; general containment, which was divided by gender; a nursery and rudimentary schooling area for children of the detainees; a psychiatric facility, which was overcrowded and the last place anyone would want to end up; and, finally, an area for the elderly who, without any family members to care for them, had been left in this facility and largely forgotten about.

It was Elise's fear of being sectioned in the psychiatric wing that made her push her doubts about herself aside. On the outside, she was a normal cleaner who was working off her debt. She wouldn't allow herself to display or even hint at her inner turmoil. Even in her deepening depression, she knew that there was a lot further that she could fall.

Every day, Elise circled the compound, keeping to herself while surreptitiously watching the other inmates. She soon realised that the few hundred people here had committed no real crimes. If they had, she reasoned, they would have been expelled from the base to meet their certain execution. As far as Elise could see, this centre held the ones who didn't quite make the contribution that was expected of them—the long-term sick, the elderly, the ones who simply could not cope for one reason or another.

This was where Elise had been stored, her markings exposing her to the reality of being adrift and unspoken for. Her first crime was to have been delirious, untethered to time or location. Her second, according to her Cytosine markings, was to have no family to vouch for her. Her third was to be too poor to pay for her medical care. These three combined had led to her current situation, which was to last for two years. She soon realised that most of the containment centre's residents would not be considered as lucky as her. At least she was fit enough to work off her debt.

All of the residents were pale, worn down and jittery. Occasionally, one of them would snap. They could be heard screaming at the walls or found near comatose in a corner. These people were swiftly dealt with and removed to the psychiatric wing.

As a cleaner working off her debt, Elise straddled the

world of the staff members and residents. She could not leave at night but she also was not held in just one room. The only person she spoke to in the first week was another cleaner. She was drawn to him; despite all the misery surrounding them, he was bright and cheerful and said hello to her every time she passed him in the corridor.

When Elise entered the staff canteen after another long, fourteen-hour shift, she decided to sit with him. The cleaning staff were segregated from the other employees and she felt foolish sitting on a separate table.

'Mind if I sit here?' she asked.

The freckled face looked up at her. 'Course, take a seat. No one else is queuing up to sit with me.'

'Been in here long?' Elise asked.

She began eating her food with just a spoon—there were no knives or forks for the cleaners or residents.

'Bit over a week, ten days.'

Elise was surprised. He was so clearly malnourished; she had thought he had been in here for years. She knew that to be a cleaner, he would have to be fourteen years or over, but he was so small that he could have passed for an eleven-year-old. She could not think of him as a man; he was too frail for that title. He was the sort of boy she instinctively knew would have had a difficult time at school, left out of all the games by the children who were concerned with status, and bullied by the meaner ones. She felt instantly protective towards him. She always had done with children who, like her brother, were treated as outsiders.

'Same here. How you finding it?' Elise asked.

The young man shrugged and lifted his spoon to his mouth. 'Same as cleaning the museum really. 'Cept I could leave there, I suppose.'

Elise leant forward. 'You worked at Cytosine's Museum of Evolution?'

The young man held his spoon halfway to his mouth and his smile was so broad it lit up his face. He took a big gulp of air before speaking. 'Was my first job. Straight into where I've always wanted to work. But I was caught walking around the museum at night a couple of times. They thought I was up to no good. They're not sure what type of no good, but no good all the same.'

Elise waited patiently while he spooned in a couple more mouthfuls.

He smiled apologetically. 'Sorry, I'm hungry today. So, then they brought me here. Apparently, I had some sort of gall bladder problem. Don't even know what one is. They removed it, and now I'm stuck here paying off the Medi-stamps.'

Elise nodded. Something was bothering her, but she couldn't place her finger on it. She pushed it aside but still felt as if there was something that she had missed or forgotten. She pushed the thought away—there was clearly quite a lot she had forgotten.

'Should be out in a couple of years if I keep my head down,' the young man continued. 'I'm Ezra, by the way.'

'Elise.'

Ezra looked around the canteen with interest. 'Never mind. Better than being expelled, eh?'

'I miss outside, don't you? It'll be spring soon,' Elise commented.

Ezra laughed and Elise stared at him.

'Sorry, I thought you were joking.' Ezra's tone changed as he ran his gaze over Elise's face. She got the impression that he was weighing up whether she was unstable. 'It ain't spring soon; that's already been and went. We're in the middle of summer now.'

Elise watched Ezra. He had enough wherewithal to stop himself from being incarcerated in the psychiatric unit if he was unhinged.

'One of us is on the wrong screen here and I know it might be me,' Elise said, after searching Ezra's face for any clues that he was unaware of his surroundings. 'I've lost... I've lost some time, some memories. But I'm not unstable if that's what you're wondering.'

'You don't seem mad like some of the others.' Ezra shrugged. 'And everyone here has lost something. I lost my parents. Who am I to judge you and what you've lost?'

Elise smiled at him. 'So, you're sure it's not spring?'

'Course I am. It was the summer solstice the day I got brought in here. Remember thinking how it was a good night to travel...ah, forget I said that last bit,' he said, glancing around.

Elise had barely heard the last bit. She had just realised that if what he said was true, she had lost over three months of memories.

TWENTY-ONE

Entering yet another forest, Twenty-Two became briefly alert to her surroundings. The smell of this one was different; it had layers that she had never encountered before.

Twenty-Two had not spoken since she had found out about Fintorian's death. It was not that she intentionally refrained from speaking in protest; it was simply that she was not aware of what was happening outside of her circular thoughts. Luca had given up trying to engage her after a week of this, but Kit would still sit in front of her and ask her questions that she did not answer. She accepted the food and water she was given but rarely finished them. She followed them every morning because she had nowhere else to go.

As they walked farther into the deepening forest, the unusual scent intensified. Blinking, she became aware of people up in the trees above her and her fingers began to twitch. She would catch glimpses of them in the periphery of her vision, brightly coloured flashes that wove their way through the treetops on wooden walkways. The tremor spread through her hands and gradually down to her legs until they bent under her weight. Without a sound, she stumbled and hit the ground.

Concentrating on the leaf mulch covering the forest floor, she did not dare to look up. She felt as if she were surrounded by an extended viewing platform again, but none of the occupants were Fintorian. They were unknowns.

Twenty-Seven carefully sat down next to her and rested his arm on her slumped shoulder. She resented this light pressure; it was a tether to a reality that she did not want to be a part of. However, she did not shrug the arm away, just distracted herself by watching a small beetle carrying a leaf four times its size across a fallen branch.

'Frack,' Luca said under his breath. 'They'll soon all be here to have a look. Kit, you stay with her. I'm going to run ahead and explain what's happened. Ask them to stop any more coming along. We need to get her into one of the tree houses.'

Twenty-Two counted the seconds, then the minutes, until she nearly reached an hour. She had still not raised her eyes. The noise died down and she felt the weight above her lessen. Kit tugged at her hand to make her stand.

'They're gone now,' he signed to her. 'They were just interested in you; they didn't mean any harm.' He didn't wait for any response. 'And we've found you a nice place to rest that I'm going to take you to.'

Twenty-Two allowed herself to be guided farther into the forest. The trees thinned out but she kept her gaze firmly on her feet, even when she climbed a walkway that lifted her off the ground.

Kit followed her into the small, wooden box she had

been presented with but she ignored him. Barely aware of his presence, she closed her eyes until he left.

Twenty-Two spent her first two days in Uracil alone in a tree house, refusing to come out. She did not find any comfort in her new pod as the ceiling was too low, but it was better than being outside where there were countless Sapiens and Medius who all stared at her.

On the third day, someone knocked at her door, awakening her from her thoughts. Believing it was her next delivery of food, she slid open the door and stood aside for them to place it on the small table. Leaving the door open, Twenty-Two sat on the floor again; she knew they would close it behind them when they left. The woman who was carrying the tray placed it on the table but instead of leaving like the others did, she sat down on the floor opposite Twenty-Two.

The woman leant back against a chair leg and ran her gaze across the room. Twenty-Two did not know why these Sapiens and Medius insisted on filling their rooms, which were already uncomfortably small, with excess furniture. Now there was an excess person in her room too.

'Twenty-Seven is doing well,' the woman said.

Twenty-Two stared through her.

'Kit and Luca told me he really came out of himself on the journey, even started signing to ask the names of new plants and animals.' The woman leant forward. 'I think he probably liked having two older men doting on him as well. They may even try him in the school in a few days' time. He's staying with Kit at the moment if you want to see him.'

Twenty-Two ignored the woman and went back to her

thoughts; in the space of three days, she had lost Dara, Ezra and Fintorian. She had no ties to this world anymore. Twenty-Seven was better away from her and with Kit.

When her stomach rumbled a few hours later, she collected the food on the tray and realised that the woman had gone.

The woman kept on visiting every day. At the end of the week, she brought a child with her. This uninvited woman sat down again and let the child crawl around the room. The infant was clearly keen to practise her newfound skills in mobility and, before Twenty-Two had time to stop her, the little girl crawled up onto her lap and begun tugging at her hair.

Twenty-Two looked down at the child. She gave Twenty-Two's hair another quick tug, clearly delighted at her own mischievousness. Twenty-Two softened towards the Neanderthal girl, and scrunched her eyes in return.

'Her name's Bay. She came with us when we left with Kit,' the woman said.

Twenty-Two glanced up at the woman for the first time. She had a thick scar running across her cheek. Twenty-Two thought this made her appear more interesting than any of the other Sapiens who had delivered her food. The rest of them all looked the same to Twenty-Two, all pointy chins and insipid features.

A prod to her chest brought Twenty-Two's attention back to Bay. With her hair scraped back from her forehead, Bay's features were clearly on display. Twenty-Two thought the little girl had the most interesting face she had ever seen. Shifting her weight slightly, she let the little girl fold up in her lap and sleep a while. She was saddened when, a few hours later, she realised Bay had gone.

The next day was different. Twenty-Two tried to drift

away from it but the respite would not come. Now that she had been brought out of her musings, she couldn't block out the constant chatter and noise of people passing her cabin. There was never any calmness or quiet here during the day. Eventually, she stood and started pacing the room, wishing someone would clear these useless items of wood from it. What was wrong with sitting and sleeping on the floor? Why did these people have to be elevated all the time?

She did not understand their ways and she did not want to. She wanted to be with Dara, Ezra, Twenty-Seven and Fintorian back in her pod. Back when the sprinklers came on at night and she was cared for.

When the same woman brought in her food, Twenty-Two sat on the floor again and tried to appear to be lost in her thoughts.

The woman sat down opposite her and took her time before speaking. 'You seem a bit better today. Perhaps not better, but a bit more alert.'

Twenty-Two tried to block out the woman's voice; she fixed her gaze on the table leg, another example of everything having to be removed from the ground.

'If you tell me what you want, then I might be able to help you,' the woman said.

Twenty-Two assessed the woman's meaning. She could tell she was genuinely interested in what her answer would be.

'I want to go back to my friends,' Twenty-Two signed.

'That's understandable. But from what I've heard, they aren't going to be where you left them. And the state that you're in, you won't make the journey back. You barely made it here. So, how are you going to get there if you don't look after yourself?'

Twenty-Two went back to staring at the table leg.

When the woman was gone, she stood up and ate all of her food even though she wasn't hungry.

Later in the day, the woman came back with another tray of food, which Twenty-Two ate without question. After she finished, Twenty-Two sat down on the floor again and waited for her to leave.

'If you're going to build up your strength, you can't just sit in here. You need to exercise too,' the woman said.

Twenty-Two said nothing, but she knew she was right.

Eventually she signed, 'I don't want to go out there; there's too many of them.'

'A short while ago, I felt the same,' the woman said, as she stood up to leave. 'I'll come and collect you at 5.30 tomorrow morning. There's no one around then. I'm Georgina, by the way.'

Twenty-Two ignored her and continued to stare at the table leg.

Over the next week, Twenty-Two would circle around Uracil with Georgina in the early mornings. Kit would often join them before going to his lessons with Twenty-Seven. Her mind was not engaged, though, and she would often drift in and out of their conversations, unaware whether they were addressing her.

She began to notice that they were staying out later and later and she began to see a few people before she made it back to her tree house. The people she passed tried not to stare, but she would often catch them glancing at her when they thought she was not looking.

By the end of her fourth week in Uracil, she had learned to largely ignore the residents she passed during her morning walks. One day, the three of them had been walking for nearly two hours when they began to make their way back. Twenty-Two was jolted out of her thoughts when a dumpy man, swathed in too much cloth to be practical, approached them on the walkway. The exertion in trying to catch up with them had caused large beads of sweat to flatten his fringe against his forehead.

Kit and Georgina tensed as he approached; he was heading straight for Twenty-Two.

'I know we're not supposed to bother you, but I just wanted to say what an honour it is to have you here,' the dumpy man said, clasping Twenty-Two's hand.

Twenty-Two examined his features before freeing herself from his grasp.

'You don't think it is an honour that I am here,' she signed. 'You think I should be grateful to you for letting me stay. The reason you came over was because you wanted to have a closer look at me.'

'What did she say?' the man said, turning to Georgina.

Georgina sighed. 'She said that she thanks Uracil for opening its doors to her.'

He smiled around at them all, as if he had personally given the order for her to remain.

Georgina did not reciprocate his smile. 'You're going directly against the Tri-Council's orders by coming over here. So, you shouldn't make this a common occurrence. Should you?'

'What? No, of course not,' he said, before clearing his throat. 'I only wanted to meet her.'

'You'd better be on your way then,' Georgina said, not giving him a chance to respond.

When Twenty-Two was settled back in her tree house, Kit stayed and ate his first meal of the day with her.

'Why was that man lying to me?' Twenty-Two asked when they had finished eating. 'And then why did Georgina lie about what I said?'

Twenty-Two was not used to being intentionally deceived in such an obvious way. In the last six months, Dara had always spoken the truth—as she perceived it to be —no matter how warped her viewpoint was. Before that, when Dara hadn't wanted to explain something, she would just stop speaking. Ezra had been so open, Twenty-Two didn't think he'd ever had a manipulative thought in his life.

Now that Twenty-Two was starting to meet more people, she could see that what they said often conflicted with what they meant. It confused her and made her distrustful of everyone.

'They often do that. Don't be annoyed,' Kit signed. 'They can't read each other as well as we can and this tempts them into hiding their meaning to get what they want.'

'But that is just wrong,' Twenty-Two signed.

'Maybe, but there are many different degrees of wrong. You should think about that before putting everyone on your "bad people" list.'

'How do you know about my lists?' Twenty-Two signed, alarmed.

'Just a guess; don't worry,' Kit signed, scrunching his eyes.

Twenty-Two folded her arms.

'Take that man you met this morning,' Kit signed. 'His reasons for coming over were because he is nosey and he probably wanted to brag to his friends that he had spoken with you. Do you want to be his friend? No. But there is no need to be his enemy. Now that we are around all these people, take the time to look at their motives. Even the best of people do not tell the truth all the time.'

'What good reasons are there for not telling the truth? There are none that I can see.'

'Because you don't want to hurt someone, or you are embarrassed or ashamed.'

Twenty-Two took a moment to consider this before asking, 'Do you always tell me the truth?'

'Always, when you ask me a question.'

'So, you keep things from me?'

'Yes, of course I do.'

'Tell me something you keep from me,' Twenty-Two signed, pulling herself up.

Kit stared at her. She tried to remain still under his gaze.

'You have to decide which pathway to take,' Kit signed. 'If you do not try to re-learn everything you have been taught, you will never be at peace. You will also alienate yourself from everyone who is trying to help you.'

Twenty-Two allowed his words to sink in but, in punishment, she did not speak to him again that day.

The next morning, Kit had a surprise for Twenty-Two. It was exactly a month since she had first arrived in Uracil and he had secured permission to take her outside for the day. Eager to get away from all of the noise and people, Twenty-Two agreed to join him.

At the beginning of their journey, Twenty-Two glanced over at Kit, surprised to see that he was not his usual contained self.

'What is bothering you?' she signed, hoping that this

wouldn't lead to a discussion about ways in which she could improve herself.

'It is my friend, Elise. I do not know what has happened to her and I am worried that she will not be welcome here anymore.'

'Why? What has she done?'

Twenty-Two watched carefully as Kit explained to her that when their depleted group of travellers had first arrived in Uracil, the welcome party had quickly been cancelled. Mistakes had clearly been made and Uracil was at risk. A public meeting had been organised to explain the temporary precautions that would be taken now that one of their own had been captured.

In the first few days, rumours had spread like wildfire. The only additional public announcement had been a reminder that capture was incredibly rare; the last time had been over fifteen years ago. This had fuelled the murmurings and hints that this would never have happened to a long-term resident of Uracil. Elise's name had become synonymous with failure.

Kit explained that scouts had been sent out to patrol a ten-mile radius for the next two weeks. The base was also under a strict blackout at night to ensure it could not be spotted from afar.

Now that it was clear that the rest of Zone 3 was not going to descend on them, the residents were allowed to leave the strict confines of the forest. But this still left the matter of Elise firmly in Kit's thoughts.

'And this Samuel? He is looking for her?' Twenty-Two asked.

'Yes, but we have not heard from him since we left. I worry for him too.'

Twenty-Two was touched by Kit's obvious concern.

She patted him on the arm. 'I hope the stars are watching over them for you.'

They walked in silence the rest of the way. Twenty-Two enjoyed the only sound being the rustle of the grass as they passed over it. Now that she was more aware of her surroundings, she took the time to take in all that the stars had to offer.

She had never witnessed their gifts in such a grounding way before. There had been only a few gently rolling mounds in the museum, but out here, near Uracil, the hills shot up into the sky, trying to touch the stars with their thanks. These unashamed tributes, which had been here longer than her own ancestors, were often gathered around deep pools of water that Kit told her were called lakes.

In the mid-morning, Kit stopped by one of these lakes. It was so expansive that Twenty-Two couldn't see where it ended. The sheer enormity of the scenery was over-whelming and she had to sit down for a moment to process what she was seeing. Without warning, she suddenly felt very insignificant, when previously she had believed that her troubles were the centre of the universe.

Kit sat down next to her before lying back in the wild grasses and staring up at the sky.

'What happened to Fintorian?' Twenty-Two signed after a moment.

'Before I tell you, you must remember that I cannot lie to you. Even if I could, I never would.'

Twenty-Two nodded her head. Even though Kit was harder than most to read, every signal of his hands and even the most minute change in posture or stance helped indicate his true meaning to her.

Kit sat up slightly. 'Fintorian was a good man to me when I behaved in the way that he wanted. I imagine he was the same with you. I always knew he genuinely cared about me, but not in a way that was for the good of me. He only cared for me out of his own desires for the museum, and his own status. Can you see that this was a possibility for you too?'

Twenty-Two thought about it. This was a possibility, but it would take more than a few words to reconfigure a lifetime of memories.

'The hardest thing about our gifts is that we do not see the whole picture if we only encounter these people in isolation. You probably only ever saw Fintorian in the company of you and Dara, is that right?'

Twenty-Two nodded.

'And what did Dara think of Fintorian?'

'She adored him.'

'And would do anything he asked?'

'Yes, of course, and more. She would have given her life if he had asked for it.'

'So, Fintorian was never in conflict with her?'

Twenty-Two shrugged, not liking where this was going.

'What I'm saying is that you need to watch people when they are not getting what they want. Also, judge their actions when they are with people who have less power than them. How do they treat those people?'

Twenty-Two considered this for a moment before nodding. It was true she had only ever seen Fintorian around herself and Dara and they both always did what he asked. 'So, what happened in Thymine?'

'Elise, Samuel and Luca agreed to help me escape. Fintorian would never have let me leave and that is how I knew he did not care for me. All the rules of the museum were in place for the Potiors' benefit, not mine.'

'Why did you want to escape the museum? Were they

not feeding you? Did they lose interest in you as well?'
Twenty-Two signed. Perhaps she was not the only one to
have been punished.

'No, nothing like that,' Kit responded.

Twenty-Two tried to push the disappointment away.

'I wanted to leave as I was a prisoner,' Kit continued.
'Another captured animal to be put on display. Fintorian
only cared about his hold on the museum and he would
destroy anyone who got in his way.'

Twenty-Two considered this point. It was true that, in
the museum, she wasn't allowed to leave or move around as
she wanted to. All the rules were designed to regulate and
contain all aspects of her existence. She was just another
captive animal, like the blinking eye and leggy-creature. It
was just that, in the end, they had been looked after and she
hadn't.

'What happened after they agreed to help you escape?'
Twenty-Two signed.

'Fintorian found us trying to leave and gave Georgina
that scar and he broke Elise's finger and thumb. He did not
lash out in self-defence or overwhelming anger; he carefully
chose to take Georgina's beauty from her and Elise's skill.
He was cruel to anyone who did not do exactly as he
wanted. I'm sorry but he was not a good man.'

Twenty-Two could not hide her feelings. She thought
of the man who waved at her from the viewing platform and
crouched down in front of her when they spoke. Did he
only do that because she was being compliant, not
complaining or asking to leave?

'What happened next?' she signed, staring at Kit.

'Georgina distracted Fintorian when he was about to
hurt Elise again. She injected a chip into him so he couldn't
leave the pod, just like the other animals. It meant he

couldn't reach Elise. He was so enraged with Georgina that he was about to snap her neck. Samuel had to kill him. Please don't hold it against him.'

Twenty-Two thought about Samuel; she only had a few memories of him from the day she left Cytosine. It seemed so long ago that she had left the museum.

'I don't know whether I can do that,' she signed. 'I would have to meet him again and decide for myself.'

'That is good enough for me. Thank you. He is like a brother to me,' Kit signed.

A murmuration of starlings flew overhead, across the lake. An invisible conductor pulled them to a stop and then instructed them to advance in a broad sweep in the opposite direction. Twenty-Two had never seen anything like it. She watched their synchronised movements until they flew over the next hill and out of sight.

'Why do you think we died out before?' Twenty-Two asked.

Kit leant up on his arm and used just one hand to sign. 'From my conversations with Samuel, I think that there were too few of us to survive the change in temperature and the effect it had on the landscape. I think you would be interested in talking to him when he gets back to Uracil. I also believe that while in some areas the Sapiens would have exterminated us, in others they may have befriended us.'

'The Sapiens are not a good species, are they?' Twenty-Two signed.

'They are not innately bad; they just tend to be led by bad people. They ignore a person's motives for wanting to lead them and instead look at the outcome they are promised. They often do not see that it is the thought process behind a desire that is the strongest indicator of a person's character.'

Twenty-Two stared up at the sky as she considered this. If the world were led by Ezra, she thought it would be a safe place to live in. But even though she did not understand the Sapien hierarchy, she thought it unlikely that anyone would give him the chance to lead. He was very short and everyone she had met seemed to place a lot of value on a person's height. She remembered that she too was considered very short.

'They are also weak when it comes to taking a person's power when they abuse their status,' Kit continued. 'They wait too long to remove these people from their positions and get into wars where thousands of lives are lost. When, really, someone who knew the truth of that person should have ended their existence long before it got to that stage.'

Twenty-Two's eyes widened.

'Please do not misunderstand me,' Kit quickly signed. 'Everyone has their darker side, me included. What I am saying is that if someone chooses to lead others, they should be judged with a higher amount of scrutiny at all times of their leadership. They may start with the right intentions but then the power may corrupt them. And if that dark side rules, if they care so little for others' lives that they are willing to sacrifice them without a second's thought, there is no reasoning with those people. The only way is to take their power or take their lives from them.'

Twenty-Two nodded her agreement; there was no room in her heart for sentimentality over a life when the stars' offerings were abused. Sitting out here, she could see that she had been given a second chance. She had to find a way of honouring this gift.

'What is the point in coming back?' she signed. 'There

are only a few of us and everyone stares as if we are from another planet. What am I supposed to do in Uracil?'

'We aren't from another planet, just another time,' Kit signed. 'You have to remember how unique that makes us; people will always look at us and that is better than going unnoticed.'

'What is your purpose then?' Twenty-Two asked.

Kit scrunched his eyes before standing up. 'I am going to learn as much as possible so I am able to judge the truth of each situation. I am also going to teach those who want to learn sign language. We need to be able to communicate with people to be heard. What is yours?'

In that moment, everything fell into place for Twenty-Two, but she did not answer his question.

TWENTY-TWO

Elise was woken by a small hand shaking her. Her automatic reaction was to hit out until she could get to her feet, but she stopped herself after the first blow made contact. No enemy would yelp like that. After nearly a month of knowing Ezra, she could recognise his yelps; no other identifying words were required.

'I'm so sorry,' she whispered. 'I didn't know it was you.'

Ezra rubbed his arm. 'That's okay; I should have known I would scare you. I just didn't know you could land a blow like that is all.'

There was the sound of more rubbing and then he tugged at Elise's arm. 'You've got to come with me. I need your help.'

Elise quickly got dressed in the dark, careful not to wake any of the other five female cleaning staff. Their communal sleeping area did not allow much privacy but they were all so tired from their day's work they rarely stirred at night.

It was a couple of hours before their shifts began so

Elise and Ezra loaded themselves with mops and buckets before slipping through the corridors, Ezra leading the way.

Every few turns of the corridor, they would pass a guard circling their well-trodden route. Elise's heart had sunk in the first few weeks of being in the containment centre; the number of guards far outweighed the amount in the museum. But she had soon learnt that, by and large, the guards would ignore them if they looked as if they were performing their duties.

Her weeks of exploring the containment centre had revealed no hidden exits, windows or doors. There was only one way out and this was through the heavily patrolled front gate, where every person passing through had his or her identification closely inspected and then swiped. She could see no way to escape and was beginning to consider the possibility she would have to serve her full two years before she got to leave.

'It's like being back at the museum again,' Ezra said, smiling at her as they slipped through the corridors.

Elise didn't have the heart to point out that, from what he had told her, he wasn't very good at moving around areas that he wasn't supposed to be in.

'Where are you taking me?' she asked.

'To see my friend.' He stopped in the hallway and turned to Elise. 'There's something I have to tell you, but you have to swear on the stars that you won't tell anyone what I'm about to say.'

'Of course I won't,' Elise said, searching his face.

'That's not good enough,' Ezra responded, pressing his lips together.

'Sorry,' Elise said, trying not to roll her eyes. Instead, she put her hand to her chest. 'I swear on the stars that I won't tell anyone what you are about to say.'

'And swear on Jupiter and all the other planets. This is important enough to warrant them being involved as well.'

Elise sighed. 'I swear on Jupiter and all the other planets too.'

Ezra gave Elise an appraising look and she suddenly felt very uncomfortable. He still thought that she had grown up in Cytosine and was an orphan like him. She felt uncomfortable misleading him but didn't know how to tell him the truth without risking the safety of her family. She didn't know how she could put any of this right.

'When I was caught, there was someone else with me,' Ezra said. 'Her name's Dara and she worked in the museum as well. She took having to leave the museum quite badly. And now she's, well...she's a bit mind jangled is the best way of putting it. I'm worried about her; she's changed.'

'What do you want me to do?' Elise asked, not sure where this was leading.

'I want you to take a look at her, see how you think she is. I think she's getting worse and I don't know whether to ask to get her moved. And if she was going to be moved, I don't know where to ask her to be moved to. The psych ward's out of the question but...but there's got to be somewhere better for her...and I owe it to...'

Ezra burst into tears before he could finish what he was going to say. He angrily wiped them away. He reminded her so much of her brother in that moment that Elise was by him in two steps. She wrapped him in her arms. His sobs wracked his small frame and she didn't say anything until he stilled.

'I'm sorry. Not very adult of me, is it? I'm not supposed to do that anymore,' Ezra said, stepping away from Elise.

Elise looked down at his freckled face. He refused to meet her gaze.

'You don't need to be ashamed of crying,' Elise said. 'We don't turn fourteen and suddenly become emotionless statues. You shouldn't be embarrassed by tears. I cried when I woke up in this place.'

'You did? That makes me feel better; you're years older than me,' Ezra said, picking up his bucket. 'You must be nearing middle-age.'

Elise opened her mouth to correct him and then closed it again. How long had she been in here? She hadn't seen her reflection since she had woken up. *What if I've lost more than three months?*

She ran to catch up with him. 'Ezra, wait a minute. What year is it?'

He turned to her and laughed. 'I like you, but you're a bit mind jangled too, aren't you? It's 2269.'

Elise tried not to appear too relieved; for a moment she had feared she had lost ten years of memories. 'Just testing.' She smiled. 'And I'm not nearing middle-age either.'

Ezra shrugged. 'You just seem so much older than me. You're so...closed and quiet.'

Elise blushed. 'I'm just getting used to this place is all.'

Ezra didn't say any more about it as he led them to the geriatric wing. When they reached the heavy doors, they held their passes against the card readers. Looking at the doors, Elise realised that none of the patients inside the geriatric wing would have the strength to push them open if they were intent on trying to move to another area. Elise wondered if the Potiors had designed the doors this way—she wouldn't put it past them.

Although marginally better than the psychiatric ward, this one always left her with a strange mix of feelings. She oscillated between being so uncomfortable that she wanted to leave straightaway and the desire to spend days in here trying to help its occupants.

Elise struggled to keep her passive mask in place as she followed Ezra down the central walkway. Rows and rows of beds were lined up alongside each other in the galleried room. A few nurses flitted between them, drawn to the more unwieldy patients. They would stand by each patient, administer tablets and wait until they were swallowed. Half an hour later, each medicated patient's agitation would subside and they would slump backwards, their eyes glazed over. After quickly checking their blood pressure, the nurse would then move onto the next one.

The patients were sprawled in various positions on top of their beds. One man was lying with his head at the base of the bed and his feet on his pillows, his gaze never leaving the ceiling fan above. Another elderly woman was crouched on her bed, repeatedly picking at a loose thread on the eiderdown while mumbling to herself. When they passed her, the woman peered up at them before shrinking away and fixating again on the loose piece of cotton. Another woman had both of her legs hanging down one side of the bed; it looked as if she were about to topple out at any moment. Bed after bed, these miseries repeated themselves in various forms and predicaments.

Elise tried not to look at anyone for too long. She did not know what was worse, pretending these people were not there or openly staring at them. She tried to smile at each one, though few saw her and even fewer responded.

'I made friends with the nurses and they let me come in and care for Dara every day,' Ezra said.

He pointed out a bed farther down that held a tiny woman. She was the right way up and neatly tucked under her sheets. Her fine, silver hair had recently been washed and stuck up from her scalp in a feathery spray.

'She looks well cared for,' Elise said before they reached the bed.

Ezra beamed his response before approaching the woman and gently shaking her awake. 'I've brought someone to see you.'

One eye opened and peered around, followed by the other. They both locked onto Elise.

'Oh, I thought it might be...' Dara trailed off.

'No, no, it wouldn't be,' Ezra said. 'This is Elise. She's another cleaner like me. Thought she could come and keep you company sometimes before and after our shifts, like I do.'

'What's your surname, Elise?'

'Cyton,' Elise responded, trying not to dwell on the fact that the first thing she was saying to this woman was a lie.

'Well, that's a start at least. If I hear another word about perfect-valley-bowl Thymine, I'll fall out of my bed and not get up again. It's all this one can talk about.'

She gestured at Ezra, who blinked rapidly.

'Do you want to visit Thymine?' Elise asked Ezra.

He shifted in his seat before answering. 'I was born there so I'd like to go back and visit. Was moved to Cytosine when I was a baby.'

'I have...I mean...I once had a friend like that,' Elise said. 'Except he was born in Adenine, no parents, like you. He always wanted to go back. I think he hoped he might have some family there.'

Ezra shrugged. 'I sometimes think there might be someone in Thymine for me. But wishing won't help anything, will it?'

'So, you both worked at the museum then?' Elise asked, trying to change the subject.

They glanced at each other before Ezra answered. 'Yes, Dara was the one I was caught walking around with late at night.'

Elise stared at them both. It seemed an unlikely friendship, but who was she to judge these things? She wondered whether Ezra looked up to Dara as the grandmother he'd never had.

'Were you a cleaner as well in the museum?' Elise asked Dara.

There was a squawk from Dara that drew the attention of the other residents. One of the men eight beds down started wailing loudly, rocking his knees to his chest. Ezra smiled nervously at the closest nurse, who glared at them and brought her finger to her lips.

'A cleaner!' Dara exclaimed. 'A cleaner!'

Ezra winced.

'Dara was a Companion,' Ezra whispered before there was another squawk.

Elise tried to still her reaction; the only other Companion she had met was Luca.

'That's a pretty rare job; had you been doing it for long?' Elise asked, trying to sound as if she were just making polite conversation.

Dara's small chest swelled up. 'I was the first in Zone 3. Well, technically second, but definitely first Companion to ever be hired in Cytosine.'

'Did you know sign language before you started or did they teach you?' Elise asked.

Dara gave Elise an appraising look. 'How do you know so much about Companions then, eh? Didn't know it was common knowledge about the sign language.'

Elise tried not to react. 'Just always been interested in the Neanderthals from school. People my age never got to see them in the museum. Made sure I picked up whatever I could from the teachers.'

'Same as me,' Ezra piped up, smiling over at Elise. 'Tell us, Dara, what were the first Neanderthals like?'

'Well...where to begin...' Dara was clearly enjoying the attention. 'I was brought in as the Companion to Nine.' She settled back on her pillows. 'The first seven had already died. It had taken the museums a while to realise that the Neanderthals couldn't cope with the isolation and Nine was Cytosine's only one left. I knew sign language already. My older sister...well...I needed it for her.'

Elise smiled at Dara, thinking of her own sibling.

'I'd no idea what work I was starting,' Dara continued. 'It was all very secretive. I'd had some difficult choices to make, fifty years old and never lived away from the home I grew up in. My parents had passed on, as had my older sister, and I didn't want to live with my brother's family anymore.' Dara blinked rapidly before staring down at her hands. 'His wife never took to me and the children followed her example. So, at fifty, I decided I wanted to live away from home for the first time. There weren't many options for Sapiens of my age so I just took the only job I was offered that provided a room as well.'

'Did they give you any training? Tell you how to deal with them?' Elise asked, lowering her voice and leaning in towards the woman.

'Not a jot. I was just given this seven-year-old girl and told to get on with it. They'd only started trying to teach her sign language the previous year. Before then, the Neanderthals had no proper way of communicating. They didn't live together and no one knew how they would have spoken to each other before. So, that's when the Potiors decided to try sign language. It was the saving of her really. She was quite wild with the frustration of it all.'

Elise was captivated; hearing about what the earliest Companions had had to go through put her own initial struggles with Kit into perspective.

'She did much better, once she had a way of expressing herself,' Dara continued. 'But she was never properly right. I think those first seven years by herself did more damage than I could admit to myself at the time.'

Dara pulled herself up against the pillows; she had slid down to being almost horizontal. Elise leant over and gently helped her.

'No point hiding the truth from myself now,' Dara said. 'So much time has passed, you see.'

'How was she not right?' Elise asked, thinking of the Neanderthals in the other bases. Perhaps they had also been neglected at an early age.

'She had no stimulation when she was young. No one to talk to, play with. A thing like that...it takes its toll. She could sit for hours and just watch a ladybird on a blade of grass.' Dara shrugged. 'Maybe she lived her life in another world, an inside world that she had made for herself.'

'What happened to her?' Ezra asked, resting his head on the edge of the bed. 'I can't remember if she was ever mentioned in my classes.'

Dara paused before answering. 'She was taken to Adenine when Eight died. That made Nine the oldest surviving Neanderthal and they wanted her in the capital.' Dara looked away. 'I was only given a week's notice before they moved her. She was fifteen. I'd had eight years with her by then...'

'You must've missed her,' Elise said, leaning over and taking the old woman's hand.

'What? Missed her?' Dara said, blinking. 'Of course I did. Even though we weren't encouraged to think of them in that way. And in a few weeks' time, I had a new baby to look after.'

'What was her name?' Elise asked, trying to brighten her voice.

Dara ignored her. 'I thought with this new one, with her being younger, that I'd have a better go of making it right... but she didn't really stand a chance, not out in the real world. They're not raised for that, are they?'

'Out in the real world?' Elise whispered. 'Why would she need to be ready for that?'

'Well, that's enough for us today, Dara,' Ezra said, standing up and stretching. 'Elise and me have got a full shift ahead of us. I'll come back later for your hair wash.'

Elise picked up her mop and bucket, despite wanting to hear more. 'I'd like to come and visit you again sometime, if that's all right?'

'Of course, dear. I ain't got anywhere else to be in this stars-forsaken place now, have I?' Dara said.

She leant forward for Ezra to adjust her pillows.

'No, I suppose not,' Elise said, giving Dara a little wave goodbye.

Elise and Ezra walked in silence out of the ward. Elise kept her head down and tried not to stare at the elderly residents who had been swept into this corner of the containment centre. She couldn't stop thinking about whether Dara's last Neanderthal had left the museum.

It was only after the heavy double doors closed behind them that Ezra spoke. 'She's not well, is she? She's so different to how she was before.'

Elise thought about it a moment before speaking. 'She's certainly very frail, but she seemed alert to where she was. She was so interesting and I think quite sweet, the way she talked about the Neanderthals.'

'Exactly! Sweet! She's nothing like what she was before. She used to be cranky and rude. She didn't try to hit me once today!' Ezra gestured upwards. 'What I wouldn't give for a swipe from that sharpened tongue of hers. It's not right, none of it is. At least when she was mocking me, I knew she had some fight left in her.'

'Maybe she's just tired, needs some rest,' Elise suggested.

'I don't know. I made a promise to someone that I'd look after her and...'

Ezra stared pointedly at the ceiling.

'We'll both look after her then,' Elise said. 'She's got more of a chance if there are two of us. But I don't think we should ask to have her moved. The only other place they would take her is the psych ward, and I don't think we could look after her as well there.'

Ezra stared at his feet. 'Thank you. I can't begin to explain how important it is to keep her going.'

Elise tilted her head. 'What did she mean? About a Neanderthal not being able to live outside?'

Ezra drew in a large breath before speaking. 'She meant nothing. Mind jangled is all. Just as I said.'

'She seemed pretty alert to me. What are you hiding?'

'Nothing. We're not hiding anything.'

Elise stopped walking. 'You can't expect me to help you all the time if you're not telling me everything.'

She was tired and her nerves were frayed. She could feel the weeks in the containment centre getting to her.

'You're a good one to talk,' Ezra said, turning on her.

'You ain't telling me the truth but I don't go prying. No one in Cytosine has your accent, but I don't say anything. Let you alone, so why can't you do the same for me?'

Before Elise could respond, he marched off to the closest cleaning closet, stepped inside and firmly closed the door behind him.

TWENTY-THREE

These were the things that Elise knew to be true: She was born in Thymine, not Cytosine, and her surname was Thanton, not Cyton. Her last memory before waking up in Cytosine's containment centre was of leaving her parents' house in Thymine.

She had to repeat these facts to herself daily or the doubts would set in. If the doubts set in, she knew it would be the beginning of her long decline. There was still much further for her to fall.

Elise repeated these few things she was sure of, or a variation of them, to herself every day as she walked to and from visiting Dara. She tried not to think about her family or friends or how she had ended up here or when she would leave. Instead, she busied herself looking after Dara, who received the attention with a quiet dignity.

Elise would sometimes see Ezra at Dara's bedside but they politely avoided each other; a distance had grown between them since their argument. Elise did not push Dara to tell her any more about her life as a Companion and Ezra had clearly told Dara not to discuss it with Elise. This left them with very little of their past to talk about; Dara's whole world had been her role as a Companion and Elise couldn't bring herself to invent stories that amounted to nothing more than lies about her childhood and teenage years in Cytosine.

Instead, they concentrated on the day-to-day ups and downs of the containment centre. Enid from seven beds down dying in the middle of the night had left them with a bleak few days; their spirits were then mildly raised when Gemma across the way began to recover from her second stroke and regained her speech. It was these events that held their attention now. Elise tried not to think of her family or friends too much; it opened up a pain in her chest that made it hard for her to breathe. The outside world had shrunk into a single burning thought that she pushed away to ease her mind; it had been replaced by the internal workings of this colony.

Today had been particularly difficult for Elise and she felt the need to speak to Dara more than ever. She had been in the containment centre for three months and it weighed heavily on her, threatening to take over. It was only an eighth of her sentence and she didn't know how she could stay in there a moment longer. She worked fourteen-hour shifts every single day. She was used to hard work, but she could not settle into the monotony of it. There were no weekends or holidays built into their schedules, no entertainment, no moments of celebration or collaboration. She woke, she worked, she visited Dara for an hour, maybe two, she ate the same food and then she slept, only waking to repeat this again.

She hadn't seen the sunlight in all this time, the overly bright, electric lights being the only illumination the containment centre offered. She had not gazed at the colour green, touched anything that felt soft or warm or felt a light breeze on her skin...these memories were all fading away and she knew she had to let them go to survive in here.

Concrete, low ceilings, doors so heavy you needed both hands to push them open...this was what enclosed her and she felt her surroundings press down on her more with every day that passed. This feeling made her pull at her collar, the stale air choking her from the inside out. She wished every day that she had never left Thymine and, more recently, she had started wishing that she had never left the safety of her parents' home to go back to the museum. If she wished her life further back in time, then the path that had led her to this place would be reversed, even if it meant not returning to help her friend. This last thought dragged her further down; even her humanity was being slowly eroded in this place.

Dara had developed a cold in the last few days that had spread to her chest and Elise could hear her hacking away as soon as she entered the geriatric wing. Elise quickened her pace and nodded to the few residents who glanced up when she passed. Walking down the line of beds, she made sure to bow her head in deference to the nurses who could ban her from visiting in an instant if the mood struck them.

Elise quietly pulled a chair closer to Dara's pillow and helped the weakened, old woman lean forward to try and clear her chest. Elise rubbed her back, feeling the knots of Dara's spine pushing through the paper-thin skin. She waited patiently for her to regain her breath. The only physical contact Elise ever had with anyone was with Dara. She had not hugged or held anyone in the entire time she had been here, except for Ezra that once. Her body had started to feel isolated from the others; she knew that if someone did try to touch her, she would shrink from them. She thought of Samuel and wondered where he was.

Once the old lady had cleared her chest, she sat back and looked at Elise appraisingly. 'You're in the depths today, aren't you?' Dara took a moment; the wheezing caused her to struggle for breath. 'Make sure that you don't get too comfortable down there or you might not be able to get back up again.'

'It's been three months today,' Elise said. 'I realised it this morning and I don't how I'm going to make it to two years.'

'Well, you've got a few options,' Dara said, leaning forward to cough again. Tears formed in the corners of her eyes. 'You either don't make it, make it out with all your marbles or make it out with less than you came in with. It's your choice.'

Elise had to smile at the truth in Dara's words. 'How does it not get to you? How does this place not seep inside?'

'It's because I know I'm not going to make it out of here. So, I refuse to let it win twice by taking all my joy as well.'

Elise snorted to cover her fear. 'Of course you're going to make it out of here. You've just got a bit of a cold is all.'

Dara stared at Elise. When she next spoke, it was laboured and the pauses between her words grew as she went on. 'I knew as soon as I woke up in this place that I wouldn't be leaving it. My time is nearly over now and that is all right with me. I'm old and I'm tired and I think I deserve a little bit of peace.'

Elise blinked, not knowing what to say. She leant over and unnecessarily plumped up the pillows again. Dara accepted the attention graciously. When Elise started to move away, Dara held onto her sleeve to prevent her from sitting back again.

Her speech slowed even further and she took little gasps between each word. 'Take...care...of...Ezra...for...me.' She held all of Elise's attention. 'He may not be the smartest bear in the woods...but he's got to be one of the kindest. And that's a quality worth preserving...wouldn't you say?'

Dara struggled to keep her gaze on Elise, who nodded her agreement. With a small smile of satisfaction, Dara closed her eyes and fell asleep.

Elise didn't move from her bedside. When Ezra came later that evening, they both sat in silence watching her chest moving up and down, her breathing becoming shallower as the night wore on.

Dara didn't open her eyes again.

At four in the morning, her chest stilled and Elise prayed to all the stars that they had granted her some peace.

Dara's passing pushed Elise further into herself. Caring for the old woman had given her a purpose that provided the human contact and kindness that she desperately needed, in a place that discouraged both. The only thing that kept her getting up in the morning was Ezra's sudden decline. She had made a promise to Dara, so all of her focus slid onto Ezra.

At first he was just late to his shifts. Elise noticed the looks the managers gave each other as they jotted this down on their timesheets. Elise tried to speak to him about it but he had steadfastly refused to talk to her since their argument. He would just shrug and walk away. Elise would try to follow but once he entered his shared quarters, she couldn't go any farther; they were for the male cleaners only.

She still tried to keep an eye on him as they went about their duties, but what she saw of him only worried her more. He had always been a diligent worker, but she would now catch him leaning against his broom handle, staring down one of the many long corridors. Elise knew that if she had noticed these bouts of inaction, then his managers would as well.

A week later, Elise stood outside the male sleeping quarters. It was the beginning of their shift and she was waiting for Ezra. When he didn't come out of the room with the rest of the men, she caught up with one of the older cleaners, a man named Harold who was mid-way through a three-year sentence. She spoke with Harold in hushed tones, both of them looking around for their managers or, worse, the guards. Harold told Elise that Ezra hadn't got up that morning, had said he was sick. Shrugging, Harold left Elise and ambled down the corridor to begin his own work for the day. He had already told her that he wasn't going to do anything to jeopardise his release in eighteen months' time.

Worried, Elise made her way to the geriatric unit. There she found one of the kinder nurses, whom she knew had appreciated the care Ezra had given to Dara. She asked if he would come and check on Ezra on his lunch break.

A few hours later, Elise waited outside the door to Ezra's sleeping area while William examined him. Pacing up and down, she dipped her head as one of the guards passed. He raised an eyebrow at her and gave a smirk. He obviously thought that she was hanging around outside the male sleeping area for another reason. Back at home, she probably would have glared at him, but in here she knew there was no point in antagonising him; the guards always came off better.

When the door swung open, Elise turned. William wore a puzzled expression.

'What is it?' Elise said, glancing around her to check they were alone for the moment.

William snapped off his latex gloves and put them in a bin outside the door. 'Well, that's just it. There's no temperature, no pain, no raised or lowered blood pressure. Apart from being very underweight for his age, there is nothing much wrong with him.'

Elise followed William as he retraced his way back to the geriatric wing. 'He should be back to normal in a few days then.'

William stared at her. She guessed that his height gene had been tweaked as he was a whole foot taller than her. 'Well, not really. If there's nothing physically wrong with him, that means either I've missed something, or it's more to do with his state of mind.'

Her feeling of elation quickly dissipated.

'And if it's to do with his state of mind,' William continued, 'then there's only one place he'll end up.'

Elise nodded her understanding—the psychiatric wing.

'Look, I have to go now,' William said, turning off towards the door. 'And don't tell anyone I did this for you. Ezra's got a lot of good in him, but they won't like me tending to a cleaner, especially as no reports will be made. Everything has to be done officially round here. I won't be able to help again and it's not my speciality anyway. Try to see if you can get him interested in something; that's my advice.'

Elise walked away slowly. She would have to become a Companion again.

TWENTY-FOUR

It had taken several months, but Twenty-Two now felt the strength that coursed through her increasing with every passing day. Her muscles were fully formed again and the power they once held was returning. She found some comfort knowing that no Sapien was a match for her.

She was also aware that this feeling of strength had the potential to be destructive and she had to hold it deep inside. She began to constantly monitor herself to ensure that she was not falling into the many pitfalls that the freedom of thought and movement gave her. Never before had she had all these overwhelming choices presented to her, pulling her in so many directions. She felt her self, her core, slipping from her grasp, and she tried to remember her key personality traits from before she had left Cytosine. Like anyone trying to assess their nature, she felt the need to ask people's opinion of her, believing that the task required objectivity. But no one in Uracil had known her longer than a few months and she did not think she would see her friends again—Fintorian was dead and it was quite possible that Dara and Ezra were as well.

She therefore spoke to no one about her internal worries. The only people she could possibly trust with these thoughts were Kit and Twenty-Seven, her own kind. But Kit had not known her from before. She visited Twenty-Seven every day, but he was just a boy who was trying to settle into a school that was completely alien to him; she knew it would be wrong to burden him with her questions.

She ruminated on what her key traits were for several days until she felt satisfied that she could present an outline of who she was. She made a list and scrolled through it most days. One point she kept on returning to was that she liked to feel useful. She had always possessed the desire to help others and this, amongst other things, was what led her to seek out the Tri-Council. She had considered trying to speak to Raul or Flynn first, but after watching them for several days she decided Faye was the one to make her appeal to.

When Twenty-Two first approached her, Faye sat quietly on her viewing platform. She made no interruption while Twenty-Two explained her need for occupation and her desire to be useful. Faye had dismissed all the other people who were waiting for her so that she could provide Twenty-Two with a private audience. Twenty-Two was grateful for this thoughtful act; she knew that Faye only left her platform to sleep and rarely gave a private audience to anyone if they didn't have a prior appointment.

After she had finished her appeal, Twenty-Two clasped her hands in front of her. She was seated on the tree trunk's carved ledge. Faye continued to sit silently in front of her on the wooden seat where she spent most of her day receiving visitors.

After a few moments' thought, she lifted her hands to sign. 'Have you not considered going to school, like Kit and Twenty-Seven?'

'I have, but that is Kit's dream, not mine. I can already read and write as well,' Twenty-Two signed.

Faye's eyes widened.

'My Companion had a fall six months before I left Cytosine and she forgot most of the rules,' Twenty-Two explained. 'She began teaching me things that she wouldn't have done if she had kept all of her memories.'

'And you are fully literate?' Faye asked, her eyes shining.

'I think so,' Twenty-Two signed, now beginning to doubt herself.

'Would you mind if I asked you to read something?' Faye handed over her screen. 'Just the first three lines, please.'

Twenty-Two glanced down, read the words and then noted them down in her mind's eye, just as she did with her lists. She then signed the first three lines of the document.

'Perfectly done,' Faye said, following Twenty-Two's hands.

Growing in confidence, Twenty-Two decided to press on. 'I wanted to ask if I could work for you, perhaps take notes of your meetings or help you with your daily chores.'

Faye blinked rapidly, but she quickly recovered. 'That is a very kind offer, but I am not in any need of help at the moment. Uracil does not agree with monitoring its residents, so I prepare only brief notes after each meeting. It may also be frowned upon if I were seen not to be looking after my own personal chores. I may help make the decisions in Uracil but I cannot be seen to have special privileges.'

Faye smiled and looked down at her hands. In that moment of apparent embarrassment and uncertainty, she was more beautiful than ever. Twenty-Two thought she could almost see Fintorian's exquisite bone structure reflected in Faye's high cheekbones.

Twenty-Two realised that her chance to work alongside Faye was slipping away; in a moment, she would be dismissed.

'I could prepare your notes for you as you have your meetings,' she signed.

Faye blinked at Twenty-Two before answering. 'It would not do for people to see someone taking notes on a screen while they talked to me about private matters.'

'It wouldn't have to be on a screen, I could remember most of the key points word for word, exactly as they say it, if necessary,' Twenty-Two signed.

Faye frowned. 'You can do that?'

Twenty-Two nodded, still not sure if it was something everyone could do or not.

'All right,' Faye signed. 'I'm going to keep talking for the next five minutes and then you are going to repeat what I've said back to me.'

While Faye talked about her favourite food—peach pavlova, something Twenty-Two had never heard of before and had no choice but to spell phonetically—Twenty-Two recorded what she heard in her mind's eye. She then scrolled through what she had written and repeated it back to Faye. She also asked about the spelling of pavlova and amended it for next time.

'Extraordinary,' Faye said, forgetting for a moment to sign. 'And we had dared to question your capabilities.'

Twenty-Two scrunched her eyes in response.

'Perhaps it would be useful if you could sit in on some

of the meetings with me, at a distance perhaps. Can you lip read?' Faye enquired.

'I can, but it's impossible to be completely accurate,' Twenty-Two signed, wanting, as always, to answer honestly.

'Well, that's better than nothing. I would be delighted if you would join me on the days that I am working. You could be an...Administrative Aid, alongside Cedric. He helps me get ready for meetings and assists with organising my appointments. You can help him prepare the seating areas for meetings and ensure we have refreshments, that sort of thing. But we will keep your other role between ourselves. Is that agreed?'

Faye fixed Twenty-Two with a clear stare.

'I can agree to that,' Twenty-Two responded, grateful that she had achieved what she had set out to do.

'We can start tomorrow then.'

For the first time since leaving Cytosine, Twenty-Two felt she had a purpose and that she was helping others again. This was on a much grander scale, as it wasn't just Dara or Twenty-Seven that she was caring for; she would be watching over the whole of Uracil. She could combine her need to help others with her desire to observe the leaders of Uracil at the same time.

Without feeling embarrassed, she allowed herself a little skip as she made her way over to Georgina's medical station. Bay would still be in nursery with the other children and they would collect her together when Georgina finished her shift.

The station that Georgina worked from was a drop-in centre for people with minor ailments. For convenience, it was in one of the tree houses, the closest location to the residential homes. The more serious injuries and illnesses were dealt with in a cabin on the forest floor that could hold the equipment that was required to treat such matters.

The door to Georgina's station was open so Twenty-Two did not knock. She approached the entrance but did not go in any farther. Tilla was standing next to Georgina, who was seated at her desk. Tilla caught her eye and smiled at Twenty-Two before leaning over and kissing Georgina on the lips.

'See you tonight then?' Tilla said to Georgina before turning to Twenty-Two. 'Didn't mean to make you blush. You're looking good by the way; all your hair is returning.'

Twenty-Two was not blushing, so she pondered for a moment how to respond. Often she found that the people she met said what was unnecessary, while avoiding what was obvious.

'Thank you,' Twenty-Two signed, knowing that Georgina would translate for her. 'I am feeling strong for the first time in a year and am also rarely embarrassed by what I see.'

Twenty-Two stared appraisingly at Tilla. She always liked the way Tilla wore her clothing, even though Twenty-Two would never swap her own knee-length tunics for such things, no matter how often Tilla pressed her to do so. Today Tilla was wearing a blood-orange skirt that trailed on the floor, so she had to pick it up once she began to move around. In direct contrast, she wore a skin-tight, blue top, which barely reached her midriff. Tilla loved bold colour and Twenty-Two always looked forward to seeing what combinations she would wear next.

'Well, I'm glad you're feeling better, and if you ever change your mind about swapping a few of those tunics, you know where I am.' Tilla cocked her head to the side before waving at Georgina. 'I'll see you later.'

Once Tilla had left, Georgina looked up.

'Sorry about that,' she signed, before rubbing her forehead.

'About what?' Twenty-Two signed.

'Never mind. I'll be ready to get Bay in five minutes, if that's okay?'

Twenty-Two did not want Georgina to feel the need to apologise for things that she should not be sorry for. 'If you are happy and she is happy then there is nothing to apologise for, is there?'

Georgina smiled. 'No, I suppose you're right. It's just I'm trying to take it slowly and in a private way, but she's got her own ideas.'

Twenty-Two knew they had strayed outside her limited knowledge of such matters, so she fell back on saying what she believed to be true. 'If you are honest with each other, you will find your way together.'

Georgina rubbed her forehead. 'Sometimes you sound so much like Kit...'

Twenty-Two did not know how to respond to this and felt that it did not require a comment whose only purpose would be to fill her side of the conversation. So, instead, she changed the subject.

'I have some news,' Twenty-Two signed, scrunching her eyes. 'I have a job.'

Georgina pulled out a tissue from her desk drawer and turned away.

'Stars, sorry,' she said, dabbing her face. 'I just got a flash for the briefest moment of how far you've come. A job, well...that's just fantastic! I'm so proud of you. I only wish that Samuel would hurry up and return with Elise so they could both meet you. They so wanted to help Kit find the other Neanderthals and see if they could lead their lives together. And then here you are with a job.'

Twenty-Two felt the warmth of a compliment spread through her. She had received two today, which was unprecedented. She had not seen either Samuel or Elise since that first day she had left Cytosine, but Georgina would often talk about them. Sometimes Georgina would get teary when she spoke about Elise, trying to guess where she was or what had happened to her. Twenty-Two admired Georgina's loyalty to her friend. It was for that reason, along with Georgina's kindness to her when she had first arrived, that Twenty-Two had worked hard at building a friendship with her.

'When do you think Samuel will come back?' Twenty-Two signed.

She wanted to decide for herself if the man who was responsible for Fintorian's death was as good a man as Kit believed him to be.

'I don't know,' Georgina signed, standing up to collect her things. 'I've finally got a message from him that a scout brought in. He told me he has been to Thymine to check on Elise's parents. He broke into their house at three in the morning to avoid detection. Nearly got himself killed by his account.' Georgina smiled. 'Apparently, Elise's father is both fearsome and unappreciative of mysterious visitors. Samuel said something about nearly being finished off by a range of kitchen implements. Once Samuel was able to calm him down, he explained that he had come to check on them at Elise's request.'

Twenty-Two held out Georgina's screen for her to place in her bag but didn't interrupt. She knew it helped Georgina to talk about her friends, as she missed them. She was always trying to hide from Twenty-Two her belief that something had happened to them.

'He did not tell them that Elise had been captured in Cytosine,' Georgina continued, placing her screen in her bag and turning around to scan the room again. 'When Samuel found out there had been no repercussions for Elise's family, he decided not to bring them to Uracil until he knew Elise was safe. He did not want to bring them to a place that blames Elise for her own capture.'

Georgina stopped signing while she looked around to see if she had remembered everything. 'He made the right choice. Uracil wouldn't be a sanctuary for Elise's family at the moment. She is held entirely responsible for what happened; they say she was being incompetent and all sorts of other things. I think it's part of the reason Samuel is staying away...'

Twenty-Two did not comment even though Georgina had trailed off. She waited to see if Georgina wanted to continue; she enjoyed hearing people's thoughts about their own lives and the lives of others. She liked to observe them to see if their words matched their true meaning. Georgina's fear for her friends was clear for anyone to read, but she tried to hide her distaste at the way Uracil had blamed Elise for her capture. Twenty-Two was fairly certain Georgina believed that Elise had been sent out to work for Uracil before she had been properly trained. She hid this belief, but Twenty-Two guessed that she might have discussed it with Luca or Kit, who were her closest friends. She had certainly never said this to Twenty-Two.

Although they welcomed Twenty-Two into their little group, she knew that they did not share everything with her. It made her wonder whether it was because they still thought of her as being too fragile, or whether it was simply that she was missing some essential composite for that type of close, almost sacred, friendship. She tried not to dwell on these thoughts; self-doubt had always been part of her makeup, but that didn't mean that she should indulge it.

Georgina walked over to the medicine cabinet and pulled on its door for the third time.

'I always have to check several times that it's locked,' she said. 'Some of the opiates in there could kill with a high-enough dosage. If someone came in here looking for medicines and opened it up, they could take the wrong dosage and...' Georgina shook her head. 'Never mind. It's locked.' She tapped her temple. 'Brain, remember that at two in the morning when you start worrying about it again.'

They went outside and Georgina closed the door to the tree house before glancing at Twenty-Two. 'You're lost in your thoughts. No time for that now; we have a very tired and possibly quite cross Bay to collect.'

Georgina linked her arm with Twenty-Two's as they made their way to the nursery. Twenty-Two couldn't help but scrunch her eyes at the gesture.

The next morning, Twenty-Two made sure she was up two hours before her first full working day began. Breakfast could either be eaten communally on the long tables or collected from the large kitchen station and taken back to the resident's room. Twenty-Two always ate in her room. Although Kit was trying to teach sign language to the residents of Uracil, only some of the population had decided to take it up. This meant that she was often in need of a translator, which made communal mealtimes very isolating.

After she had finished her breakfast and taken her

morning walk around the circumference of the island, she made her way to Faye's platform. It was the end of autumn and Twenty-Two was enjoying the change in seasons, which she had never fully experienced before. It was true that they would drop the temperature in her pod to reflect the change to autumn and then winter, but this was not the same as being outside and experiencing it in full. She had soon learnt that a change in season was not simply just an adjustment in temperature. Scrunching her eyes up at the sky, she enjoyed the feeling of the dappled sunlight dancing across her skin while she waited to be told what to do next.

A small, reed-thin man bustled towards her, his nose so hooked it almost touched his top lip. He was only in his mid-thirties but gave the distinct impression that he had always appeared middle-aged, even when a boy.

'Right, well, this is going to be a one-way conversation as I don't speak with my hands,' he said very loudly, glancing up to check that Twenty-Two was listening to him.

Twenty-Two nodded, mentally adding him to her list of bad people.

'I am Cedric. Counsellor Faye has asked me to show you how to prepare the platform for meetings.' He paused to stare at Twenty-Two. 'Why she wants you to sit in on these meetings is beyond me. But it is not, of course, for me to question Counsellor Faye's motives. Not for me at all.'

Cedric proceeded to spend an hour showing Twenty-Two how to prepare the seating area for guests and explaining what drinks should be served to whom. The more he spoke, the more confident he became in his own accomplishments. 'Of course, Michael, who is first in today and works in the agriculture division, prefers slightly cooled mint tea so that he can drink it straightaway. He doesn't like to linger. Half a spoon of honey and a small oat biscuit on the side. Three cushions for his seat, which he prefers in the shade, two for the derriere and one for the base of the spine...'

While Cedric showed Twenty-Two how to lay out this particular cushion arrangement, she took a mental note of all the names he mentioned, their positions and preferences. Cedric didn't have the time to list everyone who came to visit, as there were over two thousand residents in Uracil, but he started with the most important of the visitors. He spoke quickly and never repeated himself; it was for Twenty-Two to keep up.

When they had set up for the first guest's arrival, Faye strode into the circle. Today she was dressed in a simple gown of the palest pink that nipped in above her waist and fell straight down to the floor. As was usual for her, she wore no shoes and instead had placed delicate chains between her toes and ankles that tinkled as she moved.

She smiled. 'Good morning to both of you. I hope Cedric has begun your training.'

'I have indeed, Counsellor Faye,' Cedric said, taking a deep bow.

'Cedric, I've told you before; please don't bow,' Faye said. 'It will not do.'

Cedric reddened and Twenty-Two followed the advancement of the change in colour as it crept from his cheeks up to his forehead and laced over the top of his bald head.

'I am most terribly sorry, Counsellor Faye,' he stuttered.

He almost bowed again in apology, but managed to stop himself in time. He was left awkwardly tilting forward, which he tried to cover up by enthusiastically coughing.

'Whom do we have first?' Faye asked, taking her seat

and accepting the glass of water that Twenty-Two handed her.

Cedric glanced at his screen and reeled off the morning's appointments. 'But we start with Michael, whom I believe wants to speak with you about the harvest.'

Faye nodded and Cedric went and collected Michael. The man had been sitting patiently at the other end of the vast platform behind another wide tree trunk that helped support it. This was where all the waiting visitors were directed to sit, so that Faye would not be observed in her discussions with other guests.

Michael was also in his thirties, but he was so physically different to Cedric that they could have been from different species. He was an unenhanced Sapien, but years of hard labour in agriculture had made him strong and broad. Every step he took, Cedric had to take two to keep up.

Michael made his way around the tree trunk and took a seat on the pillows that had been arranged for him.

'Thank you for seeing me at such short notice,' he said, addressing Faye. He looked down and scooped up the glass holding his slightly cooled mint tea.

Faye smiled warmly at him. 'Of course. As Head of Agriculture, I cannot ignore your requests. Especially as I know that you would never waste my time.'

'That's true. I've always preferred to be out there with our crops rather than in the settlement.'

Michael noiselessly sipped at his tea.

Twenty-Two noticed that Michael never held Faye's direct gaze; it was clear from his body language that he was not comfortable in her presence.

'I came to ask if you could spare some hands for harvesting this autumn,' he said, briefly looking up from his glass. 'The weather looks to turn soon and if the rains are heavy they may damage the crops.'

Uracil relied upon various produce that was seeded together in the same fields. Crops were planted this way so that, from a distance, they did not have the regimented lines that surrounded the other bases. This meant that all seeding, care and harvesting had to be done by hand so that the differing plants could be identified. The method was labour intensive but it shielded Uracil from discovery.

'Of course,' Faye said. 'I can move some of the foragers over for a week. They should be better at identifying the correct plants for harvest. When do you want them?'

'Next week, if possible,' Michael said before standing. 'Should I get Raul and Flynn to agree to it as well?'

'No need,' Faye said in her warmest tone. 'They are letting me make the day-to-day decisions at the moment. They only bother with the directional decisions where a unanimous vote is required. It gives them more time for their other interests, such as speaking with the residents. They like to know the overall mood of Uracil so they can decide how we can better serve its needs.'

Faye shrugged and smiled before rising to acknowledge Michael leaving.

Michael nodded his goodbye, also turning to nod at Cedric and Twenty-Two. Pleased with the gesture, Twenty-Two returned his acknowledgement with a scrunch of her eyes. Michael's eyes widened, but he quickly recovered and gave her a smile that reached his eyes in return.

A steady stream of visitors continued throughout the day, some staying for only a few minutes, others lingering and procrastinating for as long as they could. The heads of the different divisions got their pick of the choice visiting times, while their assistants fitted in with whatever was next available.

Residents who wanted to speak with Faye would wait patiently for a gap between the meetings. They normally requested an audience when they felt they had been wronged or aggrieved in some way by another resident. Faye would try to settle the matter right there by calling on the other resident to attend. For the more serious complaints, she would schedule a hearing date when both Raul and Flynn could attend and pass judgment with her.

Twenty-Two found these meetings fascinating and she listened carefully when she was able to sit in on them. If she was asked to retreat with Cedric to the edge of the platform, she would read the lips of the speaker. From this distance, she could only accurately follow eighty per cent of the guest's conversation and she was unable to see Faye's response, but she was able to make a reasonable mental note of what had been said.

Towards the end of the day, a man entered whom Twenty-Two had never seen before. He was nearly as tall as Faye and even though he was advancing into his middle-years, he still had the strong, lean muscles of a man half his age. He towered over Twenty-Two and she knew that, despite her recovering strength, this was one man that she would not stand a chance against in a fight.

'So, this is your new Administrative Assistant,' the man said to Faye.

'Yes, she is proving to be a quick learner,' Faye responded. 'Twenty-Two, this is Thiago, the Head of Intelligence.'

'Strong coffee, no sugar, a small fruit platter and he likes to remain standing,' Cedric said, before smiling around at everyone. No one returned his smile and he shrunk back from the conversation.

'Yes, very good Cedric,' Thiago said, before turning to Twenty-Two and signing, 'It is a pleasure to finally meet you.'

'You can use sign language?' Twenty-Two responded.

'I am trying to learn,' Thiago said. 'I have been to a few of Kit's lessons. I think if we are housing more Neanderthals then I should be able to converse with them.'

'I can help teach you as well, if you like,' Twenty-Two signed, pleased that he was making the effort to learn how to speak with her.

'That would be greatly appreciated, thank you. Now, Faye, I have an update on our situation in the south.'

'Ah, good. I've been waiting for this. Both of you can go. This meeting is not to be observed as it concerns the well-being of Uracil.'

Faye and Thiago walked over to the tree with the carved seating, their heads bent in quiet conversation.

Twenty-Two watched them for a moment before reluctantly turning to clear up the final glasses. She had finished her first working day.

TWENTY-FIVE

I f Elise was prepared to become a Companion to Ezra, he was equally unprepared to accept any help from her. For weeks, she waited every morning for the male cleaners to file out of their sleeping quarters and then she would slip inside the room, hoping that her entry had not been noticed. Ezra would still be fast asleep and she would shake him awake, ignoring his grimace as he rubbed his eyes. She would then coax him into getting dressed by promising him that he would only have to keep going until lunchtime and then they would decide together whether he could continue into the afternoon. She would follow him around all morning, making sure that she did her cleaning and his as well if needed.

At lunchtime, Elise would sit opposite Ezra while he pushed the same stew they ate every day around his plate. His collarbone had begun to protrude even farther through his shirt; he was losing weight.

After a month of this, Elise snapped.

'They'll put you in the psych wing if you carry on like this,' she whispered across the table.

Ezra shrugged. 'Can't be much worse than this. At least I wouldn't have to work for free for them every day.'

Elise sighed. At least in the early days with Kit, when he made it clear that he didn't like her, he still looked after himself. Ezra hadn't showered in days and had started to provoke his managers into telling him that he needed to buck up his ideas. Elise knew it wouldn't be long before he was reported to the containment centre's higher authorities.

'You think being in the psych ward will be better than this?' she said, trying to control her voice. 'Maybe you do belong there, because you seem to be forgetting that they won't ever let you out. No one gets out of there. You'll spend the rest of your days slipping further from reality. Forgotten about until you can't even remember who you used to—'

'How's that any different to now?' Ezra exclaimed, pushing back his chair.

The commotion drew some stares. A couple of the guards started to make their way over.

'I'm sorry,' she said, reaching for Ezra and trying to pull him back into his seat. 'I didn't mean to say anything. Just calm down, will you? Don't do this here.'

She reached forward and tried to grab his sleeve again.

'It's no different to now!' Ezra shouted, ignoring Elise's efforts to quieten him. 'No different to any of my time here or outside! No one remembers me out there. *They never saw me, even when I was stood right next to them!* The only one who ever paid attention to me was *her*, but she's been gone for months. Stars knows where she is...'

Two of the guards approached Ezra from either end of the long canteen table.

Elise stood up. 'No, no, he's sorry. It's my fault. I wound him up. He'll be all right in a minute.'

The guards ignored Elise and carried on moving towards Ezra. He was still fixed on Elise and oblivious to their approach. Ezra was getting louder; several people in the canteen hurriedly moved towards the two exits—they couldn't risk getting mixed up in something that might impact their release dates.

'*And you!*' Ezra shouted. 'You don't really care about me. If you did, you wouldn't have lied to me right from the beginning. Who are you—?'

Before he could continue, Ezra was grabbed by one of the guards. The other one swiftly took a syringe from his utility belt and injected him in the neck. Ezra looked around in confusion. Before he could say anything else, his eyelids began to droop.

The guard lowered Ezra to the ground before giving him a nudge with his foot.

'He's out,' the shorter guard said. He raised his voice to an unnecessary volume for the few people remaining in the canteen. Most had scarpered at the first sight of trouble, not wanting to accidentally get mixed up in anything they wouldn't be able to get out of again. 'And you lot remember what happens when you start unscrewing like this one. If you can't keep things lidded, then you can't stay out here. No excuses. No bad days.'

With that, one of the guards picked Ezra up by his feet and the other grabbed his hands. Ezra's head lolled to the side and Elise winced as it smacked against one of the chair legs on the way out.

Her final reason for staying grounded in reality had just been hauled off to the psychiatric wing.

She tried to keep going. She woke up early every morning, got dressed and completed her shift, but without Dara or Ezra to keep her in the present, her mind began to drift back to where her predicament had begun. How had she lost three months of memories? How did she end up in Cytosine? Where were her parents? What happened to Kit and her other friends? Without any answers, she began making up more and more elaborate stories to fill in the blanks.

I lost my memories after hitting my head...I came to Cytosine to help rescue a Neanderthal...My parents were implicated in my plan to get Kit out of the museum and are now in Thymine's Containment Centre...My friends are there with them...

Round and round the catalysts and outcomes went, each more bleak than the last. She reasoned that her friends had to be in Thymine or they would be in here with her. If they *were* in Cytosine, after five months, surely they would have found some way to make contact with her. But no one was coming for her and she had another five hundred and seventy-four days to serve in this place.

Once she was released, she would somehow have to get back to Thymine, even though she didn't know the way, wouldn't have enough treated water to last the journey, had no tickets to spend on food...

It was hopeless.

Ezra had been in the psychiatric wing for three weeks and Elise hadn't spoken to anyone in four days when she noticed a nurse staring at her in the canteen. Elise looked away and lowered her head, worried that she had imagined it. She counted to a hundred and then glanced up again; the nurse was talking to one of her colleagues. It was nothing. She was getting jittery and paranoid; there was no reason for a nurse to be staring at her. *Unless I'm starting to look jittery and paranoid?* Maybe her unravelling was clear for everyone to see. No, she couldn't let that happen. She must push it away from the surface—show everyone she was fine.

Standing, Elise smiled around the canteen at no one in particular and made her way to the counter to return her tray. She continued smiling until she pushed open the canteen doors; the expression automatically slid from her features. Making her way to the cleaning cupboard, she collected the equipment she needed and headed towards the psychiatric ward. She was scheduled to work there this afternoon and she hadn't seen Ezra in a week. She was only allowed into this ward to clean; it wasn't as relaxed as the geriatric ward where the patients were no real threat. Inside the psychiatric ward, a volatile patient coming out of their most recent drugged state could do a lot of damage in the moments before they were sent back into the fog again. Precautions had to be taken.

Buzzing her card against the door, she waited for two of the guards to come and collect her. Once they had checked her ID, they waved her through. She made her way along the hallways, systematically sweeping the rubbish away, emptying her wheeled bin into the larger ones and disposing of the sacks of rubbish in the shoots. The psychiatric ward was the worst one to clean; human fluids of all descriptions were liberally splattered over the floors and walls.

A voice came from one of the side rooms, growing louder. 'Fingers and toes, fingers and toes, fingers and toes...'

Elise grimaced. She had to enter this room next to clean it.

She pushed open the door and tried to keep her eyes locked onto the concrete floor. She didn't want to disturb herself any further with what she might see if she glanced towards the occupants.

'Look, see,' a male voice chanted from one of the three beds. 'They took a finger and they took a toe.'

Elise knew that nothing would make her look at him.

'It wasn't the only thing they took,' the man continued. He shouted at the door. '*They took my chances too.* Will have taken yours as well.'

Elise knew he was addressing her.

'They take everyone's chances for children in here.'

'Shut up, Stanley,' the man on the bed next to him mumbled into his pillows.

'Took yours too,' the first man continued. '*Took yours too!*'

'I said shut up.'

The second man lunged towards the other but was held back by the straps around his wrists. Unable to move, he spat at the first man, the globule perfectly arcing and landing on his roommate's forehead.

Elise turned and ran outside before it escalated any further. In the hallway, she narrowly missed being trampled by four guards who were running towards the room she had come from. She knew that the patients would be heavily sedated and then immobilised in an isolation cell. She had to avoid getting mixed up in anything that could lead her into the same situation.

Elise moved into the next room down the corridor. This one was much more quiet and contained only one sleeping figure. Elise sighed her relief. She swept the room and emptied the bin, accidentally dropping it on her way to the door.

The figure did not stir, despite the noise, and Elise was drawn to their bedside. It was a young woman, in her twenties perhaps, although it was difficult to tell. People aged more quickly in the containment centre, particularly this ward. Her face was still, too still.

Elise stopped for a minute and watched her chest, which neither rose nor fell. Alarmed, she hurried down the corridor until she found one of the nurses.

'Please come with me. I think she needs help,' Elise said, quickening her pace back to the room.

She ran over to the bedside and turned to the nurse when she heard the doors swing open again. The nurse snorted then chuckled, before emitting deep belly laughs.

Elise's stomach rolled. She tried to still her features.

'She's dead, you stupid Sap. Been dead for hours,' the nurse said once she had recovered.

'But why...why is she still here?' Elise stuttered, unable to take her eyes from the young woman.

'We're not going to waste time taking her out of the centre now. One of the nurses will wheel her out when their shift ends.'

Elise stared at the nurse, unable to understand how she could show no compassion when someone had lost their life. The nurse glared at Elise and she knew she had made a mistake by not just continuing with her work.

'And what's it to do with you, how we do things? Who are you anyway? You're no one, nothing.'

Elise began sweeping under the dead woman's bed.

'I'll be watching you,' the nurse said before leaving the room.

Elise lingered a moment longer, staring at the woman's features. *If an act is not witnessed, it may as well have never occurred.*

Elise did not know where the thought had come from and she pushed it away. Leaning against the wall, she silently asked the stars to remember this woman.

Cleaning her way into Ezra's shared room, Elise could see that he was slumped on his mattress. Two other men were both passed out on their separate beds having recently been sedated. Elise took comfort that he was still in the shared room as it meant that he hadn't antagonised the nurses or other patients. She watched him for a moment; she wouldn't get any sense out of him in his current state. It would be hours until he came around. He was clean, so he must have taken the time to wash at some point in the last few days. She had to hold onto these little wins if she wanted to believe that there was any hope of him surviving and leaving this place.

When she turned around, the same nurse Elise thought had been watching her in the canteen entered the room. Startled, Elise looked down at the floor and began sweeping underneath Ezra's bed.

The nurse approached. Her head still bent, Elise moved around the side of the bed so that she wouldn't be in her way. But the woman came right up to her. Elise flinched. She began to hum quietly under her breath.

'Elise, isn't it?' the woman said.

Elise nodded and carried on sweeping, the humming catching in her throat.

'Thanton?'

Elise froze. 'No, no, Cyton...see?'

She held out her wrist.

'Can I see that?' The nurse grasped Elise's wrist.

Her grip was strong for such a small woman. Elise tried not to flinch.

Elise angled her wrist around. 'See, Cytosine born and bred. Orphan, no family, ended up in this place...'

The nurse peered at her wrist and then looked up at Elise. 'You've lost quite a bit of weight, most of your muscle tone and you've aged about five years, but you're definitely the one I've been looking for.'

TWENTY-SIX

Elise's stomach rolled. Her gaze automatically darted to the exit. They'd found her. She wasn't even sure who 'they' were, but she knew that her parents were now in danger.

'Shhh...it's okay. I didn't mean to alarm you,' the woman said, her large, brown eyes locked onto Elise's. 'You won't remember me, but I've come to help you get out of this place.'

Elise took a step back. The woman was so small that she could easily knock her over if she needed to get away. That wouldn't be a wise move, though; if she hurt a nurse, she'd surely end up in the psychiatric wing.

'Thank you for your offer of help, but I'm fine. I'm nearly quarter of the way through my sentence and I need to stay here to serve the rest if I ever want to leave.'

When Elise tried to step around her, the woman immediately stepped in the same direction, blocking her path.

Elise began to panic. She couldn't refuse to do anything a nurse or any other Medius in this place asked her to do. It wasn't an option. 'Please, I just want to carry on with my cleaning. I'm sorry if you thought I was staring at you in the canteen. I was looking in the wrong place.' Her voice became higher. 'Please, can I just go?'

The woman's voice softened. 'I've been sent by your friends, Samuel, Kit, Georgina and Luca. They asked me to help you. Once we get out of here, I can explain why you lost your memories.'

Elise fixed on her passive mask; inside, she wanted to shake the information out of the woman. 'I...I don't know what you're talking about.'

'Sure you do. I don't know at what point your memory was cut, but your friends all miss you.'

Elise blinked back tears. So, she hadn't been forgotten.

'Are they all right? They're not in another containment centre, are they?'

The woman smiled. 'No, they're absolutely fine. They're all waiting for me to get you out of here.'

'If they're fine, then why didn't they come for me? Why did they send you?'

The woman raised one perfectly arched eyebrow. 'Because they can't do what I can. Now, if I'm going to get you out of here, there can be no discussions, no questions, no diplomacy. You do what I tell you to do, when I tell you to do it, or I'll leave you behind. There's no point in us both getting caught up in this stars-forsaken place.'

Elise glanced down at Ezra's curled form. A line of drool reached from the corner of his mouth to the bare mattress.

'Thank you for coming to help me, but I can't leave him behind.' She gestured at Ezra. 'If he can't come with us then I'll have to stay.'

The woman rolled her eyes. 'Self-sacrificing to the end.'

'It's not just for him that I'm doing this,' Elise said,

trying to keep the annoyance from her voice. 'I'm doing it for me as well. If I leave him here, I think I'll leave a piece of myself in this place. I'll never be free of it. I made a promise to someone to look after him and if I leave him here, he'll die. There's no question about that. Why should I get to leave because I've got friends who know a feisty super-nurse? Why should he stay in here because he's got no friends out there?'

The woman smiled at Elise and leant in close. 'I'll let you in on something—I'm not really a nurse. But I am pretty super; can't deny that.'

Elise glanced over at Ezra again, trying not to get caught up in the woman's self-assured tone. 'So, can I bring him with us?'

The woman shrugged. 'We can try to get him out. But the rules still apply. No discussions from now on. I'm ditching you both if you jeopardise my safety. I'm not spending the rest of my days in here. Agreed?'

'Agreed.'

'Now, everyone's going to be wondering what I've been doing in here for so long, so you better get back to work. I'm going to take a look at your friend. Remember, no discussions or reacting to what I'm doing. It's necessary, okay?'

Elise nodded and headed over to another of the drug-addled patients' beds. She began sweeping underneath it, trying to ignore the nurse leaning over Ezra. She'd angled herself so that anyone who peered through the reinforced glass windows in the door wouldn't be able to see what she was doing. Pulling a small syringe out of the pocket of her trousers, the woman rolled Ezra onto his front with surprising ease. In the next moment, she had injected him in the base of his spine and pushed him onto his side again.

Elise tried not to react. *She was sent by my friends. She was sent by my friends.*

She didn't doubt the stranger's words. She would leave them both behind if she felt cornered.

'I need to ask another nurse to verify the situation, preferably one of the less diligent ones. What I've done is only temporary, but it's necessary. He'll come around later. We need a body to get us out of here. I was going to use the one next door, but we've had to change our plans now, haven't we?'

Elise didn't react. She hadn't even known it was possible to make a living person appear to have died.

'What shall I call you?' she asked, slightly in awe.

The nurse pointed at her name badge. 'You can call me Nurse Roseanna for the moment. Back to work now. You've got no business in this, remember.'

Elise went over to the third bed and began sweeping under it. She didn't even look up a few minutes later when Nurse Roseanna returned with a tall, bustling nurse.

'This is the one, Emily,' Nurse Roseanna said, pointing at Ezra's bed.

Nurse Emily didn't even spare Elise a glance. She made her way over to Ezra's side and briefly held her fingertips to his neck and wrist. 'No pulse. But no need to bring the recovery unit either. I've been waiting for this to happen since he got in here. Skin and bone. Hopefully, someone will finish their shift soon and volunteer to take him away. We need the beds at the moment; more coming in than leaving.'

Nurse Roseanna unfolded a small screen that hung from a thick, silver chain pinned to her shirt below the collar. 'I'm getting off in ten minutes. I can take him out, if you want?'

'Do you know where you're going?' Nurse Emily asked, briefly checking on the other two residents. 'Both still with us,' she said under her breath, a note of disappointment clear in her voice.

'Out the front, past security, turn right, follow the cliff wall for about five minutes, third winch takes him to the top of the cliff where the crematorium staff take over?'

'Yes, that's right,' Nurse Emily said, straightening up. She gave Nurse Roseanna an appraising look. 'Are you going to manage pushing him all that way? I hope you don't mind me saying, but your enhancements don't lean towards the physical side of the spectrum.' She gave an awkward laugh. 'That isn't a judgement in any way; just an observation.'

Nurse Roseanna crossed her arms. 'It's true my parents decided to provide me with gifts of a more cerebral tilt. To my own children I will grant a mixture but, like the stars, we must live with what we are given.'

'Oh, yes, of course. I fully agree,' Nurse Emily responded. 'We cannot judge each other's gifts. We should keep our eyes on our own. Petty division is an attribute of the Sapiens and one to be avoided. I was just wondering if you may need some help pushing the trolley.'

Nurse Roseanna drew herself up to her full height, which was still a couple of inches shorter than Elise.

'I might need some assistance,' she said in an offhand manner. 'Especially as he is ah...leaking...some sort of fluid. Can I take this cleaner with me?'

'What, her?' Nurse Emily pointed at Elise. 'I don't know how much use she'll be, but I don't see why not. Just to the front, mind; she can't go beyond security. I'm going back to the nurse's station to update our records.'

Nurse Roseanna nodded. 'I'll just go and collect my

things and then we'll be off.' She turned to Elise. 'You, wait here and keep cleaning. Don't go skiving off because you think you've finished your shift.'

Elise nodded and took out a spray and cloth. The two nurses left and she sprayed the glass windows and rubbed them.

Five minutes later, Nurse Roseanna returned, wheeling a trolley bed and carrying a brown satchel over her shoulder. She only spoke when the doors closed behind her. 'Spray the windows again and leave it there for a moment. We have exactly two minutes to make you look less like... well, less like an inmate that's given up on life. You brush your hair and pin it back. I'll try to do something with your face.'

Exactly one hundred and twenty seconds later, Elise rubbed the spray from the glass windows. She couldn't see herself but she knew that Nurse Roseanna had applied some make-up. Elise had brushed and pinned back her hair.

'Come and help me lift him onto the trolley,' Nurse Roseanna said, giving Elise an appraising look. 'Continue as you are until halfway through the journey. I'm going to give you a signal. You will then take this bag with you to the door to your right. Inside that room you will have ninety seconds to change into the clothes and security tag.' She tapped the bag. 'I expect your persona to change with your outfit. If you come out looking like a Sapien dressed as a nurse, I will leave you. If you act in a satisfactory manner, I will stay. We then have to get past security. If necessary, we may have to be very persuasive—'

Elise opened her mouth to interject but was cut off.

'Actually, don't flirt. I imagine you're terrible at it.' She gave a little shudder. 'Go for the young, low-end Medius who's just so proud to be asked to do anything. Even if it's pushing a dead body through a containment centre.' Nurse Roseanna widened her eyes. *'Wait till tonight when I get to tell mother all about this!'* She narrowed them again. 'You shouldn't struggle with that.'

Elise fixed on her passive mask. As soon as she got out of here, she would take Ezra as far away from Nurse Roseanna as physically possible.

A few minutes later, they trundled through the corridors together, Nurse Roseanna pushing the trolley, with Elise walking backwards and pulling it from the other end. Ezra lay under a sheet, completely covered. The security guards barely gave them a moment's notice, especially after catching the look of fixed resignation that Nurse Roseanna was wearing. Elise glanced up at her occasionally and watched the narrative playing out across the woman's features. She could almost hear her thoughts: *Why do I have to take this stupid corpse out at the end of my shift? And that Nurse Cassandra was clearly trying to avoid the job by pretending to stay five minutes longer...*

They reached a dark corner of the corridor lacking the motion-sensitive, overhead lights that usually snapped on in recognition of their approach.

Nurse Roseanna bent over to inspect her shoelace. It had come undone. 'That's all I need.' She sighed loudly. 'I think you should go now. You're just getting in the way, no strength to you. Go and find another nurse to help me while I fix this.'

Elise nodded and took the bag with her. In two minutes' time, she returned as Nurse Eleanor, wide-eyed, taller than before and disdainful of all Sapiens.

The two nurses continued round the endless corridors, a wheel on the gurney squeaking in protest. Elise developed a tick in her right eye that matched the rhythm of the wheel.

She lowered her head and hoped that Nurse Roseanna hadn't noticed it.

With her back to the route, Elise only realised that they were closer to the entranceway when the chatter around them increased. A short queue of staff members waited to exit the containment centre. They were neatly filed in front of two large, metal gates where six guards were checking everyone's ID. The air was jovial; the guards laughed and joked with the staff members they recognised.

Elise straightened and began chatting to Nurse Roseanna as they waited their turn, her tone light and her conversation even more so. The two nurses swapped places and talked about what they were doing that evening, leaning against either end of the bed. Elise was so nervous she was grateful to have the trolley to rest her hands on; without that, she wouldn't have known what to do with them.

When it was their turn, Nurse Roseanna handed over her pass.

'You're newish, aren't you?' the guard said conversationally as he scanned her pass.

'First week, but not my first time,' Nurse Roseanna answered, a slight twinkle in her tone.

Elise didn't know what Nurse Roseanna was twinkling about, but she knew she couldn't act in the same way without laughing at herself. Surely no one would think that was attractive?

The guard grinned at Nurse Roseanna. 'Might see you tomorrow then?'

'You might,' Nurse Roseanna said before continuing to push the trolley through.

'Wait up,' the guard said, the teasing quality leaving his tone. 'Who've you got with you?'

'Ah,' Nurse Roseanna said, pulling the sheet off Ezra. The guard took a step back. 'That would be the recently departed cleaner number 4837. Need to winch him up to the crematorium before I head home for the evening.'

The guard knew the routine. He gingerly felt for a pulse in the corpse's neck. He then held his hand away from him as if he wanted to detach himself from it. Elise guessed that he couldn't wait to wash his hands. He waved Nurse Roseanna through.

Now it was Elise's turn.

TWENTY-SEVEN

Twenty-Two pulled out the correct cushions for the first visitor, lined up their drink and started preparing for a rapid turnaround between meetings. She worked quickly and with minimal fuss; she took pride in enabling Faye's schedule to run as smoothly as possible.

She knew that the first guest, Sylvia, liked to spend as much time as possible in Faye's company and would stray into the time for the allotted second visit. She also knew that Sylvia was rather fearful of Twenty-Two, so she decided that she would join Faye once the appointment ran over by ten minutes and signal that the next visitor was leaving. Her presence alone would unnerve Sylvia to the extent that the mood of quiet unburdening would be broken and Faye would be able to continue to her next appointment.

After several weeks of working for Faye, Twenty-Two had met most of the key residents of Uracil. She knew their tastes, fears and worries. She knew whether they spoke with honesty, or out of fear or reverence. She had memorised all of these things, but she had chosen not to disclose this information to anyone; she only related the spoken words to Faye. She kept her impressions to herself.

Cedric's role had become obsolete; he could not compete with her near-perfect memory. He had silently withdrawn and begun assisting Faye with the more practical matters in her personal life. Faye had not objected to this change in role, despite her earlier protests. Cedric had not spoken to Twenty-Two since. She could feel his gaze burn into the back of her head when he came to collect Faye and escort her to her living quarters in the evening. Twenty-Two did not care; after only a month, she knew she had made the right decision asking to work here.

Mid-morning, Fiona, the Head of Infiltration, came to speak to Faye. Twenty-Two found her pacing on the other side of the platform. She was a tall woman who wore flat, knee-high boots that highlighted the strength in her calves. Her long, auburn hair was pulled over one of her shoulders in a braid. Twenty-Two dutifully led Fiona through to the platform and, once she was seated, handed her a cup of chamomile tea.

Twenty-Two had begun to suspect that Fiona had a problem with her nerves. Despite being the Head of Infiltration for over ten years, Fiona hadn't been on a single mission for five of them. It seemed that she always had a reason for remaining in Uracil. It appeared to Twenty-Two that Fiona was beginning to slip from the position of high esteem in which she had previously been held.

Once she had tentatively sipped her tea, Fiona began. 'Thank you for seeing me. I must be frank—' Fiona glanced around at Twenty-Two. 'Will she remain?'

'She doesn't have to if it is a private matter,' Faye said, nodding at Twenty-Two to retreat to her seat at the edge of the platform.

Twenty-Two walked away quickly and tried to look relaxed once she was seated; she found that the visitors would speak more freely if she was not staring directly at them. It reduced her ability to lip read, but increased the honesty of the spoken words.

Twenty-Two couldn't see what Faye was saying but made a note that Fiona was concerned about someone named Maya. She had not reported in for several weeks, but Fiona did not think that she had been captured. Twenty-Two could tell that Fiona's concern was genuine. Fiona then listened to Faye for a minute, the surprise clearly registering on her face. Fiona thanked Faye for the explanation and left without turning around.

Twenty-Two puzzled over this. She had never met Maya but had heard her name mentioned in passing a few times. She also worked in the Infiltration Department and was held in high regard. She had been sent on a mission several months ago but had not returned. Twenty-Two thought that Thiago had mentioned her name once to Faye, but knowing she was not supposed to observe those meetings, she had not followed the rest of their conversation. It was to satisfy Twenty-Two's desire for order that she wanted to place and categorise each resident of Uracil. Without having met Maya, there was an anomaly that niggled her.

That evening, she went to visit Kit. Out of everyone she had met since leaving Cytosine, she trusted his judgement the most. In the last few weeks, she had taken to eating her evening meal with him on the communal benches. Luca and Georgina would often join them. There was usually also a selection of the people who attended Kit's night classes in sign language. Word had spread about Kit's classes and attendance was high. It was true that some people only came so they could meet a Neanderthal, but for the majority, their interest was genuine.

Before they left Kit's tree house for the communal benches, Twenty-Two made a decision. Her desire for an ordered understanding of Uracil overrode her policy of never discussing her work. Even on this occasion, she did not say what it was in relation to, and only asked Kit if he had met Maya before.

'Yes, a few times. She was Elise's trainer,' he responded, rolling up the sleeve of his shirt. Unlike Twenty-Two, who still wore tunics every day, he had abandoned the clothing he wore in his pod and instead dressed like a Sapien or Medius in one of the other bases.

He had once told Twenty-Two that he was still getting used to this clothing and thought it unlikely that he would start dressing as flamboyantly as the Uracil residents, no matter how many years he remained there. The clothing made him look much older and Twenty-Two often had to remind herself that he had only recently turned fifteen and, therefore, was only a few months older than her. His air of quiet self-assurance gave the impression that he was in his mid-twenties. It was an impression that she believed he wanted to foster; she had noticed that he also avoided confirming his age if he could.

'Was she a good person?' Twenty-Two asked.

Kit sighed. 'I don't know. I only spoke to her a few times when I came to meet Elise after her training. I try not to judge a person's entire character on only three polite conversations.'

'Yes, I suppose so,' Twenty-Two responded. 'What do you think has happened to Elise?'

Kit's face darkened. 'I think she's been captured and is being held somewhere, probably Cytosine.'

'Do you think Uracil wants her to come back?'

Kit stared at Twenty-Two. 'I think they are divided on it. On the one hand, it is an embarrassment to them, particularly Maya, that she was captured. On the other hand, the longer she remains in the hands of the Potiors, the more likely it becomes that she will expose Uracil. Why? What do you know?'

'Shall we go down to dinner?' Twenty-Two signed, standing up.

She and Kit always sat on the floor together when they were among their closest friends. Amongst outsiders, they tried to blend in by using the elevated furniture so clearly favoured by everyone else.

Kit grabbed Twenty-Two's arm as she turned to the door. 'What do you know? Have you heard something in the meetings?'

Twenty-Two looked down at Kit's hand and he let go of her. 'I cannot talk about it.'

'If you know something about Elise then you should tell me,' Kit signed, his frustration clear to Twenty-Two, despite his fixed expression.

'I don't know anything about Elise and that's all I'm going to say.'

They walked down to dinner in silence.

The following day, Twenty-Two paid particular attention to the visit from Thiago. He had become more relaxed around her and didn't track her presence as he used to. She was now a silent figure who tidied up in the background and brought him his favourite blends of coffee.

As usual, he had left it until the end of the day to

request an audience with Faye. Carefully carrying the glasses from the last meeting, Twenty-Two silently turned to watch their bent heads as they sat on the bench carved into the tree. When she passed them, in the depths of their private conversation, she heard Elise's name being mentioned. She had to force herself to keeping walking away and not to turn around. She carried the glasses steadily to the edge of the platform, her curiosity burning away at her.

She took a chance and turned around, still holding the tray of glasses close to her chest. From this distance she could only read some of the words forming on Faye's lips but she could not see Thiago's mouth at all. She allowed herself a minute watching them, knowing fully that either one of them could glance up at her at any second. They would instantly know that she was trying to read their conversation; why else would she be staring intently at them? Her nerve broke after a minute, but she had learnt all that she needed.

She thanked the stars that it was the last meeting of the day and that she wouldn't have to see Faye again that evening. After washing up the glasses under Cedric's reproachful gaze, Twenty-Two made her way to Kit's tree house, her heart fluttering all the way.

When she knocked on the door, the voices inside stopped abruptly. Twenty-Two hoped whomever was with Kit would leave soon. She wanted to speak to him alone. Of all the times for him to have visitors, it had to be now.

Kit pulled open the door and scrunched his eyes at her. 'Come inside. There is someone I want you to meet.'

'I need to speak with you,' Twenty-Two signed.

Kit pulled Twenty-Two inside. 'We can speak later; first, I want you to meet someone.'

A very tall man made his way over to Twenty-Two. It was the man who had killed Fintorian. She immediately cooled towards him, unable to reconcile herself to the necessity of the act, despite what Kit had told her.

She looked around at the others in the room, scrunching her eyes at Georgina and nodding at Luca. There were limbs everywhere, the group of friends sprawled across Kit's small tree house. Between them all, there was only standing room left.

'Twenty-Two, it is a pleasure to meet you again. Hopefully in what will shortly be more pleasant circumstances,' Samuel signed.

Twenty-Two watched him appraisingly. 'Have you had some good news about Elise?'

Samuel's eyes widened for a moment before he quickly recovered. 'Well, actually, yes, I have. A contact of mine says she has located Elise in the containment centre in Cytosine and is close to getting her out.'

'She could be back with us in only a few weeks,' Kit signed.

'Even a few weeks is too long,' Georgina said, hugging her knees closer to her.

'Stars knows what's happened to her in there...' Luca began before glancing at Samuel and trailing off.

Twenty-Two nodded as she processed this information. She looked around at the small group of friends, who were by far the kindest people she had met since leaving Cytosine. Even Samuel radiated warmth.

Kit quickly changed the subject and she half listened to them talk amongst themselves about whom Samuel had seen in Thymine. Twenty-Two had spent months learning as much as she could about the way Uracil operated, but today she had learnt of something quite separate.

The friends slowly stopped talking and stared at her—a quiet, young woman standing in the corner of the room who refused to join them.

'Is there something you wanted to tell me?' Kit signed, turning to Twenty-Two.

'Yes, there is,' Twenty-Two responded, Kit's question bringing her back to the room. 'There is an infiltration operative who has been instructed to free Elise. Their orders are to check whether she has spoken about Uracil. After they have gathered this information and travelled outside of Cytosine, they have one further set of instructions.'

Twenty-Two looked directly at Kit while she signed the next part, so he would understand the truth in her words. 'They have been told to dispose of her.'

No one spoke for a full minute, and then all of the stars broke loose from the sky.

TWENTY-EIGHT

T he guard peered at Elise's pass before looking up at her. 'If the last one was new, then you're even fresher, aren't you? First day, indeed!'

Elise stared at the guard while she channelled Harriet back at Thymine's Museum of Evolution, a Medius who always had a chip on her shoulder for being mistaken for a Sapien.

Elise pulled her shoulders back and tried to look down at the guard even though he was over a foot taller than her. 'I can assure you that I have all the necessary qualifications. Came ninth in the year for the nursing examinations, was head-hunted by the midwifery department but decided to throw caution to the wind and specialise in palliative care.'

The guard didn't try to hide his annoyance at her snooty tone. 'You're through.'

He held out his hand for the next staff member's ID. Elise knew she would receive no warm welcome from him tomorrow if she were to return.

She took the other end of the trolley and pulled it through the floor-to-ceiling, metal gates and onto the springy, recycled-rubber path that hugged the edge of the cliff face outside Cytosine. The change in scenery was immediate. She did not allow herself to relax as she carried on rolling the trolley behind her, imagining that at any moment someone would shout out for her to stop. She could almost hear the sound of several sets of heavy boots rushing to catch up with her.

She glanced up at Nurse Roseanna, who glared at her. Elise's cover was slipping. She fixed her expression into one of mild boredom combined with annoyance as she carried on trundling the trolley along the pathway to the winch that led to the crematorium.

Similar to Thymine, the pathway at the outskirts of the settlement was the only evidence of human interference. It snaked its way next to the cliff face, grass and pebbles either side, the only sign that they weren't walking through the untouched landscape of a river that had carved its way between two cliff faces.

Elise tried not to react to the light breeze on her face. It was a crisp, early-winter day, but she wouldn't allow herself to pay too much attention to the clouds rolling above her head. She was outside for the first time in nearly five months but she had to act as if she last stepped outside that morning.

She could not remember travelling into Cytosine, but of all the bases, it was the one she had always wanted to visit. Back in Thymine, she had been told that the whole of Cytosine was burrowed into excavated tunnels in the sheer cliff face. Glancing around briefly as she tried to guide the trolley, she could see this was only partially correct.

Up above her, stretching so high that she couldn't see the top, was a vast cliff face that had several walkways zigzagging across its surface. These walkways were bolted into the rock and meandered horizontally along the cliff, leading to various cave mouths stretching all the way up the side. In complete diametric contrast were the slender winches and zip lines used to transport goods that raced vertically up the cliff's side.

The entranceway to the containment centre was dug into the base of the cliff and it confirmed her suspicions about why she hadn't seen any natural light for the past five months. Beyond the entranceway, in the distance, lay the low-level roofs of a few official buildings and the glass roof of Cytosine's Museum of Evolution. All of the low-slung, residential housing followed the curved path of the river that had dug out the channel between the cliff faces thousands of years ago.

Unlike the wild-flower-covered roofs of Thymine, the houses here were made of blocks of mud and hay that were shaped to be perfectly circular. They had small, pointed roofs that looked like hats pulled down low over the ears of the buildings. The mud walls were covered in small pieces of flint that allowed the one-storey buildings to merge visually into the pebbled shoreline of the riverbank.

There were a few low-slung buildings at the top of the cliff face, but these were hidden from view by their sloped grass roofs, partially dug into the ground. The slim, horizontal windows were pointed towards the edge of the cliff, away from any traveller's eyes. From only a few miles away, there was no visible trace of Cytosine. Just as Thymine was constructed to lessen its impact on the valley bowl, Cytosine burrowed into and hugged the edges of the canyon.

Two miles from the settlement was the gentle sea to the south of Zone 3. Gulls sailed by above Elise's head, riding the air currents. She swore she could smell the salt from where she was. This access to the sea was essential for all the bases as it carried the sailboats transporting the bi-annual delivery of manufactured goods. In return, it collected the medicines and other scientific-based commodities that Cytosine produced.

While taking in her surroundings, Elise carried on chatting to Nurse Roseanna as they wheeled the trolley farther away from the settlement. The disposal of bodies, as with the containment of prisoners, was naturally kept as far away from Cytosine's residential area as possible. They had passed two of the winches to the right of the containment centre and had not seen anyone for the last ten minutes of their journey. Elise could feel herself finally beginning to relax.

Nurse Roseanna stopped at the edge of the path and glanced around her as if she had lost count of the number of winches; Elise matched her expression of confusion. A look of recognition came over Nurse Roseanna's features and she pushed the trolley towards the side of the cliff and straight into some bushes. Elise followed, not sure how they were going to avoid sending Ezra up to the top of the cliffs when they came to the third winch. Glancing along the cliff face, she couldn't see it.

Nurse Roseanna took a syringe out of her pocket. Before Elise could say anything, she slammed it directly into Ezra's heart and pushed the plunger down.

Within a moment, Ezra took a gasp of air and sat up. He stared at the two women, his confusion clear.

His gaze then locked onto Elise. 'Oh, it's you.'

'I thought you were friends,' Nurse Roseanna said to Elise.

'We were, but perhaps not at this exact moment,' Elise responded.

Their rescuer delved around in her brown bag and

threw some clothes at them. Her mood had suddenly changed. Elise wondered if it was to do with her exaggerating her friendship with Ezra.

'We don't have time for this ridiculous deviation. You have ninety seconds to change or I'm leaving you both.'

Ezra opened his mouth to protest but was cut off by Nurse Roseanna's glare. 'We got you out. You'll either be caught or die if you don't come with us for the first part of the journey. I'll take you wherever you want to go, but we need to leave the vicinity of Cytosine now. You can't come back either.'

Ezra closed his mouth and nodded.

No one said another word. The three of them got dressed in less than ninety seconds and set off at a slow jogging pace towards the woodland to the north of Cytosine.

Elise had always prided herself on her fitness, but it was soon clear to her how much of her stamina and conditioning she had lost while in the containment centre. After half an hour of jogging, she began to feel light headed and had to ask Roseanna if they could slow down for a while. With a brief nod, she reduced her pace to a very brisk walk. Every few minutes, she would glare at them both to check they were still following.

'Who is she?' Ezra whispered to Elise when Roseanna was far ahead enough to be out of earshot.

'She was sent by my friends to help me escape,' Elise said, after Roseanna had turned around to check on them again. 'Look, you were right. I haven't been entirely honest with you about who I am. But I couldn't be while I was in there.'

With that, Elise began to explain in small snippets who she was and what her last memories were. She stressed that she had no idea how she had gotten to Cytosine, explaining that she had had to hide who she really was in the containment centre.

By the time she finished, it was starting to grow dark and she could barely see Ezra's features.

'So, you were a Companion in Thymine?' Ezra asked.

She was about to answer when Roseanna stopped abruptly. She waited for them both to catch up. 'We have to find somewhere to sleep for the night.'

Without any further explanation, she led them into the edge of the woodland. Elise glanced around and then followed.

Once they had settled down for the evening, Elise offered to help build the fire, explaining to Ezra it was something that she had learnt back in Thymine's Museum of Evolution. For the evening's meal, they shared some rabbit meat that Roseanna left them to hunt for and a vegetable broth. Ezra did not speak to Elise again until he explained that he was tired and was going to settle down for the night.

Elise's initial elation at being free had started to dissipate. She suddenly felt very weary.

Settling down by the fire, she stared at Roseanna. 'What's your real name?'

The woman looked up at her. 'It changes all the time; just call me Roseanna. Look, I'm sorry about snapping at you back there, but I just wanted to get us clear of Cytosine. I had to get you both moving.'

Elise glanced over at Ezra, gently snoring, curled up under the trunk of a nearby oak tree.

'I understand,' she said. 'But can you start telling me what's going on now? Where are Kit and Samuel? When will I get to see them? Why have I lost three months of memories and what happened in that time?'

Panic set in as she spoke, the enormity of her situation hitting her. She wasn't safe yet. She'd lost half a year of her life in a containment centre and, at the moment, only the stars knew what had happened to her beforehand. She certainly didn't.

Do I want to know? The thought popped into her head uninvited. She had heard of people suffering from amnesia when what had happened to them was too painful to recall. Maybe this was why she couldn't remember anything.

Roseanna smiled. 'If I tell you what happened, you might not believe me. But I'll give it a try. How many bases are there?'

'Four,' Elise said, without having to think about it. 'They were named after the four bases found in DNA: Cytosine, Thymine, Guanine and Adenine.'

She had been taught this since her earliest years in school, her history lessons split into the Pre-Pandemic and Post-Pandemic years. One of the core subjects of the Post-Pandemic years chartered the development of the four bases and the steps the Potiors took to bring order back following a turbulent period of history.

'Say it again,' Roseanna said, peering closely at Elise's face.

'There are four bases,' Elise said slightly louder.

Why was she being asked to repeat such basic information?

Roseanna stared at her. 'What if I told you there were five?'

'Then you'd have to explain yourself because I only know of four,' Elise responded.

'What is your last memory before finding yourself in Cytosine?' Roseanna asked, still watching Elise carefully.

'I'd left my parents house and was heading back to

Thymine. I was going back to help Kit. I knew I had to leave Thymine but didn't know where I was going to take him.'

Elise inadvertently yawned and stretched her arms out.

'I think you should get some sleep.' Roseanna stood up. 'I'll watch over you.'

TWENTY-NINE

Elise woke with a start. There'd been a noise. She just wasn't sure if it had been in her dream or if she had actually heard it.

Before she could remember where she was, a body landed on top of her chest, making her cry out. Pushing the weight off her, she scrambled to her feet and tried to get her bearings. Reaching down to the ground, she felt out a figure that was slumped by her feet. Guessing it was Ezra, she pulled at his arm to try and make him stand.

'Get up!' Elise whispered, trying to work out what had happened.

It was nearly pitch black and the only light came from the nearly extinguished fire—the moonlight couldn't fight its way through the heavy tree canopy.

Ezra struggled to his feet.

He gulped at the air. 'They were going to hurt you.'

'Where are they now?' Elise whispered, turning and peering into the darkness.

There were so many shapes and outlines that she

couldn't tell what she should be focusing on. A distant owl hooted, making her jump.

A moment later, they were plunged into darkness. Someone had kicked dirt over the only source of light.

Elise tensed and switched into her favourite blocking position, one her father had taught her.

She turned to face the sound of footsteps racing towards her. Whoever it was, they weren't trying to cover their location anymore. She braced and then kicked out. She made contact but, to her dismay, it wasn't hard enough. She had only glanced the side of their torso. They moved away.

There was complete silence.

A blood-curdling scream came from Ezra, only a few feet away from her.

Elise flipped around and stumbled blindly towards him.

'Stay right there, Elise,' Roseanna said.

Elise groaned. How foolish they'd been to blindly follow a stranger into deserted woodland.

'I know you can't see anything, but I'm guessing you know what this means,' the woman said, her voice calm.

There was a gurgling sound from Ezra; his airway was being restricted.

'What do you want?' Elise shouted.

'I want you to kneel down on the ground and keep talking so I know where you are while I deal with him.'

'I'm kneeling down; just don't hurt him. It was me you came for.'

'I've read your file, Elise. Your weakness always has been your self-sacrificing nature.'

There was another strangled, gurgling noise from Ezra.

'*Don't hurt him!*'

'Don't worry. I'm not an animal. I'm just tying him up. '

Elise's mind whirled as she decided what to do. When

she heard Roseanna approach, she tried to still her breathing.

'Keep talking, Elise, or I'll go back to him.'

When Roseanna was only two steps away, Elise pounced. She grabbed for a leg and pulled it with all her force. The yelp let her know that it was probably Ezra's leg that she had gotten hold of. She hadn't realised that Roseanna had brought him with her. He fell heavily, but at least he was now on the ground.

Elise rose, straining to listen for the sound of footsteps. A hush descended over the forest.

The cracking of a twig had her twirl around, but too late. She had never trained with her father in the dark.

Roseanna leapt onto Elise's back. The force pushed her to the forest floor.

Trying to haul herself back to her feet, Elise felt a rope being laced around her neck. On her front, she tried to turn around so she could fight back, but the weight was too much. Her arms were pinned by Roseanna's legs. She had never felt so helpless.

She tried to cry out but there was no noise, just a thick gurgling. She strained to hear whether Ezra had gotten to his feet but there was no movement from him either.

Bright specks burst across her vision; at any moment, it would be over. She weakened and stopped struggling, concentrating instead on the stars flashing, guiding her to the end.

When she woke, her tongue felt as if it had grown out of all proportion. There was tightness around her neck and every breath drew the pain up through to her head and back down again.

She opened one eye and saw that she was level with the forest floor. She opened the other.

Panicked, she pushed herself unsteadily to her knees. It was daytime; she could see clearly now. She tried to stand. Her vision blurred for a second and she stretched out to find something to steady herself. Her hand felt the smooth bark of a silver birch tree and she held onto it for a moment.

Once the dizziness had faded, she glanced around. Behind her, Ezra lay slumped on the ground. Stumbling over to him, she crouched by his side. She held her ear to his mouth—he was still breathing.

Gently shaking him, she whispered, 'Wake up. We have to go. It's not safe.'

There was no response. She shook him more firmly, panic rising. Where was Roseanna?

Ezra let out a groan and his eyes blinked open. He gave a small start when he came face to face with Elise.

'We have to go,' Elise said, once she knew that she had his attention. Her voice was raspier than usual and it hurt to speak.

'What happened to your neck?' Ezra asked.

They tensed. Footsteps approached.

Elise began to tug Ezra to his feet but he was frozen with fear. Panic swept through her and bile ran up her throat into her mouth. She stood up and strained to lift Ezra, a dead weight in her arms. A sob escaped her; the steps were getting closer.

She wasn't going to be able to lift him. Lowering him to the ground, she turned around to face whomever was approaching.

Peering through the trees, at first Elise thought a child

was walking towards them. As they got closer, she realised it was a woman.

Elise took a step back and tensed. Roseanna had been small, but Elise had stood no chance against her.

The woman smiled broadly at Elise and her fear was inexplicably allayed.

'Who are you?' Elise called out.

'I'm Maya. I'm the one who saved both of your lives.' The woman was only a few feet away now. 'Samuel sent me. I met with him a couple of months ago; I've been trying to locate you since then.'

'Just stay there. I've already nearly been killed by one person who was supposedly sent to rescue me.' Elise bent down to Ezra and his eyes locked onto hers. 'Please get up,' she whispered to him. 'I need your help.'

He nodded at her and stumbled to his feet. Once he was standing, he pulled his jumper down past his waist and turned to face the woman.

'Samuel told me he's sorry for throwing a rock at the chameleon display,' she said.

Elise froze and her heart beat rapidly in her chest.

'He says it was a crass way of getting you to open up to him and he wishes that he'd just waited and earned your trust,' the woman continued.

Elise didn't move. 'Samuel said that? You know Samuel?'

'We knew you wouldn't remember me, so I asked him to tell me something only the two of you would know about. He told me he threw a rock at the glass chameleon display in Thymine, which forced you to reveal your quick reactions to him. Clever but, in that moment, not so very kind, perhaps?'

Without her realising it, thick tears began to fall down Elise's face.

'I'm sorry that it's taken so long. But please know that you have been missed.'

There was something familiar about the woman's tone.

'Can you please do something for me?' Elise asked.

The woman took a step forward and then stopped, her gaze searching Elise's features. 'Of course. What is it?'

'Would you please tell me what the stars has happened?'

Beside her, Ezra nodded his head in vigorous agreement.

Elise sat quietly and listened to Maya recount the story of what had followed after she left Thymine. It was strange to hear her own tale; she felt distanced from the woman who had travelled to Uracil with optimism and hope.

It was just a brief outline, as Maya would only recount what she knew to be true. Elise only interjected to ask where her parents were and if they were safe. She was satisfied when she learned that Samuel had visited them and touched that he would put himself in danger to do so. He was clearly a better friend than she remembered.

Still feeling weak, Elise settled back on Maya's sleeping blankets while she learnt about Uracil. She had offered to work for the Infiltration Department—that was what had led to her capture. She was surprised to learn that Maya had been her trainer and tried not to regret the weeks of valuable tuition that she had lost.

Elise searched the woman's face; there was certainly

something familiar about it, but she couldn't recall a single memory of meeting her before.

'I'll tell you one thing,' Maya said. 'You would've had more of a chance against Septa if you were able to remember what I taught you.

Maya had dressed her wounds and was now making them a thick stew over a small, crackling fire.

'So, that's Roseanna's real name?' Elise asked.

'Yes. She's one of Uracil's best fighters. When I found her on top of you, I only had minutes to deal with her.'

Maya shrugged.

'You killed her?' Elise asked.

Maya glanced up from stirring the stew. 'No, no, I knocked her out. While she was unconscious, I took away her memories of the last couple of weeks. Then I moved her a few miles south of us. That's where I was coming back from. She'll wake up disorientated but, not remembering the last two weeks, she'll try to locate you in Cytosine again.'

'You took away her memories?' Elise asked. 'Like what happened to me?'

'Yes. We gave you a bracelet with a capsule in it. You asked me if it was a suicide pill when I first told you to wear it.'

Maya chuckled.

Elise automatically circled her wrist. The bracelet had been removed in her first days in the containment centre, but the action felt familiar. She had no idea where it was now.

'The blockers are formulated to disrupt your recall of memories for a pre-selected period of time. It isn't exact, but can be narrowed down to within a couple of weeks. I set it to erase all your memories of Uracil so you couldn't betray us.'

Elise opened her mouth to protest.

'It had to be done. Uracil is too precious. We don't tell the new recruits about what the blocker does exactly, as we fear they won't take it. But soon you'll understand that thousands of lives are worth more than one person's memories.'

Elise had begun to understand that already.

'Anyway, you only lost three months,' Maya said, smiling. 'If I take my current blocker, I'll lose sixteen years.'

'So, you gave Septa a two-week blocker?' Elise asked.

She was trying to limit her questions as it hurt to speak, but there was still so much that she didn't understand.

'Yes, I always carry a few on me. Useful items.'

'If she was trying to kill me...' Elise said, not sure how to ask the question.

'Will she try again? Should I have disposed of her instead?'

Elise nodded without meeting her gaze. She didn't want to spend the rest of her life looking over her shoulder.

'Septa is part of the Infiltration Unit, just like you and me. Don't get me wrong; I never really liked the woman. She's always thought that, because she's younger than me, she's better. But Septa is still a colleague and she was just following her orders. Removing her recent memories, it gives us time to escape.'

'Who gave her the order?' Elise asked.

Maya stared at Elise. 'Septa takes her orders from the Head of Infiltration, who takes her orders from the Tri-Council. No one else has that sort of power.'

'But, why?'

'I don't know.' Maya scooped out some of the broth and bent to taste it. 'I didn't even know there was an order out on you. When I realised that you were no longer in the containment centre, I started tracking you. It was thanks to your friend over there that I found you. If it wasn't for him screaming at such a high pitch, I wouldn't have been able to pinpoint your precise location.'

Elise glanced over at Ezra. He was sitting at the base of a tree away from the fire. Maya had steadfastly refused to discuss anything to do with Elise's lost months in front of him. Elise was to tell no one about Uracil.

'What are we going to do about Ezra?' Elise asked.

'Well, I think you're going to need some company while we decide how long you can live outside the bases for.'

'You don't want me to go back to Uracil?'

Maya laughed. 'If you went back to Uracil, you'd be arrested on the spot.'

Elise thought for a few moments, rubbing her forehead. She felt as if years had passed. 'Well, I'm not hiding from them and Septa. I want to know why they sent someone after me. Something's very wrong and I don't want to hide away like a dirty secret. People need to know what's happening. If an act is not witnessed, it may as well never have occurred.'

Maya looked up. 'That's Raul's saying. From the Tri-Council. You must have a couple of leaked memories coming through.'

Elise pulled her hair away from her face; she'd known that phrase had come from somewhere. And the more time she spent with Maya, the more relaxed she felt in the woman's company. She didn't think she was another Roseanna.

'If you want to swap one prison for another then that's your choice,' Maya said, shrugging.

Elise could tell that Maya lost little sleep over other people's decisions.

'If Uracil's as precious as you're making it out to be, don't you think its people have a right to know that someone's giving out orders to kill one of its residents?' Elise asked.

Maya sighed. 'Yes, I suppose so. But be prepared to lose this fight. You're a newcomer. No one's going to listen to you.'

Elise pushed aside her doubts; she wasn't going to live in the shadows. She had been captured—and that could only be her fault—but it surely didn't justify sending an order to assassinate her. Even the Tri-Council must have known that it didn't, as the order had been kept secret. Elise fixated on the logic of the last point and mulled it over for a moment.

'Please let me take Ezra with me. He's got nowhere else to go,' Elise said, glancing over at him.

'No,' Maya said. 'I cannot just bring back random strays with me. Uracil's closed to new residents.'

'If he can't come, I won't go back with you.'

'Fine by me.'

'He has nowhere else to go,' Elise said more firmly.

'I have to act in Uracil's best interests.'

'Then why did you let me live? You went directly against an order!' Elise said, her voice rising with frustration.

Maya's eyes widened. 'I...I had made a promise to Samuel. His mother was my best friend. If he ever found out that I let you die...' She shook her head. 'Perhaps I can sneak you back into Uracil, find Samuel and you can plan your next move together.'

Elise thought about it for a moment. 'No, it has to be

done in the right way. As soon as I do something under-hand, I lose all credibility. They will use it against me. I have to face them head on.'

'It's your decision...'

Maya trailed off as Ezra walked over, carrying his bag. 'Don't worry. I've not come over to listen in on you. I'm just telling you that I'll be off now.'

'Safe travels,' Maya said.

Ezra looked crestfallen.

'Where will you go?' Elise said, rising to her feet.

'I'm going to Thymine. I've got friends there.'

'Are you sure?' Elise asked, trying to read his features.

Ezra pulled himself up to his full height. 'They were heading to your museum actually.'

'Thymine's Museum of Evolution?' Elise asked. 'Why would you want to go there?'

'Well, Twenty-Two had nowhere else to—' Ezra glanced at them. 'Forget I said that. Which way is Thymine? Just point me in the right direction and I'll be off.'

Elise grabbed Ezra's arm. 'You know Twenty-Two?'

Ezra shifted his feet. 'I was helping her escape when I got caught. I'm pretty much her only friend now that Dara's died. And she's definitely the only friend I've ever had. She got away, should be in Thymine now.'

'Oh, frack,' Maya muttered.

THIRTY

It was with some satisfaction that Twenty-Two was able to finally catalogue the last missing residents of Uracil. Standing at the edge of the platform, she watched from above as the young woman was led away to the cabins that held Uracil's prisoners. On Faye's orders, the guards had waited until it was dark before escorting Elise around the edge of the settlement. She would not be heard from until tomorrow.

Twenty-Two recognised her from their brief meeting in Cytosine but Elise had visibly aged since then; Twenty-Two suspected from her countenance that she had altered internally as well.

Thiago had been summoned by Faye to meet with Maya. No one else had been notified of their arrival. Twenty-Two was instructed to sit at the edge of the platform; she watched carefully as Maya recounted the events that had led her to locating Elise a month ago.

'I tracked them from Cytosine without much difficulty,' Maya said. She was standing with her hands firmly clasped behind her back. 'I heard a scream and was able to pinpoint their exact location. That is when I found Septa on top of Elise. She was using a ligature from behind to asphyxiate her; Elise was face down on the ground. If I hadn't intervened she would have died within moments.'

Twenty-Two noticed that Maya had positioned herself so that she was closest of the three to the exit down to the forest floor. She declined to move from this position, despite Faye's request that she be seated.

'How can you be sure it was Septa? You said it was dark,' Thiago questioned.

'After she lost consciousness, I checked her identity and moved her to another location. It was Septa.'

'How did you come to be there? Your last orders related to a collection point near Guanine,' Faye said, leaning forward.

'I had agreed to assist Samuel in extracting Elise from Cytosine.'

'You take your orders from Samuel now?' Faye said.

Maya dipped her head. 'No, always the Tri-Council. But there was a gap between my missions...I was trying to help.'

'You had no right to be there,' Thiago said, standing up.

Maya took a step back. 'I've never had to remain in my last location between missions before. I thought you'd want one of our captured agents recovered?'

Faye joined Thiago. 'And that is right. We always need to know when we have a rogue agent.'

Maya stared at Faye. 'Rogue agent?'

'Someone has clearly been compromised. We will have to think upon this,' Faye concluded. 'An accusation of this nature against an agent is unprecedented. Witnesses will be summoned. Until Septa is brought in, do not discuss this with anyone or leave Uracil. That comes from the Tri-Council.'

Maya had no visible reaction to this order other than to give a brisk nod. She retreated from the platform without making any noise and Twenty-Two watched her until she was out of sight. It frustrated Twenty-Two that Maya gave so little away; she wanted to know more about this missing piece of Uracil.

Samuel had first told Twenty-Two about Maya after she had reported the order for Elise to be disposed of. Following the group's initial panic, he had reassured them that if anyone could help rescue Elise, it was Maya.

He had asked if Twenty-Two could continue to work with Faye and the Tri-Council. Twenty-Two had agreed but told him she would not become a spy; she would observe what was said but would only report matters that related to Elise. She could not lie—would not lie—for either side. It would go against the very essence of her moral code.

Since then, she had watched the Tri-Council and Uracil's highest-ranking residents even more closely, but nothing new had emerged. She had begun to wonder if she had misread the movement of Faye and Thiago's lips.

Before she could update Samuel on Elise's arrival, she had to collect the final traveller from the other side of the platform. She had noticed the boy who looked like Ezra as soon as he had arrived, walking slowly behind Maya and Elise. She had not dared to run over in case she were mistaken; it was too much to hope for.

Once she got closer to him, she suddenly became nervous. Seeing this person from her past in an alien setting unnerved her. It felt as if the two jarred and she couldn't remember how she had previously been so relaxed in his company. She knew she was a different person now; her naivety had ebbed away, leaving a brittleness he would not have seen before.

When Ezra turned to greet her, his grin had never been so wide; he couldn't contain his excitement and bounced on the balls of his feet. Twenty-Two scrunched her eyes, not allowing her concern for his diminished appearance to cross her features. She wondered if she had been that thin and wrung out when she first arrived in Uracil.

Standing in front of him, she could not meet his gaze. 'I'm so sorry you were captured. I'll do everything I can to help now that you are here.'

'The sign language is a bit rusty, but I'll change that soon enough,' Ezra responded. He scratched the side of his head. 'Might need some help with settling in. Can't think it will be easy getting used to living in a tree.'

Twenty-Two scrunched her eyes, pleased that Ezra would accept her help.

She was conscious that Faye had been waiting too long, so she beckoned him to follow her. The moment he saw the seven-foot-tall, shimmering, golden Faye, his mouth dropped open.

'This is your friend, I believe,' Faye signed to Twenty-Two.

'Yes, he is the one who tried to help me escape,' Twenty-Two signed, showing Ezra to the carved seating in the trunk of the tree.

'I understand that the only reason Maya brought him to us was to let me decide whether he could stay,' Faye signed. 'As he claimed to be your only friend and aided your escape, she thought the decision was too important to be made by a member of the Infiltration Department.'

Ezra glanced between the two women, watching their hands intently. He did not appear disgruntled at not being included. Twenty-Two realised that this was probably because he was used to being talked about rather than to.

'I know he wouldn't normally be able to stay,' Twenty-Two signed, taking a seat slightly closer to Faye than Ezra. 'But he's a hard worker. Very resilient and also kind—'

'You don't need to do that,' Faye interrupted. 'His attributes do not need to be laid bare like some spreading of wares on an emporium tabletop. I will let him stay. As a gift to you. You've been such a help these past few months that I think a reward is in order. I'm sure I can persuade Raul and Flynn to agree.'

'Thank you,' Twenty-Two responded, dipping her head slightly. She stared at Faye's hands long after she had finished signing.

'I will speak to Raul and Flynn later today,' Faye said, her tone indicating that she had finished both with the matter and with them.

Ezra grinned at Faye. 'I'd be honoured to stay in Uracil. Thank you very much.'

'A job will be required, but I am sure you can arrange something suitable,' Faye signed to Twenty-Two.

'Thank you for this gift,' Twenty-Two responded before standing. 'I will take him to one of the guest tree houses now. Before we find him a permanent home.'

Faye nodded and smiled, her beauty lighting up her face. Ezra blushed and made a deep bow to Faye before grabbing his bag and scurrying after Twenty-Two.

'Well, this is a turn up,' Ezra said. 'There being a fifth, super-secret base. And you're here too!'

Twenty-Two scrunched her eyes at her friend.

Leading him across the walkways, she noticed how Ezra tried not to look down and instead gripped the edge of the handrails as he walked beside her. He was focused on peering at the strange, wooden houses with their woollen outer coatings, steaming chimneys and solar panels that stretched their way up to the forest canopy.

Hurrying along, she didn't speak until they were inside the guest cabin closest to the spiralled walkway down to the forest floor.

Closing the door behind them, she went and sat down, cross-legged, on the floor. Ezra stayed by the door, clutching his bag to him and glancing around.

'And this is for me?' Ezra said. 'I can stay here?'

'Yes,' Twenty-Two signed. 'You can stay here as long as you want until we find you your own tree house. It will look pretty similar to this one.'

Ezra broke out into his broadest grin. 'This is a million times nicer than that airless room I had back in the museum. Maybe a billion, even.'

Twenty-Two scrunched her eyes, pleased that her friend was as cheerful as she had remembered him to be. Her version of a smile slowly faded as she realised that it couldn't last.

'Would you sit down, Ezra? I've got something to say. And only sign your response if you don't mind.'

Ezra's brow wrinkled but he sat down on the floor in front of her.

'You don't mind me being here, do you?' he signed.

'Mind? Ever since I left Cytosine, I've thought about where you and Dara might be. To know you're safe is a sign from the stars themselves that they have been watching over me.'

Ezra drew back from her and Twenty-Two realised that he was hiding something.

'Then what is it?' Ezra asked.

'Things aren't as safe as they seem,' Twenty-Two signed slowly, so that Ezra could clearly understand her meaning.

'I know that,' Ezra signed. 'I was there when that fake-nurse spy tried to kill Elise. Maya said that it was Uracil's Die-Council who had ordered it.'

Twenty-Two was taken aback. Perhaps Ezra wasn't as naïve as she had thought. He was used to living under pressure. She had an uncomfortable realisation that it was she who had been unaware of the ways of the world, not him.

'Just as long as you know what you're getting into if you stay here,' Twenty-Two signed.

'No different to out there, really. At least here they might not put me in prison to pay off an operation I don't even remember needing.'

'Let's hope,' Twenty-Two signed, leaning forward to pat his knee. 'Is there something you want to tell me?'

With no warning, Ezra burst into tears. Twenty-Two scrambled across the floor to his side.

'I'm so sorry,' he half-hiccuped when his sobbing had subsided. 'I tried so hard to keep her going—Elise did too—but she died in the containment centre.'

Twenty-Two let Ezra go and sat down heavily next to him. She'd suspected something had happened to Dara but hadn't let herself get carried away until she heard it from him.

She squeezed her eyes shut and willed the tears to come for once, but of course they did not. Her heart felt heavy in her chest and her limbs began to ache under the strain of it all. She wrapped her arms around her knees and rocked herself gently for a while, just as Dara had done when she was a young girl.

While she tried to comfort herself, she listened to Ezra recall his time in the containment centre. He spoke in a matter-of-fact way, as he always did; there was no added drama to his tone or self-pity. She had a feeling that this wasn't entirely for her benefit and that he needed to speak about it, to unburden himself of the past few months and the guilt he carried about Dara's demise.

When he had finished and had been silent for a few minutes, Twenty-Two turned to him. 'I want to thank you for caring for her. For making her last few months as comfortable as you could in the worst circumstances. For bringing a bit of her old self back to life in her final weeks. I couldn't have asked for any more from you.'

Ezra stared pointedly at the corner of the ceiling as he furiously blinked away the tears. Twenty-Two did not move closer, acknowledging the embarrassment clearly radiating from him.

'I would like to introduce you to some of my new friends; they are friends of Elise as well,' she signed, watching the tears slide down his freckled face. She wanted to comfort him but knew that wouldn't help him at this moment. 'My oldest friend meeting my newest.'

At this, Ezra gave a grin that showed all his teeth and nearly stretched to his ears.

Making their way to Kit's cabin, Twenty-Two pointed out where the most useful walkways were located and encouraged him to try one of the zip wires the next day. They walked close together, the familiarity of their friendship having returned.

When she knocked on the door, the voices inside stopped talking and it was a few moments before Kit slid it open, his features fixed as always. Without saying anything, he pulled her inside. With no hesitation, she grabbed Ezra and tugged him through the door.

The small room was crowded and there was nowhere to sit. It was also so warm that she had to stop herself from moving over to the window. Why had no one opened it? She looked around at the strained faces. Luca was standing guard by the door. Georgina was vigorously bouncing Bay on her knee; the baby was delighted at the unexpected game. Samuel's face couldn't be seen as he resumed peering down at his feet with his head in his hands. She recognised a few other faces, including Tilla and Maya's. No one spoke.

'I wanted to introduce my friend Ezra to you all,' she signed after a moment.

Ezra smiled at each of them. 'Pleasure to meet you all and thank you for having me.'

The room was silent.

It was Kit who took action first, stepping towards Ezra and taking his hand briefly. 'I'm glad you made it out of Cytosine and I'm sorry to hear of the time you spent in the containment centre.'

As if Kit's kindness awoke them from their thoughts, the distracted occupants of the room each remembered themselves and greeted Ezra in turn.

'What has happened?' Twenty-Two asked Kit when everyone fell silent again. She glanced over at Maya. 'You know that Elise has arrived?'

Kit nodded.

'Nothing's happened,' Luca said, before drumming his fingers against the wall.

Kit stared at Luca. 'She can be trusted.'

'We don't know short-stuff, do we?' Luca signed.

'Watch your tongue,' Georgina interrupted. 'You've been bitter for the last month, knowing it's your precious Faye who has done this.'

'You just hate her because she's beautiful,' Luca snapped.

Samuel raised his head. 'That was uncalled for. Stop it, all of you. There can't be any more fighting between us. We have to remain united.'

Twenty-Two watched the faces as they slowly nodded their agreement.

'Sorry,' Luca mumbled.

'You will be if you carry on like that,' Georgina responded, holding both her hands up to Samuel when he glared at her.

'Don't mind me,' Ezra said, bouncing on the balls of his feet. 'I can see you've got a bit to deal with at the moment and that doesn't mean that I have a right to know. Being new and all.'

Georgina moved over on the bed and waved him across to join her. In a moment, Bay was sitting contentedly on his knee while Georgina asked him about his journey.

'Is it because Elise has arrived?' Twenty-Two signed to Kit.

'It's Elise and Faye,' Kit signed to Twenty-Two, so that only she could see. 'We think that Faye tipped off Cytosine's Museum of Evolution that Elise would be breaking in that evening. It was all a set-up to get rid of her.'

'But why?' Twenty-Two signed. 'Why have her captured and then have her rescued only to be killed?'

Kit glanced over at Samuel. 'Faye wants Samuel away from Uracil, preferably in another zone if possible. She could see how he felt about Elise and thought he would want to remain in Uracil to be close to her. Samuel suspects that she's done something to their father as well; he hasn't been heard from in two years.'

Twenty-Two was shocked. 'How does he know this?'

'He's had his suspicions for a while about how Elise got caught. It was a straightforward mission and, under normal circumstances, she should have been fine. When he learned from you that one of Uracil's infiltrators had been sent to assassinate Elise, his suspicions about her initial capture began to grow.

'Last night he attended a private meeting with Faye in her sleeping quarters. I went with him and I read her. She would never say anything to incriminate herself but she speaks only with power in mind. She wants Samuel gone and will do anything to achieve it. But we have no proof.'

Twenty-Two ignored the mumble of agitated voices around her as they carried on with their separate discussions.

'You're sure of this?' Twenty-Two signed. 'That she is responsible for Elise's capture?'

'As sure as we can be, but we'll never have proof. We know that she ordered Septa to free and kill Elise, thanks to you. It's likely that Septa will now be painted as a rogue agent or worse...Elise will be. You were in the museum that night; was there anything different?'

Twenty-Two only had to think about it for a moment before answering. 'Yes, there were so many guards patrolling that night. Normally, Ezra and I could go a whole evening with only meeting one or two workers; sometimes, we would see no one. We spent our evenings exploring the museum; he would teach me what he learnt at school about our history and the Sapiens. But that night, we barely spoke. It seemed everyone was out patrolling. The Director was there and the Collection's Assistant. No one was sleeping.'

'Exactly. They knew something was going to happen. But Faye is too careful, nothing written down, everything verbal,' Kit signed.

'I could tell them all. I could tell them everything I've seen her say. Including them discussing the order on Elise's life. I can remember it all,' Twenty-Two signed.

She could feel Uracil closing in on her, the Sapiens' mistakes of the past being repeated time and time again. What would happen to her species if Faye were allowed to continue to act in this way?

'Even if you told the whole of Uracil what you heard, no one would believe you. Who would believe a Neanderthal new to Uracil over Faye?' Kit signed, his movements conveying his agitation for once.

'I have to go,' Twenty-Two signed, suddenly feeling light-headed. 'Please walk Ezra back for me?'

'Of course. Are you all right?' Kit signed.

'Yes, yes, just tired. I'll see you tomorrow.'

Head down, she made her way back to her tree house as quickly as she could, her thoughts whirring. She had known from the minute she had begun watching the Tri-Council that Faye was the one she had to pay the closest attention to. Raul and Flynn were much older than her and seemed weary of their roles. They only continued out of a sense of duty and were clearly relieved that Faye had offered to take over the bulk of the work.

Twenty-Two had stuck close to Faye and silently observed all of the meetings. She had been displeased to see Faye dispense with the rules she had initially set for herself. Cedric conducted all of Faye's personal chores for her now and she had begun to refuse to meet with residents who had aggrieved her in some minor way. Without an audience, those residents were permanently silenced, a step that cut off their access to resolution and justice. Twenty-Two had wondered where these adjustments to her moral code would lead Faye but, despite all of this, she had never suspected how far Faye might go.

It was not until Twenty-Two witnessed the discussion about the order on Elise's life that she became fully aware of how far across that line Faye had strayed. She soon realised that the discussions with Thiago were where the real damage was done. The acts that no one else could observe.

If Faye could make that order, then what else could she do? Tip off Cytosine that Elise would be in the museum on the night of her capture? Remove her own father from power to make way for her own reign?

The Sapiens wanted proof of these two last acts, but the more Twenty-Two thought about it, the less she believed it was required. She had proof of the first act and that in itself showed a preferred way of dealing with these situations. Did someone else have to die or escape near death for a precedent to be set? Was another person's life worth that surety?

Kit had said that people in power had to stand up to a higher test than those without it. Twenty-Two knew that Faye had failed that test and action had to be taken before someone else's life was risked or lost.

Changing direction, she walked with her head down, grateful that the rain had driven most people indoors. It was late and she passed no one. Checking she hadn't been followed, she entered one of the tree houses and, with a bit of brute strength, took what she needed. She then returned to her cabin to wait for the depths of night to come.

At 3am, she slipped quietly out of her room. She walked quickly and with her head down, a large, hooded jumper pulled over her face. Pausing outside Faye's sleeping quarters, she went around to the back door where no one could see her enter.

Slowly pushing open the door, she waited a moment to assess the situation.

Faye had recently changed sleeping quarters to a tree house that was larger than most, with several separate rooms. Silently entering, Twenty-Two turned to close the door behind her before making her way across the smooth, wooden floorboards. She made no sound with her bare feet. Crossing into the small hallway, she moved towards the second door to the right, where she knew Faye slept.

Her heart began beating faster and, for a moment, she dithered. Was this the right thing to do? She internally shook herself; this was no time for doubt. She was about to face a woman who was stronger and faster than her. A woman who had the power to call guards to her side in a moment, who would then arrest Twenty-Two without any need for proof or evidence. Isn't that what she had done to Elise? Faye had been given both physical and custodial powers that she had abused and would abuse again. This was right.

Pushing open the door with one hand, Twenty-Two waited a moment before entering. She took a deep breath before taking a step forwards. Although dark, there was the faintest hint of moonlight seeping in from the edges of the window around the lowered blinds. Used to moving around in the darkness in her pod, Twenty-Two counted three steps to the bed where she could see a figure lying on their side.

Twenty-Two lightly ran her finger over the sleeping woman's arm before she located the largest of her prominent veins—her lean body weight meant that they bulged under the surface of her skin.

Pulling the syringe out of her pocket, Twenty-Two

made a silent plea to the stars before carefully angling the needle into the vein and pushing down on the plunger.

It was only a second before Faye woke. 'What? What is going...? You! Get away from me!'

With that, she flung Twenty-Two across the room.

She landed heavily against some shelving. Pain sparked across her lower back. She didn't know if she had injected enough of the opiate or how long until it would take effect. All she knew was that she had to get out of Faye's cabin.

Scrambling to her feet, Twenty-Two leapt the two steps to the door and skittered into the hallway. She could hear Faye's footsteps following but she didn't dare turn around.

Sprinting towards the back door, Twenty-Two rushed out and stepped neatly to the right of the doorframe, where she remained.

Her heart raced. It wasn't supposed to be like this; Faye was supposed to pass away gently in her sleep, not catch Twenty-Two mid-act.

A second later, Faye threw open the door, slightly unbalanced, the drugs already taking hold.

Without hesitation, Twenty-Two took one step forward and, with all her strength, pushed Faye over the bannister of the walkway.

She knew she would remember the pressure of Faye's body leaving her fingertips for the rest of her life. A crunching noise caused Twenty-Two to involuntarily shiver. Peering over the side, Twenty-Two watched the still body. She was unaware how long she remained there, but she didn't once take her eyes off the lifeless figure below.

She had broken the final rule.

Three hours later, Twenty-Two stilled her expression and answered the hammering at her tree house door. Calming her features, she pulled it open and stood aside for Kit as he rushed in.

'It's Faye; she's dead. They found her an hour ago, beneath her sleeping quarters. She fell,' he signed.

'She is definitely dead?' Twenty-Two signed.

'Yes, Georgina was one of the nurses called to check on her. She broke her neck...the angle—she went head first, they think.'

Kit sat down on the floor and Twenty-Two sat opposite him.

'You are not surprised,' Kit finally signed.

'I will hide it from the others, but not from you,' Twenty-Two responded.

Kit stilled his own features. 'What have you done?'

'I did what everyone else was too weak to do. Faye ordered the death of Elise. We are certain that she tipped off Cytosine about Elise's arrival, which had the consequence of Dara and Ezra being arrested and, ultimately, Dara's death. She had to be stopped.'

'You acted out of revenge,' Kit signed, leaning forwards.

'No, I have watched her for months. I asked for that job so that I could be near the ones in power and watch over the residents of Uracil. It took a while, but I eventually learnt that underneath her beauty was an abomination. She only acted for the accumulation of power. She had no real warmth, no kindness and no pity. You could see that as well. Everything she did was for the benefit of herself, either in the immediate future or stored for later.'

'That does not make what you did right.'

'You said yourself that these Sapiens are weak, that they

do not take the power from the ones who have it when they should. I did what no one else could. I acted.'

'We cannot ever be certain she tipped them off about Elise or that she killed her father.'

'That is true. But I can be certain that she made the order against Elise. Maya has confirmed what Septa did. She's not a rogue agent; she acted under Faye's orders.'

'That is also true,' Kit signed. 'But you should never have acted alone; it was not your decision to make. Uracil is in chaos.'

'Let it be. It is better there is no ruler than a corrupted one.'

Kit stared at Twenty-Two before dropping his head into his hands.

'Stars, you were by yourself for too long,' he signed with one hand.

Twenty-Two did not know what he meant; she had very few memories of being alone.

'It is not your fault,' Kit continued. 'Fourteen years of confusion and isolation. It is so damaging—' Kit dropped his head again.

'I am not damaged,' Twenty-Two signed. 'And I was not alone. I had Dara and now I have Ezra. I did the right thing.' She watched Kit for a moment. 'Are you going to tell the others?'

Kit glanced up before dropping his head into his hands again. 'I don't know. This position you have put me in.'

'If you think it is the right thing to do, then I will accept it. But I will never regret my actions. I stopped history from repeating itself as it has done countless times before.'

'That may be true,' Kit signed before dropping his hands into his lap.

They sat there together for an hour before Kit finally

looked up at her again. Twenty-Two had not noticed the passing of time; she was used to it from being in her pod. An hour could be blinked away if necessary; it was a mere matter of adjusting when your thoughts resurfaced.

'I am not going to tell the others, but if you do something even close to this again, I will stop you myself,' Kit signed. 'This power of judgement can be all-consuming, so I will watch you to make sure it doesn't destroy you. For what has been done to you, I believe you deserve one more chance. Perhaps you have already served your prison sentence for this act.'

Despite the strength of her righteousness, Twenty-Two was relieved that she would get to see Ezra again, and choose what she ate and drank and where she went. 'I promise that I will not act again in this manner without speaking to you first.'

'You promise on the stars?'

'I promise on the stars and all our ancestors who once lived under them.'

THIRTY-ONE

E lise circled the wooden cabin. Although small, it was clean, warm and had a private bathroom. Her pod back at the museum and sleeping quarters in the containment centre had been far worse.

It wasn't her surroundings that were niggling her; it was trying to guess what the Tri-Council's next move would be. She had known that she would be arrested as soon as she arrived in Uracil and she had to prepare for whatever might follow. She calmed herself. She had faced much worse with fewer allies. Unless Maya had also been arrested, it was likely that her friends now knew of her arrival. She would have to be patient for the moment.

It was still dark outside and she had only slept for three hours after arriving in Uracil the previous night. She knew no one was likely to come for her until the morning, so she occupied herself practising some of the exercises Maya had shown her on their journey to Uracil. Although they had trained together for an hour or two each night, she still had far to go until she regained her former strength and agility.

During the long days travelling across Zone 3, Maya

had spoken with Elise about how Uracil had been founded, who the leaders were and also its rules. Elise had learnt about Samuel's family, how his father had been on the Tri-Council and his sister had now taken that position. She listened carefully, aware that she was replacing some of the memories she had lost. The more she learnt, the further it confirmed that she was making the right choice by returning.

When daylight began to filter into Elise's cabin, she stopped mid-stance. She had heard a shout. It was followed by two others. Within a matter of minutes, she could hear people running past the cabin. Her only view out of the cabin was through a skylight; there were no windows to the side. She realised this was the restricted view the Neanderthals had suffered all their lives. No chance to see immediate events unfold, only what the sky presented to them.

The shouts and harried voices carried on for the next hour. Elise tensed when she began to hear crying and wailing. Something had happened, something important enough to disturb most of the residents.

She began to pace up and down the cabin. Moving continuously, she reassured herself that her arrival was a coincidence, not the cause of the disturbance. She was not important enough to warrant this reaction. After another hour, she stopped still and tensed. The door opened and one of the guards stepped inside. He looked at her warily and his gloves glowed a blue colour.

'Sit down on the chair in the corner. Hands underneath your legs,' he said.

Elise obliged, reasoning that it was better to be remembered than forgotten at this early stage of her captivity.

'You have some visitors. Stay on the seat the whole time or I'll be forced to restrain you.'

Elise nodded and watched as the guard slipped out of the room again.

A few minutes later, two men entered. Both were swathed in long sheets of clothing. Despite searching her memories, she did not recognise them. She was uncomfortably aware that this didn't mean she had never met them before. She felt at a disadvantage.

The third person who entered was Samuel. She smiled up at him, but did not move to greet him; she knew she was being watched. Maya had hinted to her on the journey that Elise's relationship with Samuel had changed in the three months she had lost. Maya had refused to say much more and told Elise it was for her and Samuel to discuss. She didn't want to replace Elise's memories with false ones. Elise knew that, a few months ago, she would have blushed at such revelations, but she was changed now; her thoughts were focused on the Tri-Council.

Samuel spoke first. 'Elise, this is Raul and Flynn. They are two of the three members of the Tri-Council. You met them before when you were last in Uracil, but they also know you will not remember them.'

Elise was grateful to Samuel for not leaving her to guess whether she had previously met the two men. She tried not to stare at their clothing, but she had never seen anyone dressed like them before. For a brief moment, Elise wondered whether Samuel was angry with her for being captured in Cytosine.

Elise nodded her greeting. Raul and Flynn perched on the edge of the seats that Samuel had brought in for them. These were the men who had ordered her assassination. She had to face them head on.

She glanced over at Samuel and he gave her a smile that reached all the way to his eyes. No, he was not angry with her for her failure. Having him there to witness this exchange strengthened her resolve; he would do what he could to help her.

'Elise, we have met before, but please do accept our apologies for your current situation. We were not aware of your arrival yesterday,' the Sapien-looking man said.

Elise nodded. 'I knew it was likely that I'd be arrested if I returned to Uracil, but what happened to me is too important to remain hidden. Septa was ordered to kill me and I don't think that many people knew about it. Whatever my failures, I struggle to believe that Uracil would agree with that order.'

The taller man, who looked like a Medius, stood up. 'You are right. Those are the actions of the other bases, not the ways of Uracil. I can assure you that myself and Flynn were unaware of the situation. We believe that Septa may have been a rogue agent.'

Elise was careful not to react to this assertion.

Raul started walking up and down the length of the cabin with his hands clasped behind his back.

'Maya has confirmed your story and this cannot be ignored. Especially following this morning's events.' Raul glanced at Samuel. 'And you are quite sure that you cannot remember anything of the night you were in Cytosine's Museum of Evolution?'

'No, nothing,' Elise responded. 'My first memory is of waking up in the recovery room following my operation.'

Samuel stared down at his feet before meeting Elise's gaze again.

'So, you remember nothing about the circumstances of your ah...capture?'

'No,' Elise said.

'That is a shame; your testimony would have been useful,' Raul continued.

'That's not fair, Raul,' Samuel interrupted. 'You know she cannot remember anything and the drugs are designed to make it that way. You've already spoken with Twenty-Two and Ezra. They confirmed that the museum was heaving with guards that night.'

'I was merely highlighting that without—'

'Enough, Raul,' Flynn said. 'We have to face the obvious. Septa was no rogue agent. That is the easy way out. The evidence is circumstantial but still overwhelming. The Tri-Council left too much power in one pair of hands. We chose to have three leaders in the beginning to prevent such things and we have neglected to uphold that wise decision.'

Flynn stood and all of their gazes followed him as he paced the length of the cabin. 'Thiago is to be questioned next. I have known him since he was a child. Without Faye by his side, he will confess to everything to save his own skin. We cannot hide ourselves from the truth anymore, just because it is the easier path to take.'

Raul looked mournfully at Flynn before speaking. 'You are right. We did not build this settlement so that it would slide into being indistinguishable from the other bases.' He turned to Elise. 'You are free to go. The circumstances of your capture are likely to be revealed shortly and it is safe to say that it is unlikely that it was your fault.'

Elise had several questions but allowed herself only one. 'What happened this morning?'

'We will leave Samuel to explain that to you, for it is his news to tell,' Flynn said, before crossing to the cabin door. 'You can continue working for the Infiltration Department if you want, but rest assured your family can come to Uracil whatever you decide to do. We used to allow all the residents to bring family members in; it kept the residents content and far less likely to betray Uracil. It was a mistake to alter that decision. It is the very least we can offer after what you have suffered in the containment centre.'

Once they had left, Elise turned to Samuel, who was keeping his distance by the door. 'Can we leave this room and go for a walk? I can't remember the last time I was free to move around where I wanted to. Today feels like it should be spent outdoors.'

Samuel smiled broadly.

They set off and Samuel gave Elise a tour of the island, pointing out the landmarks. He did not take her into the centre of Uracil, leading her instead around the edge of the lake. Elise listened quietly as he filled her in on visiting her parents and his months of searching for a way to secure her release.

'And now you're here and you're still you,' Samuel concluded, glancing over at her.

'That place didn't break me but it has changed me. We can't ignore that.'

Samuel was silent.

'All those months in there have made me sure of what must come next. We have to stop hiding away. We have to show everyone in Zone 3 what is happening right underneath their noses in the containment centres. Show them that the stars did not make the Potiors. The Sapiens and the Medius made them. And it's time they were stopped.'

Elise could see out of the corner of her eye that Samuel was smiling.

'I agree,' he said. 'If we keep on hiding the truth, we are complicit in what is happening to people in the other bases. We have to stop relying on spies and fearing our detection. A new era is required.'

Elise hadn't been sure what to expect from him. She stared at the ground as they continued to walk along the shore of the island. 'Thank you for everything you have done and for sending Maya to help me. Without her I would have died.'

Samuel cleared his throat and tapped his forehead. Elise smiled. She had missed his awkwardness and was pleased that he had not changed.

'I did everything in my power to secure your release,' he said eventually. 'I am only sorry that it took so long. But there is something I have to tell you.'

He stopped walking and sat on a fallen log, positioned so that it overlooked the misted lake.

Elise followed, not liking the sound of this. She did not sit down and remained standing in front of him. 'Is it my parents, my brother? Should I bring them to Uracil right away?'

Samuel looked up. 'No, no, nothing like that. I promise you, they were fine when I saw them. They've had no difficulties since you left; it seems that your quick thinking convinced the authorities that they were not involved in Kit's escape.'

Elise sat down heavily, relief flooding through her.

'It's not about your family. It's about mine,' Samuel said. 'It was my sister who ordered that Septa free you from the containment centre and dispose of you afterwards.' Elise opened her mouth to speak but Samuel cut her off. 'We also believe that it was my sister who contacted Cytosine's Museum of Evolution and told them a spy from Thymine was coming. That is why they were waiting for you. They knew you were there to look at Lab 412. They thought you had been sent by Thymine's Museum of Evolution to spy on Marvalian's new project. He is so paranoid about the other bases discovering what he is doing that he fell for it straightaway. When they caught you, you had already taken your blocker and appeared completely insane. They probably believed that you couldn't have made the journey from another base and were an unlikely spy. They couldn't expel you, so they put you in the containment centre instead.'

Elise stared out over the lake. 'Maya already told me that the Tri-Council gave Septa her orders, but in a strange way I'm pleased my capture wasn't my fault. It sounds silly but I thought I'd failed, that everything that happened afterwards was down to my inexperience.'

'I'm so sorry, Elise,' Samuel said. 'I'm so sorry for everything that happened to you in there.'

Elise pushed down her feelings of sorrow and loss. 'You're not responsible for your sister's actions. No more than I am. We're separate people. The only thing I don't understand is why your sister would go to such lengths to get rid of me. I can't mean much to one of the leaders of the Tri-Council.'

Samuel blushed. 'That would be my fault. You and I became...close during the time that you lost your memories and my sister didn't want me to have any ties to Uracil. She wanted me to leave. Perhaps she was paranoid that I might start asking questions about what happened to our father. Ultimately, she decided to remove my ties, so that I would have no reason to stay.'

Elise tried to process what Maya had hinted at. She had always admired Samuel, but had never allowed herself to think of him in that way. A Sapien and a Medius? It wasn't possible.

'I don't expect anything of you,' Samuel said hurriedly. 'You lost the weeks we spent together and I don't want you to feel obliged to follow the same path as before. But know that I will be here to help you if needed. And even if you require only friendship from me, I will happily provide it.'

Elise's heart ached for him. He was so clearly trying to not add to her burdens. She knew then that her capture had hurt him more than she could have imagined.

She took a breath. 'Something led me to you before, so it may lead me there again. Perhaps all that is needed is a bit of time, a bit of distance from what has happened...what happened to both of us.'

They were silent for a few minutes.

'Where's your sister now?' Elise asked uneasily.

Samuel pushed his hair from his forehead. 'She...ah... she died this morning.'

Elise didn't know what to say. 'But how? She's similar to a Potior, isn't she?'

'Was similar to a Potior. In more ways than one.' Samuel stood up. 'We should go back. It's pandemonium in Uracil. There's no precedent for this type of thing and everyone is up in arms.'

They walked into the woodland in silence, but Elise needed to know more.

'How did she die?'

'She had a fall, over the side of one of the walkways,' Samuel said.

Elise stared at her boots as they crunched through the undergrowth. 'And she was enhanced, like a Potior?'

'Yes, she had similar enhancements to me, and a few other additions,' Samuel said, looking away.

'And how likely is it that you would accidentally fall off anything?' Elise asked, staring straight ahead.

'I know,' Samuel responded.

They carried on walking in silence. When they approached the centre of Uracil, Elise noticed that people were following their progress in the treetops above, trailing behind them along the walkways. She began to feel uncomfortable and glanced at Samuel for reassurance, but he was staring straight ahead. In the clearing up ahead there was a line of guards.

They stopped. Elise could feel the air humming with anticipation.

'That's the one,' someone yelled from above.

A few others joined in and shouted across to each other, alerting their neighbours to their presence.

Bolstered by the crowd, someone threw a branch at them from high above. It hit Elise squarely on the back and she stumbled forwards. Turning, she reached for Samuel and he pulled her back towards him.

'Don't let them get away!'

A crowd was also gathering on the forest floor.

Samuel addressed the guards. 'Let us pass.'

One of the guards stepped forwards. 'We think you need to be questioned, about what happened to Faye.'

'I told you, I was asleep at the time,' Samuel replied in a calm tone, loud enough that the crowd could hear him.

'She couldn't have fallen without some help. And who is the most likely person to take her place on the Tri-Council?' the guard said, also addressing the audience.

The crowd cheered and hollered.

'I don't want a place on the Tri-Council. The position should go to a vote,' Samuel responded.

He moved closer to Elise as the people on the ground started pushing towards them. There were around a hundred of them now and they were closing in. Elise felt someone jab her between the shoulder blades.

Her gaze swept over the other two hundred people who were standing farther back and watching the events unfold.

They were not moved enough to help her. She wished she had her sling, but even with it she knew they stood no chance against these odds.

'*A life for a life*,' someone shouted above them, clearly willing to call out instructions but not brave enough to come down to the forest floor.

Elise felt the crowd push closer to her. She didn't recognise any of their faces, even though she tried to make eye contact with each person. Their expressions ranged from outrage to fear to heady excitement. The woman directly in front of Elise pulled her lips back from her teeth and the noise she released was almost a growl.

In the far distance, Elise thought she saw a girl dressed like Seventeen run away from the clearing. Guessing it was Twenty-Two, she hoped that she had escaped the mob; they could easily turn on her next.

Someone grabbed Elise's arm and she shook herself free. Another tried to hold onto Samuel but he pushed them away, knocking over two other people at the same time.

With their backs to each other, Samuel and Elise continued to defend themselves but the crowd was growing in assurance. Someone grabbed Elise's hair and pulled her to the ground—she wished that she had kept it as short as it was back in Thymine. Samuel tried to free her but at that moment six guards grabbed him, pulling him to the ground. Their gloves glowing, they raised their fists above him in unison. Elise could only watch in horror as Samuel, one of the strongest men she had ever met, curled up into a ball.

'*Quieeeeet!*'

The voice boomed across the clearing and everyone froze. Elise scrabbled back to her feet, helping to pull Samuel up as well. She kept hold of his hand for reassurance, not caring that he didn't like to be touched. Elise turned to the man standing on a plinth at the edge of the clearing.

'I never thought, when I first helped remove the trees from this clearing, that I would one day witness such acts,' Flynn boomed over the crowd.

He paused for a moment and seemed to meet the gaze of every person looking up at him.

'*It was him who did it*,' someone shouted from the crowd. 'We didn't want him to escape.'

'It had nothing to do with Samuel,' Flynn responded. 'You have no evidence, no proof and you act like a pack of savages. I am ashamed to call you brother and sister today.'

'How do you know it wasn't him?' someone else shouted out from above.

'Because we've received a confession. From someone who is neither Samuel nor Elise.'

There were some mutterings in the crowd and people began glancing at each other. As quickly as the pack mentality had bolstered them, they now appeared defeated and alone.

'Back to your homes. We will have another public meeting this evening and myself and Raul will address everyone's concerns. There will be a great deal more transparency in Uracil as we go forward.'

The crowd started to disperse. No one looked at Elise or tried to signal an apology. Samuel stood his ground, still holding onto her hand as they watched everyone move away.

Elise only let go when she spied Kit, Luca and Georgina pushing towards them. She ran over and before she could help herself, she was hugging each of them in turn.

Georgina burst into tears. 'I've been so worried for you.'

'Looking skinnier than ever, Thanton. Going to have to feed you up,' Luca said, putting his arm around her.

Kit's features appeared strained for once.

'What's wrong?' Elise signed to him.

'It is Twenty-Two; she has told them that she killed Faye,' Kit signed.

'But why would she say that?' Samuel signed. 'We must speak to Raul and Flynn straightaway.'

Kit grabbed hold of Samuel's sleeve and pulled him back. 'She told them she killed Faye because she did. And she did not want to see you blamed for it.'

'Where is she now?' Elise asked.

'They have taken her to one of the cabins. They would not let me follow.'

'I always knew she was unhinged.' Luca said. 'Why would she kill Faye?'

'Because she knew what Faye was,' Kit responded. 'She knew Faye had tried to have Elise killed. And, in her own way, Twenty-Two thought she was preventing more deaths in the future...maybe she was.'

The friends looked at each other.

'What will they do with her?' Elise asked Samuel.

'If she has confessed and it's true, then she will be imprisoned in one of the cabins on the island. There is strong mitigation for a more lenient sentence, but no defence. She cannot take the law into her own hands, no matter what Faye has done.'

'Whatever they decide, I will be standing by her,' Kit signed. 'I am sorry that she did this to your sister, Samuel, but she thought she was doing the right thing. Maybe in previous or future times, it would be viewed that way as well.'

They were all silent as they waited for Samuel's response.

Samuel pushed his hair back from his forehead. 'After what happened to Twenty-Two, back in Cytosine, no good will come from us abandoning her now. She has already been neglected for most of her life. I will stand by her too and help how I can.'

'Thank you,' Kit signed.

'I will as well,' Elise said and Georgina nodded her agreement.

They all turned to Luca.

'I can't,' Luca signed. 'What she did was wrong. Seventeen was in the same position and she would never kill anyone. I can't help. She deserves everything she gets.'

With that, Luca turned and walked away from the group.

Silence descended.

'Come on,' Elise said after a few minutes. 'Let's get Ezra and check that he's all right. We can find out when Twenty-Two will next be allowed visitors. I think she'll want to see him first.'

They all nodded.

Elise glanced upwards and caught her image in one of the mirrors hanging from the top of the canopy of trees; she almost didn't recognise herself in the brief, scattered reflection. Drawing her gaze away, she joined her friends as they made their way back into the centre of Uracil.

EPILOGUE

Elise sat by the lakeside with her companions, their backs to Uracil. The only person missing was Luca, who had recently spent all of his time training as a guard.

Public meetings had been called every night for the last week following the death of Faye. Order had begun to return under Raul and Flynn's prominent supervision, but Elise made sure that she never walked alone outside, even during the day. She wondered whether she would ever feel safe in Uracil again.

'What about Tilla?' Elise suggested, as they ran through the names of possible candidates.

The upcoming elections had been announced the night before and the group were determined to help elect someone to the council they knew to be an ally. If Uracil was going to be the safe harbour that they required, they needed support from the leadership.

Georgina smiled at the suggestion. 'Tilla is influential in her own way, but she has no interest in politics. She could rally people around a candidate, but I think even she would agree that she shouldn't stand as one.'

Ezra took a gulp of air. 'I still don't see why Samuel can't stand.'

'That's very kind of you, Ezra,' Samuel said patiently. 'But it would cast suspicion on us if I were to replace my sister. Besides, I need to find out what happened to my father and to do that I need to be mobile. To be on the Tri-Council would mean never leaving Uracil.'

'One day there will be a Neanderthal on the council,' Kit signed.

Elise agreed, but she knew that day hadn't yet come.

'How was Twenty-Two today?' Georgina asked Ezra.

They each took it in turn to visit Twenty-Two in the afternoons but the morning visiting hour was always Ezra's.

Ezra blinked rapidly. 'Good, I think. Perhaps too good, if that's possible. She seems almost settled.'

'We'll do everything we can, I promise,' Samuel said. 'Her hearing is in two weeks and she will plead guilty. But with heavy mitigation, perhaps it will only be a few years before she is free again.'

Kit stared at Samuel over Ezra's bent head and a silent communication passed between them. Elise knew that Kit worried about Twenty-Two as well. Further incarceration would only hinder her transition into the outside world.

'Maya?' Georgina said.

'I've already tried,' Samuel said, gazing up at the sky. 'She takes the same view as me; she wants to be free and mobile. She would feel caged up and frustrated in that role.'

His words stung Elise and she tried not to think about what they might mean. In the last few days, she had been watching Samuel closely, considering whether what she had felt before was possible again. To hear that he wanted to be free made her wonder if he had already changed his mind about her.

'There is someone else,' Samuel said. 'His name is Michael; he is one of the heads of the Agriculture Department. He approached me when I first returned to Uracil to convey his support after Elise was captured. He was very kind to me. I think he always distrusted Faye, and from what I know of him, he is one of the most solid, honourable people I have met. Most of the residents admire him and the tales of his arrival in Uracil back when he was fourteen have always secured their respect.'

'I do not like suggesting this, but I think I should meet with him a few times,' Kit signed.

'I agree, but I didn't want to ask,' Samuel responded. 'This decision is too important for us to get wrong.'

They all nodded.

Elise leant back and stared up at the sky; it reminded her of being in Kit's pod back in Thymine. 'Sometimes I wish I had the power to pick up those I care about and transport them to a safe island away from all of this. But then there are people who don't have anyone to do that for them; they shouldn't be quietly forgotten.'

She blinked up at the sky as she thought of her parents and brother. She had surprised herself by voicing her thoughts out loud.

'Are you tired of it all, Elise?' Georgina asked.

Elise knew that Georgina had been worrying about her since she had returned to Uracil. She had scheduled a medical check up and made sure to visit Elise every day, gently encouraging her to talk about her time in the containment centre.

'Tired?' Elise said, after thinking about it for a moment. 'Not so much. I think that, after a few weeks of rest and some training, I'll be ready.'

ACKNOWLEDGMENTS

I have a few people to thank who have helped me along the way with words of encouragement, reading through the drafts and putting up with my endless requests for feedback. Many thanks to Lee, Jo, Darryl, Julie, Lorraine, Adam and lastly, but certainly not least, Michael Alexander Kee Shin Flowing Seed Tim Li Ting Chung.

ABOUT THE AUTHOR

AE Warren lives in the UK. A not-so-covert nerd with mildly obsessive tendencies, she has happily wiled away an inordinate amount of time reading and watching sci-fi/fantasy. She is interested in the 'what ifs'. The Base of Reflections is her second novel.

She is currently working on the third novel in the 'Tomorrow's Ancestors' series.

You can contact her through a variety of modern ways:
    Twitter: @amauthoring
    Goodreads
    Facebook
    aewarren.com
    info@aewarren.com

24909500R00208

Printed in Great Britain
by Amazon